The Lion's Den

ALSO BY EMMY ELLIS

DETECTIVE ANNA JAMES
Book 1: THE PIG PEN
Book 2: THE LION'S DEN

DETECTIVE TRACY COLLIER
Book 1: GUTTED
Book 2: CRUSHED
Book 3: SKINNED
Book 4: GRABBED
Book 5: SUNK
Book 6: CRACKED

DI BETHANY SMITH
Book 1: THE COLD CALL KILLER
Book 2: THE CREEPY-CRAWLY KILLER
Book 3: THE SCREWDRIVER KILLER
Book 4: THE SCORCHED SKIN KILLER
Book 5: THE STREET PARTY KILLER
Book 6: THE CANDY CANE KILLER
Book 6.5: THE SECRET SANTA KILLER
Book 7: THE MEAT HOOK KILLER
Book 8: THE BLADE KILLER
Book 9: THE SLEDGEHAMMER KILLER

DETECTIVE CAROL WREN MYSTERIES
Book 1: SPITE YOUR FACE
Book 2: HOLD YOUR BREATH
Book 3: GUILT BURNS HOLES
Book 4: BEST SERVED COLD
Book 5: BLOOD RUNS DEEP

DETECTIVE ANNA JAMES

THE
LION'S
DEN

EMMY ELLIS

Joffe Books, London
www.joffebooks.com

First published in Great Britain in 2024

© Emmy Ellis 2024

Cover art by Dee Dee Books Covers

ISBN: 978-1-83526-595-6

PROLOGUE

Burying a body in the dark was harder than she thought, even though she'd done it several times, but just enough light came from the windows of the houses behind her cottage that her surroundings presented as recognisable things, albeit silhouettes. The stone shed at the bottom of the garden with the sloping roof, once used as a toilet back in the old days. The hump of the rockery with its various bushes. The looming pine tree to her left that shielded her from view, though the neighbours' homes on that side were separated by an alley anyway. As for the others, they'd have to crane their necks from their top floors to see what she was doing. She'd switched her cottage lights off, so she was safe.

The hole she'd dug was deep enough now, she knew that from experience. She reached her arm in to double-check, and the ground pressed against her armpit with her fingertips touching the earth. It pained her to think of putting the body in there, even though it had been shrouded in plastic sheeting then a blanket. She didn't like using tape to ensure the package stayed intact. It seemed obscene, not right, but what else was she supposed to do?

She couldn't have refused to do this. The burying. The death had been her fault, so he'd said. That had been made clear during their argument afterwards, tears blurring her vision, her hands curling tight, but never defending herself even though she could. Her abuser had refused to accept responsibility, insisted that his punches and kicks hadn't sealed the person's fate, it was what *she'd* done. Yes, she'd brought the victim into their lives, so technically, if she hadn't done that, he wouldn't have had to do what he'd done.

But it was easier to take the blame.

It saved another balled-up fist flying into her face.

Her jaw ached from where his thump had landed — the first one anyway. Such a meaty fist, packed with power. One of her teeth had broken this time, a lower molar, half of it breaking off. She'd swallowed it, not wanting him to see what he'd done. The bruises were bad enough; he crowed over them every time they appeared on her skin.

It still bled, her gum. The taste of blood would forever remind her of this night. The choices she'd made. Ones she'd continue to make, even though the result was . . . this. Every time.

She patted around on the grass, touching the bundle, then dragged it towards her and placed it in the hole. She stared down, even though she couldn't see it. Memorised the darkness, what the scene looked like, so she could torment herself with it in the years to come. A penance, perhaps. A punishment. Although it wouldn't stop her from doing it again. Her plan would work eventually.

She'd be in trouble if he found out she'd spoken to any-one about this. Yet she'd disobeyed him again, as she so often did, regardless of his threats. She'd confided in a neighbour — well, some of it, not the burials. They both worked in the same place, so it was easy to whisper to one another. She wished they could be friends, but he'd told her she couldn't have any. Friends were trouble, he'd said.

He'd make no bones about telling the police what she'd done if she stepped out of line. She had to do as he said or she'd find cold cuffs around her wrists. And the shame, everyone shaking their heads at her as she was guided down the front garden path and into a waiting police car — she wasn't sure she could handle that.

What had brought her to this? She thought the grass would be greener on the other side. Turned out it wasn't. The pain, the pure agony. It would always be this way because she wouldn't stop, she would go through this again.

Some would say she was warped, and they might be right. She didn't understand herself, so how could anyone else? There wasn't a particular reason why she disobeyed him, knowing the consequences, just that she craved the danger, the excitement of it all, the tears. Even if it meant burying people. Even if it meant losing a tooth.

She took a deep breath and leaned forward, her fingers linked to create a circle with her arms. She lowered it over the mound of mud behind the hole and drew it towards her. The thud of it hitting the bundle tore at her soul, and her eyes stung, her heartbeat raced, and her throat tightened into a lump.

She was cruel to put herself through this.

Cruel to do this to the victims.

She continued until the hole was filled. Tomorrow, she'd plant flowers to mark the spot, a riot of colour, of blooming life, which would remind her that what lay beneath had no life at all, same as all the others. She wished she could make her abuser pay, but she didn't have the energy to fight back. At this moment her whole world had no meaning.

She was stuck here, always.

And she kind of liked it.

She dragged herself indoors, closed the curtain across the back door, tugged on the set at the kitchen window. She didn't want to see outside when she turned on the lights. It was too raw, her crime so stark and in her face. Time enough to face that in the light of day. She'd grieve for a bit, give it a while, then do it all over again.

"Remember, not a fucking word."

She jumped at the sound of that voice but should have known those words, or similar, would come. As if she didn't *know* she had to keep this quiet. The story he'd concocted, one that would see her at the police station in the city, was so plausible she didn't think anyone would believe the truth. Of what had *really* happened.

Punches. Kicks.

Resigned to her fate, welcoming the burn of what she supposed was shame, she went to grit her teeth, then remembered the broken one, how much it would hurt. "I won't say anything."

"Make sure you don't, else you know what'll happen. I mean it, this is the last time. If it happens again, you don't want to know what I'll do to you."

"Then let me go. I wouldn't have to do it if you didn't keep me here."

"Let you go? Not a chance. You're mine. No one else is allowed to touch you."

She smirked inwardly at that.

If only you knew . . .

"Make me a coffee, will you?" he said. "You've been ages."

She filled the kettle and placed it on the hob like an automaton. What she really wanted to do was sink to her muddy knees and scream. Cry. Let the wrenching sobs bark out of her. Say she wanted out of this madness. Beg to be allowed to do what she wanted. To be free to make her own choices, be married to someone who loved her.

Have children.

That brought on a sharp clench in her chest, her lungs refusing to allow any air in. The skin on the back of her neck prickled, like it always did when she was being watched. Then came the raising of the hair on her arms, the goosebumps, the shudder that crept through her.

She coached herself through it, to become calm. He would enjoy her suffering, revel in it, and remind her of it in the days to come, months or years even, so the pain was as fresh as it was now, the scab picked off, revealing the rawness beneath.

Cruelty was his pastime. Mind games. Control.

And she let him do it.

The kettle slowly began shrieking and she set about making the coffee, wishing she could throw it so it scorched his skin and scalded an eye. Give her enough time to rush past and make it to the front door. To find someone who'd harbour her while she phoned the police and told them everything. She'd be free then, although the guilt would always be with her. But she reminded herself no one would believe her, and the thought of going to prison—no.

No.

She waited to be told she could go and have a bath, to strip off her clothes — murder clothes — and scrub herself clean, get the sin off her. But it lived inside her now, and she'd never be free of it.

Never.

CHAPTER ONE

In the darkness of a Yorkshire winter evening, Toby Potter stared at the body by his feet. Albert Frost was going to go mad about this. Well, he would, wouldn't he? The dead woman was his wife.

Toby had known for years he'd snap one day, but he hadn't expected it to be tonight. He'd lashed out, no red flags in his mind, no whispering conscience like before. Instead, the rush of anger had overtaken his judgement, and after he'd whacked her once he just kept going.

He scoured his memory for confirmation that he hadn't been seen by more than one driver on his way to the honesty table in the lay-by near Upton-cum-Studley. He'd walked there from the village, as many tended to do, and he'd taken a deep breath at the sight of Maureen Frost, filling her carton with eggs then putting money through the slot in a wooden box. She was the last person he'd wanted to see, and the same went for her husband.

They didn't get on.

Bad blood ran deep. It skewed the mind.

Evidently, it made you kill people.

If she'd have ignored him, she'd still be alive. Shame that she'd reverted to type and just had to say something.

"I'd be surprised if you ever pay for anything," she'd sniped, "seeing as you like diddling people."

It was one of many insults she'd thrown his way over the years. But she was right. He *had* cheated someone out of their money, but if she hadn't done what she had he wouldn't have had to strike that deal. And fancy her saying that to him. Had she forgotten what he'd held over her for decades? There was still time for him to open his mouth to Albert, or did she no longer care?

But none of that had entered his mind at the time — only now, when it was all over. Instead, he'd gripped his heavy walking cane, sick of the way she always had to get a dig in, thinking the deal meant he'd let her get away with it. The cane had smacked into the side of her head before he'd had time to stop himself, and the crack of it against her skull, the heavy thud when she'd gone down to her knees, the smash of each egg as it had sprung from the carton to land on the ground, had unlocked all the pent-up rage inside him.

Once he'd started, he couldn't stop.

Her blood splashed onto the tarmac of the lay-by, a strange colour in the glow of the streetlamp, which cast its ghostly orange aura over the scene. Once he'd battered her to death, he'd dragged her to a field on the edge of Hawthorn Farm, close to the road but many metres away from the farm-house with its single glowing light upstairs, and the outer houses of the village were farther off than that. No cars had come by since that one when he'd first set off to collect his eggs, and he supposed, if the driver came forward to inform the police, he could say he hadn't gone to buy eggs at all, he'd only been out for a stroll. That wasn't unheard of; he regularly rambled, and many would back him up there.

He caught his breath from lugging Maureen across the earth. She'd always been on the curvy side, a squat bulldog with a loud mouth, and as dead weight she'd been heavier than he'd thought. He'd loved her once, unsure what to do with all that giddy lust and excitement coursing through his veins.

Funnel it into his dreams or push it out into the open?

He wished he'd never chosen the latter.

"I'd have changed things if I could," he told her as he crouched, his boot soles digging into the ground. "So you never saw Albert, never knew he existed. But you went and fell for him, didn't you? Daft cow. And look where it got you. No kids because he wanted you all to himself. A life of drudgery because he thinks women belong at the kitchen sink or flat on their backs." He resisted stroking her hair. "Your old man's a hard taskmaster, and you had to dance to his tune, didn't you? He changed you, but then you know that. I saw all those secret looks you gave me. You wanted help but were too proud — and scared — to ask me for it in case I turned my back on you like you did to me. He changed you into a spiteful bit of baggage, something he lugged around with him. I tried to warn you about him, but you didn't listen."

In the light of the full moon, Maureen's wrecked face stared up at him. Her lips, parted slightly, had a heavy stream of blood coming from the corner.

What had her last thought been? Had she regretted treating him the way she had? Or had that second blow rendered her incapable of thinking *anything*?

"Did you *ever* love me, Mo?"

He wanted her to answer, to say she *had* loved him and how sorry she was for how she'd behaved towards him, but it was too late for all that now. Any goodwill she'd felt towards him he'd never know. He'd ruined any chance of a reconciliation years ago, and anyway there wouldn't have been one unless Albert was six feet under. Despite her being gobby, Maureen wouldn't have dared go against her husband publicly, but in private was another matter. It seemed Albert was exempt from her particular brand of venom. Everyone else had to suffer, though. He'd moulded her into a waspish bint.

"You won't be able to be cruel to anyone anymore." Toby sighed. "It should have been him I killed, then we could have talked, you and me, and settled our differences. Been a couple again."

He was kidding himself. After the deal had been struck, she wouldn't have come back to him even if he'd paid her.

Come the morning, a dog walker would likely find her. Toby didn't want to get caught; he should hide her body in the woods, or maybe take her onto the remote moors — but he *wanted* her found. She'd been horrible to him, no question, but the candle he'd held for her still burned bright, and he didn't think she deserved to be left to rot. At least if someone discovered her, she'd be taken care of. A post-mortem, undoubtedly — he watched the telly, he knew how it went with unexpected deaths — but she'd be with people who cared. Out here, foxes didn't give a stuff about you, and he couldn't bear the idea of her being so alone with animals gnawing on her flesh.

Why did you kill her, then?

He huffed at that internal voice, one he listened to regularly when he'd messed up. It always spoke sense. "I didn't know I was going to. It happened so fast . . ."

He bent over and gripped her wrists, glad he'd put gloves on before he'd come out. It was nippy, so no one would think it odd that he had them on, the same with his woolly hat with the bobble on top. He dragged her farther into the field, away from the hedge, so she'd be seen better, not dismissed as a pile of discarded clothing. A quick glance at the farmhouse, and he was satisfied that the couple Vernon Brignell had roped in to run the farm, now he was in prison, wouldn't be able to see him from there.

That had been a shock, Vernon admitting to killing his first wife and burying her on his land. Maybe there was something to the saying that the apple didn't fall far from the tree, because his son, Matthew, had turned out to be a killer an' all.

But he couldn't think about that, not now. And there'd be time enough when he got home to ponder whether he'd be caught for killing Maureen. He *deserved* to be caught, he should pay for what he'd done, and, although he regretted not being able to make peace with her, this was for the best. He couldn't be tormented by her now. He didn't have to sit and hope the days passed quickly, endlessly waiting for Albert to die so he could step in and be her shoulder to cry on while she mourned.

"Goodbye, Maureen."

He took his boots off and walked towards home with the hedge as a shield, the drivers of passing cars, should they come this way, unable to see him. Without letting his bloodied cane touch anything but his gloved hand, he plodded on, past the farmhouse in the near distance, then farther, to the other end of the field, where he entered the village via an alley that connected to it. A lone lamp post stood at the end, lighting up the pavement in an amber splash. He checked the houses and, with no one else about, scooted across the road to another alley ahead. The back of his house, visible to the right and next to the alley, beckoned him.

His socks, wet from the damp grass, slapped against the tarmac, and he paused at the edge of the high wooden fence flanking his garden to peer out into the street. Again, no one around, so he hustled into his house via the side door. The warm, lit kitchen reminded him of how alone he was, how alone he'd always seemed to be, and, with no Maureen to catch his eye anymore, only Albert, life appeared bleak.

He took his socks off and carried them and his boots into his workshop at the back of the house. It used to be a dining room when he'd lived here as a child. The blood on his walking stick was an issue, but he didn't want to wash it — the police did things like look in your drains if they had reason to believe you'd murdered someone. The idea of them scouring his house to find evidence of what he'd done brought on a shiver, and he contemplated what to do. Had he planned Maureen's death, he'd have set something up, but he was working off the cuff. He didn't dare put the cane down either.

"Bloody hell! You're such a stupid bastard."

He spied a bit of green tight-weave tarpaulin on a shelf, the remnant off a roll he'd used to waterproof his shed roof in the summer. He opened it up and placed it on his workbench — awkward when he still held the cane and his boots — and put everything on top of it. He found a block of wood he'd cut off a plinth recently, balanced the cane on top, and cut it into several inch-wide pieces. He stripped off and added his coat, shirt, trousers, underwear, gloves and bobble hat to the pile, then wrapped the whole lot in the tarpaulin, everything that had touched the blood safely inside. The block of wood. The saw. Taking a roll of black bags out of a drawer, he placed the package of sin inside.

He just had to work out where to put it tomorrow. The dump in the nearest city of Marlford wasn't an option; you had to register your car there, and they had cameras everywhere. He supposed, if he weighed the bag down with pebbles from next door's back garden when they went out in the morning to take their mutt for a walk, he could go and drop it in Jubilee Lake.

For now, he stowed the black bag inside his tool cabinet and went for a shower. Afterwards, he pottered into the hallway, switched the light on and eyed his row of canes in their varnished pine stand, one he'd crafted himself. Thank goodness he had several of them. Folks around here knew he needed to use one, so if he was questioned by the police, and they knew an implement the shape of a cane had been used, he'd direct them here, saying, *Look, I've got a fair few of them.* One spot was empty, so he took his large umbrella from the coat cupboard and propped it in there.

"That's better."

A miaow came from upstairs, and he looked up. Mr Baggins, his longhair ginger tom, stared down at him from the landing, and an awful thought struck. What if those hairs had transferred to Maureen's clothing?

Sickened by fear, Toby shuffled to the kitchen and put the kettle on. Tea always calmed him, and he'd think better with a steaming cup in front of him. Drink made, he took it to the table and sat. Smiled. Thought of something that would get up Albert's nose, adding a layer of pain to the blow of finding out his wife had died.

"Yes, I'll say that, then," he told Mr Baggins, who had wandered in and was circling his food bowl. "It'll fuck him right up."

CHAPTER TWO

DI Anna James stood to the far side of the tent, staring over at the body on the grass. She and DS Lenny Baldwin wouldn't be allowed closer until the plaster casts of two footprints had been done. Whoever had left the deceased here hadn't thought things through. With the recent rain, their weight had left distinct, side-by-side impressions in an area of bare ground. The field was dotted with patches of mud here and there, maybe where people stood waiting for their dogs to have a run. It wasn't supposed to be used for that though. It had been created as a haven for insects, and in the summer it would be a riot of wildflowers, where bees and butterflies could thrive. But Robert and Diana were too old to run people off the land, and sadly some of them didn't give much of a toss about following rules. At least they picked up the dogshit, so that was something.

"I know her," Anna said. "Not well, only to nod to, but it's Maureen Frost."

The last time Anna had seen her had been in the pub up the road, the Jubilee, named after Jubilee Lake in Marlford. The weekly quiz had been on, and her husband, Albert, had crowed loudly when they'd won. As always, Toby Potter had cast the couple a dark glance, which had been swiftly returned along with a middle finger from Albert. Anna had noted way before then that there was discord between the trio, but she'd never bothered asking why. She preferred not to get involved unless the job required it. Her introverted nature didn't allow for it, although she played well at being an extrovert at work. How could she not when she dealt with members of the public?

It's exhausting, though.

"Ah, she's one half of *that* couple," Lenny said. "The ones who win all the quizzes and get 'house' at bingo."

"That's them."

Lenny had been with her a few times so had borne witness to their behaviour. He sometimes stayed over at her place if he'd had too much to drink.

Anna had to ask herself if Toby wasn't the only one to have the Frosts on their shitlist. Did someone else bear a grudge? Or had Maureen been killed at random? A chance attack on a quiet country road?

A shout came from outside the tent. "Blood by the hedge!"

"Maybe she was put there first after the attack," Anna said to Lenny in response.

"So we could be looking at someone who isn't strong enough to carry her straight here from the lay-by. Or they put her by the hedge, then changed their mind."

The SOCO who'd been doing the plaster cast peeled the now solidified rendering off the ground and popped it in an evidence box. "I'll get out of your hair." He stood and left the tent.

Lenny recapped the conversation they'd had when they'd arrived on the scene. "So she was killed in the lay-by, going by the blood spatter and broken eggs, carried to the other side of the hedge, then brought here."

Anna nodded. "Seems so. The broken eggs — was she attacked from behind? Or did she see them coming at her, panic, and send the eggs flying? Hang on, we'll soon know a bit more."

The pathologist, Herman Kuiper, entered the tent and began his initial perusal. His man bun was skew-whiff today — it was most unlike him to not have his hood up — and his eyes appeared bloodshot and somewhat red-rimmed.

"Are you okay?" Anna asked. "Only, your hair's out in the open."

"Family death last night," he said, his Dutch accent thicker than usual. He raised his hood.

"What the hell are you doing *here*, then?" Anna blurted. She could kick herself sometimes at the way she was so direct. Sometimes, the words were past her lips before she could think to keep them inside. "Sorry, that came out harsher than I meant."

"I know you well enough by now to take it the way you intended. Thanks for your concern." Herman glanced at her over his mask to put her at ease. "I can't stay at home. I'll think too much. I'm going back to Holland next week for the funeral — it was my grandmother — but in the meantime I'll keep busy with this poor woman." He gestured to the body.

Maureen would be a similar age. Was Herman thinking of the parallel?

Bless him.

"She was hit with something cylindrical and long," he said. "If you look closely, you'll see the curved indents in her head."

Anna stepped forward and studied the marks. She hadn't been prepared for this kind of violence when she joined the police force. All she'd wanted to do was stop crime, and her first sight of a scene like this had brought home just how brutal people could be, how brutal her *job* could be.

"A pole," Herman added. "A heavy one."

"Like a tyre iron?" she asked.

"Hmm." Herman pressed Maureen's arm gently. "Rigor's well set in, so she's been here a while. Overnight, I'd say."

"I don't need you to look for ID." Anna folded her arms to ward off the chill. This winter was shaping up to be a right pig. "I know who she is."

15

"You can get on, then."

She sensed Herman needed to be left alone — she knew *that* feeling well enough — but one of the photographers came in. Perhaps picking up on the mood, Wayne didn't greet anyone and got on with snapping pictures.

"We'll leave you to it," Anna said and walked out.

She stared over at the hedge. Several SOCOs crouched, one placing markers to indicate where the blood was, another holding a pair of long tweezers, ready to collect anything of significance. A hair. A fibre.

Anna approached Steven Timpson, the lead SOCO, and was glad of her face mask as a sudden gust of wind tried to snatch at her cheeks. The hedge rustled ominously and she shivered. "Anything?"

"It's still as we thought when you first arrived. An attack in the lay-by. She *must* have been buying eggs — I doubt anyone else would have dropped them."

"Unless they were the attacker's."

"Could be. We've bagged the wooden money box — her prints might be on it if she wasn't wearing gloves — and the table will be taken down to the lab an' all, as will the egg carton and the mess that was made."

"I got Karen to sort house-to-house." Anna assumed the desk sergeant had done what she'd asked by now, but, being in the tent, she hadn't seen whether any police cars had gone into the village. "But there's someone who sprang to mind immediately when I saw it was Maureen Frost, so we'll go there after we've visited her husband, Albert."

"Do you know them well?" Steven asked.

"No, I just see them in the Jubilee from time to time, plus the little shop." Having to repeat the conversation got on her nerves, but she reined in her temper, which had been with her since she'd been woken at the crack of dawn by the shrill ringing of her phone.

Karen had been far too chipper when she'd relayed the news of the murder — not that she revelled in death, she was

16

just a morning person. Anna and Lenny shared snippets of information with her, and vice versa, promising to keep it a secret. Trading gossip was frowned upon in the force. Anna loved Karen to pieces, but by God could she be annoying first thing. Who woke up as chirpy as that? It always took Anna a good hour or two before she could put on her happy face.

She glanced at her watch. An hour to go, then.

She told herself off and shook away the irritation only a good coffee could fix. She hadn't had time to get one earlier. Maybe Albert would let Lenny make one at his place.

"So you don't know how her old man's likely to take it?" Steven said.

It took Anna a moment to remember they'd been having a conversation. "Sorry, a distinct lack of caffeine in my system. He seems a bit smug, so it could be difficult. Then again, his wife's dead. What I don't understand is why he didn't report her missing — Karen checked for me, and there haven't been any mispers since yesterday morning. Some bloke went off on a pub crawl with his mates and forgot to tell his missus. Herman said rigor is present, so Maureen's likely to have been killed last night."

"Maybe he's used to her staying away without saying anything to him about it."

"Strange, don't you think?"

"Then she could have been going somewhere, and that's why he wasn't alarmed when she didn't come home."

"True. Okay, we'll be off now. You'll let me know if you find anything?"

Steven nodded. "I always do, don't I? *Try* and have a good day . . ."

"You too."

Anna turned to look for Lenny. He'd just left the tent — he clearly hadn't gauged Herman's mood, then — so they walked over to a second break in the hedge and stripped out of their protectives, placing them in the designated bags. As they were quite a few metres from the lay-by, she didn't insist on fresh shoe covers and led the way to where everyone had parked their cars on the verge. Herman's stood out, a nice blue sporty number. The woman who'd found Maureen sat in her silver Audi with a PC Anna couldn't make out because the windows were fogged.

"We'd better have a quick word," she said.

"I thought you wanted to go see the next of kin."

"I do, but as we're here . . . Saves us coming back, doesn't it? Then she can get on with her day."

"It's not likely to be a nice one."

"No."

Anna knocked on the driver-side window and waited for it to sail down. A pale-faced woman in her thirties stared back at her, blue eyes wide and blank from shock, her brown hair in a tight ponytail like Anna's. PC Ollie Watson sat in the passenger seat with a Dalmatian on his lap. Anna pushed down a laugh. Ollie's trousers were filthy with muddy paw prints.

"Can we get in for a chat?" Anna asked and held up her ID. "I'm Anna, and this is Lenny. You are?"

"Cordelia Stubbs. Yes, get in."

Anna and Lenny settled in the back, Anna behind the passenger seat so she could see Cordelia's expression — not that she thought the woman had killed Maureen, but it was better to be safe than sorry.

"How come you drove here?" Anna asked. "Don't you live in the village?"

"No, I'm in Marlford, and this is the only field where we seem to be allowed to let the dog off, although I've just been told this one is out of bounds, too. I had no idea. There are no signs up."

"We?"

"Me and my husband. It was my turn to take Spotty out today."

Spotty. "Okay, so what time did you arrive?"

"About seven. I left home at quarter to. That gives me half an hour to let Spotty have a run. I get home by about quarter to eight, have a quick shower, then go to work."

"Explain exactly what happened."

Flapping a limp hand, Cordelia indicated the break in the hedge that Anna and Lenny had used, the second one down from the village. "I parked, nipped through there, then let Spotty off the lead. He ran away, as usual. It was still dark, so I switched my torch on and saw a lump. That's what it looked like at first. Just a heap of clothing. So I walked up to have a nose and saw . . . saw it was an old woman. I phoned the police straight away."

"Did you recognise her?"

"No. The blood . . . I was nearly sick."

"I can imagine. It's a shock and a half for anyone. Do you ever have reason to go to Upton-cum-Studley?"

"No, why?"

"That's where the deceased lived."

"Right. I only ever come out as far as this field."

"Have you already given PC Watson a formal statement?"

"We tried," Ollie said, "but Spotty seems to like me."

The dog licked his face.

Anna smiled. "Okay, perhaps go down to the station, then. Karen will have some dog treats. She keeps them by for the K9s." At Cordelia's frown, she clarified. "A sergeant and our police dogs."

"Oh. I'll have to ring in to work first, say I'll be late."

Is she like Herman? Goes to work to keep her mind occupied even though something horrible has happened?

Anna said her goodbyes and strode to her car with Lenny.

Inside, her seat belt on, she asked, "How come you stayed in the tent?"

"I felt sorry for Herman. He seems broken."

"Of course he is, his grandmother died. Bloody hell, Lenny, get your head together, will you?" She drove off. "Can

19

you get hold of Karen for Albert's address, please? Oh, and for Toby Potter's place."

Lenny got on with it, and, by the time he'd finished, Anna had pulled into the Jubilee car park. Upton-cum-Studley wasn't that big, so they could walk to the houses, but then she remembered how cold it was. Probably best to take the car after all.

"Albert's is just over there. Number two." Lenny pointed to a row of wavy-topped white cottages opposite the pub. "Not far to go if you've had a skinful. Handy, that."

Anna laughed. She undid her belt, reached into the back for their coats and put Lenny's on his lap. "Are you ready for this?"

"No."

Anna grimaced. "Me neither."

CHAPTER THREE

Back out in the cold, Anna shrugged her coat on and zipped it up. Lenny joined her, and they trotted over the road. Going by Albert's grey hair, she supposed he was retired, and hoped he'd be in. Mind you, it was still early, so they might even get him out of bed. She knocked on the door, dreading the kind of reception they'd get if his behaviour in the Jubilee was any indication of his personality.

Albert flung the door open. Liver spots dotted his pink cheeks, freckles in between, and his eyes were glassy. Perhaps he'd not long got up. His hair, slightly tousled on one side from a pillow, reminded Anna of her father's. He was in a tartan dressing gown and matching slippers. He gave her the side-eye.

"What do *you* want?" he groused, keeping the door open only a little bit, maybe so the heat didn't seep out.

"Can we come in, Albert?"

"Didn't know you knew my name."

Anna smiled. "I live in the village, as you're aware. Nearly everyone knows everyone. And if you don't know my name, I'm DI Anna James, and this is my partner, DS Lenny Baldwin."

"I've seen him in the pub with you from time to time." Albert frowned and gave her a glance of suspicion. "What do you need to come in for?"

"I've got some bad news. It's about Maureen."

"Hmm, she's run off with that Toby Potter, I'll bet. I should have known she would eventually. What's he done, killed her?" Albert's laugh produced puffs of white condensation in the cold air.

"Why would he do that if she ran off with him?"

"Long story, and I was only joking. She went to her sister's. Gloria. So, what's the bad news? Did she have an accident on the way or summat? How come it's taken you all this time to let me know?"

"It's better off said inside." Anna took a step forward to show him she wasn't taking no for an answer.

Albert sighed, opened the door wider and trundled off through a doorway at the end of the hall.

Anna glanced at Lenny, pulled a *he's an odd one* face, then followed the old man. He stood at the kitchen sink, thankfully filling a kettle, then put it on to boil.

"Park your arses." He motioned to a small table with four chairs.

Anna sat, but Lenny remained standing by a larder with its door ajar.

"Lenny can make the drinks," Anna said. "Come over here with me."

Albert lumbered across, out of breath. "Chest infection," he said by way of explanation. "Can't get rid of the bloody thing, even with antibiotics. I'll have pneumonia next, you'll see." He plonked himself down and wheezed. "Getting old is a right bastard."

"Sorry to hear you've been unwell." Anna steeled herself to proceed. "You said Maureen went to her sister's. Last night, was it?"

"Yep."

"What time was that?"

"About eight or thereabouts, like usual. Gloria lives in Marlford, and this time of year they go to the Christmas market and stay until late. A tradition of theirs. I was surprised Mo hadn't texted me to say what she'd bought, she usually does. I just thought she was knackered and had gone to bed." He frowned. "Come to think of it, she hasn't rung me this morning either."

"Is that something she'd normally do?"

A darkness swept over Albert's face, screwing up his features. "Yes, she knows the rules."

Rules? Blimey. Should we be looking at him for this? "Where were you when she left?"

"In the pub over the road. I had to do the quiz on my own, which pissed me off. Maureen's the one you need when it comes to geography. I still won, though."

"What time did you leave?"

"After last orders."

"Do you know if she'd have stopped off in the lay-by to get eggs on the way?"

Albert nodded. "Yep, she gets them for Gloria whenever she nips over to the city."

"And she left home in a vehicle?"

"Well, she wouldn't walk all the way to ruddy Marlford, would she!"

"She might have done. Some people do." *So where's her car?* "What make did she drive?"

"It's a Ford Focus. Grey." He rattled off the number plate as if he knew she'd ask for that next.

Lenny wrote it all down.

Albert sniffed. "What's this bad news, then? I've asked that already, but you ignored me. That's rude, you know."

The kettle clicked off, and Lenny got on with making coffee.

Anna took a deep breath. "Maureen was found in the field behind the lay-by by Hawthorn Farm. Her car wasn't there."

"What?"

"She's dead, Albert. I'm so sorry."

"Dead? What do you mean, dead?"

"We're treating it as murder."

Albert's eyes bulged. "Mur — No, that's not right."

"I'm afraid it's not a mistake. I recognised Maureen straight away."

Albert didn't display the usual emotion people did when she delivered bad news. No crying, no shouting. Had he already known she was dead? Had he gone to the Jubilee for an alibi and arranged for someone to kill her?

"You don't seem all that upset," Anna said.

"I'm not going to break down in front of you two, and how I take the news is my business."

"Your behaviour could make us think you had something to do with it, though."

"I bloody didn't! What a load of tosh."

Lenny brought two cups over and placed them on coasters. He pointed to the door and made a phone shape with his hand to let her know he'd ring in about the missing vehicle. Anna nodded to him, then switched her attention back to the old man.

"Do you need a moment before we continue?" she asked.

"No, get on with it. Then you can sod off and do your job instead of sitting here drinking a pissing brew."

"I'm doing my job by being here," she said gently. "I have to build up a picture so I know what to do next. Is there anyone you can think of who would want to do this to Maureen?" She drank some coffee, her body and mind thanking her for it.

Albert stared at his cup. "That Lenny fella didn't make it right. It's not strong enough. Maureen knew how to fix my coffee. I trained her." He blinked. "The only person we have a problem with is Toby Potter. I said that when you arrived, or weren't you paying attention? That's the trouble with you women, you need a man to step up and show you where you went wrong."

24

Anna chose to ignore that. "Why is there a problem?"

"He was seeing her before me."

For as long as Anna had lived in the village, Albert and Maureen had been an item. "And when was this?"

"Nineteen seventy-three. I came to live in Marlford in my twenties, started work at Cribbins. Met her there."

Cribbins. The chocolate factory dominated the skyline on the outskirts of the city. It brought to Anna's mind a certain Joshua Cribbins, grandson of the owner and a member of the Northern Kings gang. A man who'd made it clear he fancied her. She was attracted to him, but that way led to madness. As a police officer, it wasn't on for her to go out with a gang member, one much younger than her to boot. Would the factory owner remember any spats the trio had had in the past? Maybe they ought to pay him a visit to check.

Anna took another sip of coffee. It *was* a bit on the weak side. "So he was upset Maureen finished with him, is that what you're saying? And he's still annoyed about it fifty years later?"

Her last big case, involving Matthew Brignell, had the same theme — a man keeping quiet for two years and then letting rip — but waiting *fifty* years to do something about a grudge? Really?

"Let's just say there's bad blood and be done with it," Albert said. "He gives us filthy looks in the Jubilee during quizzes and when we play bingo. Can't stand it that we win more often than not."

"I've noticed."

"There you go, then, you've seen his attitude for yourself."

"I've also seen *you* giving *him* filthy looks, the same for Maureen. I'd say the animosity goes both ways, wouldn't you?"

"Yeah, but I wouldn't have killed Mo, would I? *He* would."

"We'll be speaking to him soon. Just out of interest, why would he kill her? Was their split acrimonious?"

"Acri-what?"

"Was it a bad split?"

25

"He was arsey, I'll say that much. Came up to me at work the morning after she'd told him, all puffy chest and bunched fists, and he had a right old go. I told him he must have a small dick and that was why Maureen had come to me. He took a swing at me, I ducked and told him to fuck off. End of story."

"Except it wasn't the end, if there's still hostility half a century later."

"Haven't you ever fallen out with someone? Come on, you must know how it goes."

She understood how it went, yes, but no, she'd never let spats continue years into the future. Maybe because her friends weren't that argumentative. Lenny was her only friend really, and they got on like a house on fire. Her parents were gentle, no enmity there. And as for the men in her life — Anna hadn't met anyone she'd want to dive into a proper relationship with, and marriage didn't appeal. She liked living alone, doing whatever she wanted without someone picking fault.

"Do you have anyone who can come and sit with you?" she asked. "A son, daughter?"

"No kids. I didn't want the buggers."

Anna saw an opportunity to test the waters. "Did Maureen?"

"At first, but I soon got that notion out of her head." He shifted his eyes away from her. Had he just lied?

"Was there anything else she gave up in order to please you?" *Shit, I didn't mean to say that out loud.*

Albert didn't seem to think anything of it. He was a blunt speaker, too, she supposed. "Plenty, but that had nothing to do with her being murdered." He pinched his bottom lip. "I still can't get over that. Maureen was a spiteful mare, but surely that doesn't mean someone would want to finish her off."

"Spiteful?"

"She said it how she saw it. I taught her that."

26

What else did you teach her? "Was she not like that before you *taught* her, then?"

"No, she was a bit of a wallflower, or so she liked people to think. You don't get anywhere in this world by merging into the background, and if she was going to be on my arm then she needed to get a bit of a backbone."

"Did you bully her?"

He shrugged. "Some would call it that, but *I* call it making her a stronger person."

"Apart from Toby, is there anyone else she may have offended?"

"Enough to kill her? Nah. How did they do it anyway?"

Finally, he wants to know. "She was struck with what the pathologist thinks is a pole."

"A pole?" Albert slapped the table. Some coffee sploshed out of his cup and dribbled down the side onto the table. "There you go, then. It's Toby. He used his walking stick."

That would work, providing it was heavy like Herman said. Bloody Nora . . . "Okay, we'll leave you be for now. We might have to come back and ask a few more questions." Concerned by his lack of tears, Anna stood. "Are you sure I can't call anyone for you?"

He glanced at the clock on the wall. "Nope, the pub opens in half an hour. I'll get myself dressed and go over there for breakfast. Plenty of people to keep me company, although if I see that Toby . . ."

"I'll ask him to stay away for the time being, although, if he hasn't done anything, I don't see why he should. Taking your grief out on him when he could be innocent . . . I wouldn't advise it."

"Or what, you'll do me for having a go at him? It's been a long time coming. We should have cleared the air properly years ago."

"If you could refrain from starting anything, I'd appreciate it. Getting lairy won't solve anything."

"No, but it would make me feel better."

27

Anna reached for her cup and took another couple of fortifying sips. "Thank you for the coffee. The pathologist will be in contact for the formal identification."

She left him to it and caught Lenny's eye in the hallway, where he stood against the wall by the stairs. She jerked her head for him to follow her to the car and, once inside, let out a long breath.

"Thought I'd stay out of the way after I rang the station," he said. "You were doing okay on your own."

"Any news on her car?"

"Yep, found half an hour ago. Burnt out. Maybe the killer pinched it, or else joyriders took the opportunity to nick it from the lay-by."

She sighed. "We'd best get round to Toby's. Can you give the others a ring and let them know the score? They should be at the station by now."

DCs Peter Dove, Warren Yates and Sally Wiggins formed the rest of Anna's team, led by DCI Ron Placket.

As she drove, she pondered the fact that nothing had come out of the surveillance on Peter. He'd belonged to the Northern Kings as a kid, before leaving to join the police force. Anna had spotted the tip of a crown tattoo on his inner wrist, which had alerted her to the fact he might well still be a gang member. Intel had told them the tattoos had been a recent thing among the Kings. They were keeping an eye on him at work, while two pairs of officers from the Kings surveillance team had been watching him at all other times in shifts. Having a possible mole in the camp left a sour taste in Anna's mouth.

The surveillance team had seen Peter in a car with Trigger, the Kings' leader. Peter's excuse was that he'd been given a tip-off about an ex-King called Smithy, but Anna didn't believe it. All right, the intel had been solid, Smithy *had* been caught with a shedload of drugs at his place, but she felt Trigger giving Smithy up had been a cover for Peter. Anna had also spotted him chatting to another King member, nicknamed

Wheels, in the pub he ran, the Kite. It all looked a bit suss. However, Peter seemed clean at the moment, so did that mean he knew he was being observed and was acting accordingly? Anna was just waiting for the opportunity to catch him in the act.

She swerved into Toby Potter's street and parked outside his house. It stood beside an alley. Beyond that, another street and an alley that led directly onto the big field where Maureen had been dumped. Not a stretch to think he had killed her, then scuttled home along there. Coupled with the killer using a walking stick, it might well be him. But he was a spindly old man — did he have the strength in him to wallop Maureen like that? Drag her body from the lay-by? Was that why she'd been left by the hedge and then moved again? Was Toby out of puff?

"Only one way to find out," she said.

"What was that?"

She smiled at Lenny. "Talking to myself again."

"*Tsk*. Right, the team are looking into things. Peter said he and Warren will go to the chocolate factory."

"So you guessed I'd want to look into anyone who worked with Maureen and her men?"

"I can read you like a book."

She smiled and hoped he couldn't.

Because that would mean he'd know she fancied Joshua Cribbins right back, and that would never do.

CHAPTER FOUR

Toby shuffled to the front door. Mr Baggins almost tripped him up. "Sod off to your bed." He gave the cat a gentle nudge with his foot. "Who's this, then, eh?"

Many people came knocking, usually to ask him to cobble something together in his workshop — a pair of bookends had been his most recent project, made to look like two piles of novels. He'd even painted titles and author names on the spines specific to what the buyer liked to read. He was proud of his work and how he put his heart into it. If you didn't have pride in your creations, your achievements, you weren't doing it right.

He didn't have pride in killing Maureen, though.

He swung the door open and smiled to hide the dip of his stomach upon seeing Anna on the step, a man beside her. Under normal circumstances he'd be genuinely pleased to see her, but Anna was a copper, everyone in the village knew that.

"Hello, there." He stretched his smile wider. "What sort of thing are you after?"

"Sorry?" she said. "I'm not with you . . ."

"A bird box? A table? Candlesticks? Something like that?"

Mr Baggins hadn't gone to bed and was currently winding himself around Toby's ankles. He couldn't exactly kick the moggy away in front of these two, so he suffered in silence.

"I make things out of wood." He tittered. "I thought you'd come to commission something."

"Err, no." Anna flapped a hand at his house. "We could do with coming in actually. For a little chat. We're here in a professional capacity."

"Oh! Well, in that case, come in. Would you like a coffee? I have a pot on."

"Please. This is DS Baldwin, by the way — Lenny."

Toby led them into his kitchen, surreptitiously looking around to check for any blood he might have missed when he'd cleaned up last night. Some must have plopped off his cane, and he hadn't noticed until Mr Baggins had licked at a spot on the floor. Horrified, Toby had disinfected the whole room. He was glad he hadn't used bleach now. Anna would have smelled it.

Satisfied he'd done a good job, he got on with pouring from the carafe of coffee. "I won't be a second."

Chairs scraped behind him, and his stomach rolled over. Should he be asking what they wanted? Would non-killers do that? He wasn't sure, so he opted to keep his mouth shut. That was the best bet, wasn't it? He carried the cups over, annoyed that Mr Baggins had followed them all in. Toby was still paranoid about cat hairs being left on Maureen, and the animal being in here would maybe draw their attention. He wanted to pick him up and shove him outside in the garden, but *that* would draw attention, too.

Bloody hell.

He sat opposite the officers and smiled, pleased now Mr Baggins had finally sloped off round the side of the fridge-freezer to his bed. "What can I do for you?"

"Firstly, can I ask you to bear with me on the questions," Anna said. "They might seem strange to you at first, until I explain the reason why we're here."

"Okay . . ."

"Tell us about your relationship with Albert and Maureen Frost."

Oh God. They know, don't they?

Toby prayed his cheeks wouldn't betray him by turning red. Maybe he should react as he would have done if he hadn't murdered Maureen. Truthfully, like people would expect from him. It was no secret that he disliked the couple.

"Don't talk to me about *those* two," he huffed out. "They upset me years ago, and I'll never forgive them for what happened."

"What *did* happen?" Anna sipped some coffee.

She seemed happy with the mix of arabica and robusta, which he blended himself in his bean grinder.

He drew his mind back to the question. "Me and Maureen, we were going to get married. We'd planned the date and everything. Planned our whole lives, in fact. Children, the lot. Then *he* came along."

"Albert?"

"Yes. Look, I've never hidden how I feel about that man, not since he took Maureen away from me. He ruined my life. I've never been with a woman since. She was my soulmate, so there was no point trying to find another."

Anna appeared to feel sorry for him, and he revelled in it. Not many people got it; they didn't understand. He'd lost count of the times folks had told him to get a grip and move on.

"So when he 'took' her from you, how did that go down?" she asked.

"We were on a date, me and Maureen, and she wasn't herself. She hadn't been for a good while, but I'd put it down to women and their monthly troubles. We were in the cinema, and I could tell she wasn't watching the film. So I said we'd go for an ice cream over the road at a parlour that used to be there, and I asked her outright what was wrong. She said she'd been seeing Albert behind my back, they'd gone further than

32

they should've, and that we ought to end it because she didn't love me anymore."

Lenny wrote in a notebook.

"I was shocked to say the least," Toby went on, all those old feelings rushing back. "I begged her to change her mind, told her just what sort of man Albert was. I'd heard things from other people at the factory, like how he was in the frame for stealing the produce — someone was nicking boxes of chocolates from the packing area and the thefts had happened not long after he'd started working there. She wasn't having any of it, defended him, she did, and I knew by the look in her eyes I'd lost her. Six weeks later, they were married. She'd only known him three months, yet she'd known me for years. We grew up together."

"That must have been horrible," Anna said.

"It was, so, as you can understand, I held a grudge. Getting on that bus of a morning, the free one put on by the factory, it was torture. It picked us lot up from the village, then made stops in Marlford. He'd get on outside the Kite, and they'd sit next to each other at the front, kissing and all that business, rubbing my nose in it. Then Albert and Maureen moved into that cottage opposite the Jubilee after the wedding, and I couldn't get away from them. Always there, they were, in my face. I've learned to live with it over the years, but it doesn't mean I have to like it."

"What about during the quizzes and bingo? I've seen how you all stare at each other."

"Albert likes to lord it over me, always has, and he gets Maureen to do the same, more so when they win. She's changed, she was never spiteful when she was with me. From what I can gather, Albert's always ruled the roost. Don't get me wrong, I'll never get over what she did to me, but despite all that she doesn't deserve being treated like she's his property."

"Tell me about when you confronted Albert."

They've been to his. He's told them. I bet his version's different to mine.

33

"I went up to him and called him out on it, said I knew what had been going on. He shouted something about me having a little dick and that was why she'd left me. Maureen had never seen it, so that was a load of rubbish, but it told me she'd seen his. I felt sick that he'd coerced her into doing that. Taking her virginity. I told him I was surprised she'd got herself involved with a thief. He didn't like that, so he took a swing at me. I ducked, our line manager came over to break it up, and that was that."

"We were led to believe you took a swing at him."

"He would say that, wouldn't he? Go and see Bruce, he'll tell you what's what. There was a report made and everything. Witnesses."

"Bruce?"

"The owner of the chocolate factory."

Lenny took his phone out and typed a message. Toby tried to see what he was writing, but his eyesight wasn't all that without his glasses. He'd forgotten to put them on.

"Where were you last night?" Anna asked.

The change of direction threw Toby for a moment. "I went for a walk like I usually do of an evening."

"Where did you go and at what time?"

"I started off on the road towards Marlford around five to eight." *There's no point in lying, that driver might come forward.* "I was going to get some eggs but realised I hadn't brought any money out with me, so I cut into the field and walked around the whole thing. I'm a rambler, in case you didn't know. I regularly forage for blackberries and the like in spring and summer, and I enjoy a long trek. I came back via the alleyways."

"I know the ones you mean. Did any vehicles pass you?"

"There was one car. Can't tell you what make it was, but I think it was black. A woman with dark hair was driving. She glanced across at me as she passed beneath a streetlamp, the first one out of the village." *Am I being too specific?*

"How old was she, would you say?"

34

"Now here's the thing. I'm not good with ages anymore. Anyone younger than fifty, well, I don't know. I see some young kids driving, and they don't look old enough."

"So she was under fifty?"

"Yes."

"Did you glimpse any of her number plate?"

"No."

"Where did you enter the field?"

"There are breaks in the hedges, aren't there? So the first one as you come out of the village."

"Before the lay-by."

"That's the one."

"Did you take a cane with you?"

Again, she'd thrown him. He nodded to cover for the twist in his gut. "I always do."

"May I have a look at it before we leave?"

"You can. I have several. Made them myself."

"Oh right. Did anyone see you walking around the field?"

"I'm not sure. Maybe ask Robert or Diana? I know they were in because there was a light on."

"It's been raining a lot lately. Did your shoes get muddy?"

Once more, his stomach rebelled, clenching, squeezing. "I was on the grass. I didn't go near the hedges where there's mud patches." He racked his brain for which shoes he'd worn prior to last night when he'd tromped around that field. "I can show them to you if you like. One minute."

He got up and went into the hallway, praying at least a speck of mud had attached to the soles to prove he'd walked there. He fished them out of the cupboard and checked. Mud was wedged against the inner part of the heels.

He returned to the kitchen. "Here you go. I go there a lot. Vernon never minded. Robert and Diana have never said anything either."

"We'll have to take these." Anna pulled some gloves out of her pocket, snapped them on, then took the shoes. She studied the soles, and her shoulders sagged.

35

He recalled his boots digging into the earth when he'd crouched to speak to Maureen. Had they found prints? Was Anna upset because these shoes had no treads?

"Are you all right?" Toby sat and sipped some coffee.

Anna placed the shoes upside down on the floor, likely so she didn't lose any dirt. "Yes, I'm fine. I'm just wondering why you'd wear these sorts of shoes for a 'ramble' in a wet field."

"I should get some boots really."

"The mud has dried so much that there's the risk of it crumbling off. I'd have expected some dampness to be there, seeing as it's so thick."

She's going to catch me. She's too clever. "Why do you need to take my shoes?"

She snapped her lips together. "We should really take your clothes and coat as well, whatever you were wearing last night."

Toby panicked. "The clothes have already been washed," he lied. "But as for the coat, you can have that, not a problem."

"It doesn't matter if they've been washed. Could you go and get them, please?"

Toby, his whole body shaking, ambled into the utility room to fetch a set of clothing from the pile he'd laundered yesterday. He returned to the kitchen and placed them on the table.

"You must do your washing early," Anna said, eyeing them. "For those things to already be dry."

"I get up at seven. I have a tumble dryer."

Anna leaned towards the pile, her cheek close. "There's no heat coming off them. How long is your wash cycle?"

Oh, she was getting on his nerves now, a regular Miss bloody Marple. "I have a quick-wash option." He calculated how long it would need for the clothes to now be cold. "Fifteen minutes, then an hour in the dryer."

She seemed to tot that up in her head and gave a quick nod. "Can we look at your canes now?"

"Certainly." Toby led the way and hoped he didn't show any signs of being frightened.

They all gathered around the stand.

"I made this," he said.

"It's lovely." Anna studied it. "Pretty carvings. You're very talented."

"Hmm, my dad taught me woodwork. He was a carpenter." Toby pointed to the cane with an extra-large crook. "I used that one." A glob of dried mud had stuck to the black rubber stopper on the bottom. "I suspect that's dried because of the stand being beside the radiator, same with the shoes being in that cupboard there, but I'm sure you'll find it'll match the mud in the field. That's what you want to do, isn't it? Would you mind telling me why now?"

"Let's go and sit down."

They went back to the kitchen, and Toby prepared himself to appear shocked and devastated. Mr Baggins crept out from his hiding place and wailed near his food bowl. Anna sat and stared at him, and Mr Baggins stared back. He had that look about him where he was going to attack, and Toby shot up to usher him out into the hallway.

He closed the door on him. "He's a nasty piece of work — a stray I felt sorry for. He claws at people for no reason."

Anna took another mouthful of coffee, then put the cup down and smiled at him sadly. "I'm sorry to have to break this to you, but Maureen's body was found in the field this morning."

A great wave of grief welled up inside him, like it would had he been hearing about her death for the first time. Perhaps guilt had nudged his emotions into coming out. Or maybe he'd distanced himself so much from the murder, it was as though he hadn't done it. A wail worthy of Mr Baggins tore from Toby's mouth. His throat pulsed with a torrent of sobs, and he clutched at the edge of the table, his head going dizzy.

"No, not Maureen. No!"

Anna winced. "I'm so sorry."

"What was she doing in the field? She's not a walker."

"We believe she stopped off to get some eggs and some-one attacked her. The pathologist thinks the weapon is a pole of some kind, hence me asking about your cane."

"Oh my God, you don't think it was *me*, do you?"

"We have to keep an open mind. Did you see anyone else while you were out? Maureen left her cottage at eight. Did you hear or see her car go past, perhaps after the other one went by, or before?"

"Maybe . . . I could have been distracted, off in a world of my own. Come to think of it, yes, I *did* hear another car, but I was at the end of the field farthest from the village at that point. Oh no, do you think she was killed while I was walking?"

"It's possible. Did anything else seem off?"

"No, nothing at all." He sniffed and cuffed snot on his sleeve.

Anna got up and ripped off a piece of kitchen roll, and handed it to him. He blew his nose and smiled at her, his lips wobbling.

"I can't believe this is happening."

Anna sat. "It's a shock, I know. She was on her way to stay with her sister in the city."

No, she wasn't.

"Her car was taken," Anna continued. "Do you think that might be the one you heard?"

"I only heard the one, so that might have been Maureen's arriving or being driven off, but that would depend on the time. It takes me half an hour to walk around the whole field, so it would have been about eight thirty when I heard it. I got home at nine."

"The timings don't work. You both left home around eight, her in a car, you on foot."

"Then she must have gone past before I got to the road. I left at five to eight and didn't go down the alley, I went through my street and came out by the pub, *then* I went down the road. She'd have gone by then."

38

That was the truth. He hadn't seen her until he'd reached the egg table.

"Right, that's straight in my head now," Anna said. "Thank you for clarifying."

"I'll never get over this. Have you been to see Albert? It'll be him. That temper of his has finally got the better of him. He's always short with her, barking out orders."

"Yes, we've seen him."

"Did he send you my way? Is that why you're here?"

"We're here because I was aware of the animosity between you."

"It wasn't me, I can promise you. I'd never do anything like that."

"Do you need someone to come and sit with you?"

The image of the black bag containing all the bloodied things burned a hole in Toby's mind. Having someone here would prevent him from getting rid of it. He'd been consumed by his thoughts. That was why Mr Baggins had been clamouring for his breakfast; Toby had been too busy mulling things over to feed him. He still had to nip next door and collect those pebbles — Yvonne and Wilf hadn't gone out yet. Panic overtook him. What if he couldn't get rid of the bag in time? What if Anna went next door to check if they'd noticed when he'd got home last night and they didn't bother taking their dog out at all because she'd messed up their routine?

"No, I'll be fine. I wouldn't want to inflict my grief on anyone."

"Lenny will nip out and get a couple of evidence bags, then we'll take your things, all right? Sorry to have to do that, but I'd like to eliminate you from the inquiry."

"But if the mud matches, won't that make me a suspect? I was there, I've admitted that."

Lenny left the house.

Anna sighed, stood and stooped to pick up the shoes. "It's just something we have to do. If I could offer a bit of advice:

39

avoid the Jubilee for the time being. Albert is going there for breakfast."

"What? When his *wife* is lying dead in the dirt?" Toby shook his head. "He really is a cretin."

Going by Anna's face, she seemed to agree.

Toby rose and, on shaking legs, went out into the hallway with her. He took an old coat from the cupboard. Lenny was busy putting the cane into a long, clear bag — he had gloves on, too, and this was all getting a bit *real*. Once he'd secured it, he bagged the shoes and coat. Anna walked back into the kitchen. She emerged with the clothes and passed the pile to Lenny, who slid them into yet another bag.

Anna stared at the other canes. "Could you get by using that umbrella as a walking stick?"

Toby nodded, knowing what she was going to say next.

"It's best we take all the canes."

He wafted a hand absently. "Do what you need to do."

Lenny nipped out again, probably to collect more bags.

Anna took her gloves off, turned them inside out and put them in her pocket. "They'll be returned to you as soon as possible. It could be a few days."

Toby wanted to tell her they wouldn't find anything, those canes were clear of any blood, but he thought better of it. Lenny came back and put the other sticks into bags, and they left. Lenny put everything in the boot and phoned for someone to collect them, his voice loud enough that Wilf and Yvonne next door might hear him.

Anna walked up their garden path.

Shit.

"An officer will come by to take a formal statement," she said across the dividing hedge.

Toby nodded, worrying about when that would be — he had to get his hands on those pebbles — and closed the door, scuttling into the kitchen to get a glass. He sat on the stairs and carefully pressed it to the wall. As he'd thought, Anna asked them if they'd happened to hear Toby coming back last night.

"About nine," Wilf said, his rumbling tones carrying well. "He's always gadding about in that bloody field."

Toby breathed a sigh of relief.

He was safe.

For now.

CHAPTER FIVE

Albert finished off his full English and sipped his coffee — that crap the copper had made was an abomination, gnat's piss. He browsed the local free magazine, *Marlford Views*, which he'd picked up from the little shop along the way before entering the Jubilee. They were supposed to be delivered to every house but, as usual, he hadn't received his. He had a sneaking suspicion the paperboy hated him and deliberately didn't pop one through their letterbox. Albert didn't like him, not after he'd chased the lad up the road that time he'd nicked some of Maureen's prize roses from the back garden. The cheek of him, sneaking round there, even using little pruning shears to snip the stems.

Albert took a moment to ponder the parallels between himself and Vernon Brignell, only *he* wouldn't be so stupid as to end up in prison. And besides, he hadn't killed anyone. With Maureen dead, if things ever came out regarding the past he could blame her. A dead woman couldn't dispute any accusations. Couldn't defend herself.

Despite what had happened, Albert was determined to keep to his routine so he didn't go off on one. He couldn't get angry at her anymore, so was at a loss on what to do, but

God, was he angry. What was she like, getting herself killed like that? He'd taught her about keeping safe, but she clearly hadn't remembered a thing he'd said.

Yet conversely, he enjoyed it when she slipped up and had to be reprimanded. She'd certainly slipped up last night, yet his anger had nowhere to go; he couldn't take it out on her. She wasn't here for him to slap about, so that fury would have to be directed at someone else when the time was right.

Albert planned to save it all for Toby.

That man deserves a fist in the gob.

Mrs Glynn, the woman who owned the shop, had given Albert a look of sympathy when he'd gone up to her counter to collect the magazine, but she hadn't breathed a word to him about Maureen. It was obvious she knew — there were coppers everywhere, and one was currently at the bar talking to the new landlord, Ian Sykes.

Likely checking whether I was in here last night.

Albert had had plenty of opportunity to kill Maureen over the years, God knew she deserved it at times, but he'd never gone down that dark path. If he had, he'd have had no one to bully, no one to make his meals, do his washing, open her legs for him. He'd moved to Marlford from Worksop fifty years ago to distance himself from a woman he'd almost strangled to death in a blind rage because she wouldn't behave, and he'd promised himself he'd be a bit savvier in future, keep everything behind closed doors. And he had. Maureen had been the perfect woman in that regard, hiding whatever he'd done to her. He'd taught her to obey him, to be cruel to people he disliked so she'd bear the brunt of their hatred instead of him, and life had been good.

Until now.

There was washing in the laundry basket in the bedroom, and he had no idea how to work the machine. She'd lied, saying she was up to date with her chores — one of the stipulations for him letting her go away for the night. She'd have known he'd check and find out she'd fibbed, anticipated the punch he'd give her for bullshitting him when she got back. He should have stopped letting her go to Gloria's years ago. It was one privilege too many. That would have been a lesson to her.

Hindsight.

Albert returned his attention to the magazine. Those drug users had made the headlines again. What was it they took? Spice? Gone were the days when only weed was on offer. Albert had smoked a fair few reefers in his younger days, before he'd met Maureen — he'd blamed the dope for the strangulation episode. These kids today, taking that stuff so they wandered around like zombies half the time, it was a disgrace. Seemed the police were doing bugger all, as usual.

The door opened, drawing his attention.

Wilf came in and made a beeline for Albert. "The police have been to ours. Hang on while I get a coffee."

Albert waited for him, his stomach knotting. Maybe the police were speaking to everyone in the village. It would make sense. But if not, had they gone to Wilf's because he lived next door to Toby and they suspected it was him? Toby had told him once that he'd take Maureen away from him; the words had been muttered one night in this very pub. Had he meant permanently? Had he bided his time all these years?

It got Albert to thinking whether Toby and Maureen had been seeing each other behind his back. Toby had sounded quite sure he'd succeed in reclaiming what he thought was his. After all, Maureen had had no trouble going behind Toby's back years ago, so she'd had it in her to be deceitful. As proved by the big secret Albert and his wife had shared. Yes, she'd been deceitful, all right.

He wanted to belt her. Clobber her senseless for putting these thoughts in his head. It aggravated him that there was no one to answer to his questions. He'd have to ask Toby, and that would sting, dent his pride.

Fuck's sake.

Wilf came back and sat opposite. "Sorry to hear about Maureen. Anna told us what happened. What are you doing in here? You should be at home."

"I like to stick to my routine, you know that."

"I bloody wouldn't. I'd be right upset if it was my Yvonne."

"Well, it isn't, and no two people grieve the same way, so keep your opinions to yourself."

"I was only saying . . ."

Albert glared at him. "What else did Anna talk about?"

"She asked what time Toby got home last night. He was out on one of his walks."

"What time *did* he get back?"

"Nine or so. He went round Vernon's field, same as always, so she said. I didn't see him from my attic window like I usually do, though."

"You and your bloody train set. Fancy playing with toys at your age." A touch of jealousy tinged Albert's words. To have a whole attic kitted out and be able to go up there for hours, shoving life away, would be bliss. He'd been too focused on keeping Maureen in line to do something like that, and he'd always resented her for it. If she'd behaved properly, he could have had some time to himself.

Wilf's mouth dropped open — God, he was offended, the big baby. "Sod off."

Albert narrowed his eyes, already mentally and emotionally moving on from that conversation. Trains and attics, Maureen's recalcitrance, something to think about another day. "So, Toby was around when Maureen copped it."

"Yep."

"Did Anna say if he heard anything?"

"No."

Frustration bubbled. Albert didn't like not being in control, and right now someone else was at the wheel, steering his life. "He must have."

Wilf shrugged. "Not necessarily. If he was at the bottom of the field, he's not likely to have heard sod all, is he?"

45

"But she'd have screamed, had to have done."

"Maybe it sounded like an animal."

Albert couldn't dispute that. Many a night creature let out weird noises. "She was battered with a pole." He'd shocked him. Feeling smug, he sucked in his bottom lip, then let it pop back out again. "A *walking stick*, I reckon."

Wilf's face dropped. "Oh. Shit."

"Yeah, oh shit."

"Now you mention it, I did see the bloke Anna was with put some things in the back of her car. Think his name's Benny."

"It's Lenny."

"Right. Two coppers in uniform came to collect it all and then drove off."

"What things?"

Now Wilf looked smug. "Cane-shaped things."

Albert's anger raged. "There you go, then. Toby said he'd take her away from me, and he's bloody gone and done it."

"You can't go around accusing him." Wilf blew on his coffee.

"I bleedin' can. Why would they need to take stuff from his house if he wasn't anything to do with it?"

"Dunno. Anna asked if we'd been out last night, wondered if we'd seen a car with a woman driver. Said she's under fifty. Maybe it was her who did it. Maureen had a tongue on her. She could have pissed umpteen people off."

Albert shook his head. "Sorry, I don't buy it. Toby of all people happens to be out walking when she's attacked? Come off it, pal."

"I see your point, but you're better off keeping your thoughts about Toby to yourself. Let Anna deal with it. She's a good copper, she is."

"Hmm, we'll see. What else do you know?"

"Not a lot." Wilf held up a hand and waggled it towards the bar. "Excuse me," he called to the PC, "can we have a word?"

The officer came over, all imposing gaze and clipped mouth. "What's the issue?"

"This is Maureen's husband. Anna's already been to see him and me. We were wondering if you had any news."

"Nothing as yet, I'm afraid."

"A load of old bollocks," Albert muttered. "You're probably not allowed to say." He waved him off.

The PC sighed and returned to the bar.

"A fat lot of good he is," Albert said. "I wonder who found her."

"Anna didn't tell you?"

"No. It might have been Toby, going back to the scene of the crime."

"Nah, he's been in all morning. I heard him pottering about in his workshop."

"I bet he's been planning this for years. He's been going for his evening walks in that field so word gets round that's what he does, so it wouldn't look weird if he was out there when Maureen was killed."

"He's got to be a bloody patient man if he can wait that long. I remember when Maureen finished with him. It was fifty years ago!"

"Yeah, well, I'm here as proof you can hold a grudge for years. I can't stand the bastard."

"Fair enough."

They drank their coffees for a while, Albert mulling everything over. He'd get back at Toby at some point, but he had to plan it right. Bumping him off now, when Maureen had only just passed away — well, it would be suspicious, and fingers would be pointing straight at him. No, he could play the long game, too, and he would. One day, when all this had died down, he'd get rid of the thorn in his side once and for all.

I should have done it years ago.

CHAPTER SIX

Toby had been on tenterhooks ever since Wilf had gone out
alone earlier. Had he been told to go into Marlford police
station and give a statement? No, he hadn't taken his car, he'd
walked — without the dog.

Mr Baggins clawed at Toby's leg, sinking his talons into
his skin.

"Ouch! You spiteful little . . ."

He quickly left the living room and fed the cat to stop
it attacking him further, then returned to the front window
and stood behind the net curtains. Two PCs had come half
an hour ago, and currently they were speaking to the neighbours at their front doors. Hilda, on the other side of Wilf's
house, trotted past dragging her blue polka-dot shopping trol-
ley behind her, off on her usual yearly trip to the Christmas
market. She'd be getting the bus — if it was still running.

The police might have cordoned the road off near the lay-by.

The slam of a door drew his attention to the right. At
last, Yvonne was off out with their dog, the yappy Florence,
an ankle-biting Yorkshire terrier that barked at Mr Baggins
every time the cat jumped over the low dividing fence to prowl
their back garden. Wilf and Yvonne usually walked Florence

round the village, and it took them over an hour because they stopped and spoke to all and sundry, so Toby had heard.

He waited for her to go out of sight, then looked at the officers. One of them was getting into a police car, the other trying to extract himself from Elizabeth Kettering, her with the recent blue rinse — she liked a good gossip, that one. He wished she'd shut her mouth for once so the man could leave. Anna must have let them know she'd spoken to Toby and Wilf, as neither of them had knocked on their door.

"Let him go," he muttered. "Bloody woman."

Finally, the PC waved at her and then joined his colleague in the car. It drove off, and Toby breathed a sigh of relief, although it was soon eclipsed by the enormity of the task ahead.

After changing from his slippers to his gardening Crocs, he dashed out the back and took his small wheelbarrow from the shed. He hauled it over the fence. Since no one was at home in their row of three houses, he didn't have to worry about being watched. Tall trees at the bottom of their gardens shielded their homes from the cul-de-sac behind, so he was all right there an' all.

Toby collected the little set of steps from his workshop. Stepladders always brought back memories of the past, an incident he hadn't seen but had been told about in confidence. He shuddered and climbed over the fence, then lifted the steps over for when he had to go back the other way. He pushed the wheelbarrow to the rockery; it had so many pebbles in it they wouldn't be missed. He quickly but quietly placed them in the wheelbarrow so they didn't clunk on the metal base. Once he'd filled it, it occurred to him that he wasn't sure how he was going to get it back over the fence. It would be heavy.

"Sodding heck."

He pushed it there, frustrated that the wheels had created lines in the grass; he used the soles of his Crocs to smooth them out. At the fence, he tossed the pebbles over, sweating and out of breath by the time he'd chucked the last one.

49

Wheelbarrow, steps and Toby now back in his garden, he filled the barrow again and took it down the side of his house to the door that led to his kitchen. There, shielded by the high fence on the alley side, another thought slapped him. All those pebbles, plus the tarpaulin package inside the black sack, would likely rip the bag because of the weight.

He stared at the sky. "God, help me out here, will you?"

He huffed off inside, went upstairs to his bedroom and fetched a suitcase from the top of his wardrobe. Thank the Lord it wasn't one of those hard-shell ones but material. The water in Jubilee Lake would soon penetrate it, dragging it to the bottom, where it would hopefully stay forever, or at least until after he'd died. It wasn't like he'd care about getting caught by then.

He took it outside, filled it with pebbles and added the tarpaulin and its contents. He zipped it up and wheeled it into his workshop ready for tonight when it got dark. He had no intention of putting it in his boot now. With the police around, people were bound to be nosing out of their windows. Elizabeth would have seen Anna and Lenny coming to his house, so she'd be keeping an eye out, or maybe she'd be on the phone, ringing her cronies to spread gossip. She might have seen Lenny putting the evidence bags in the boot, *and* those PCs arriving to collect them.

Not for the first time, he cursed living in a village where everyone thought they knew your business. It didn't do a murderer any favours.

But then again, not everyone *knows what goes on around here. The stories I could tell . . .*

CHAPTER SEVEN

At the Cribbins chocolate factory, Peter Dove put on an outfit that reminded him of forensic gear, except he had to cover his bald head with a hat much like a shower cap instead of the usual hood. He was glad to have Warren Yates with him, because he had a feeling the other DC on the team, Sally Wiggins, was watching him, listening to everything he said.

Or maybe that was his paranoia.

He'd been nervous ever since he'd got into Trigger's car outside the Horse's Hoof, the pub the police drank in after work. Two men had been smoking outside, and Peter was convinced they'd been observing him. He'd passed on his concerns to Trigger, who'd thought up a convenient excuse: he was giving up an ex-King. But Peter didn't think Anna had bought the story, even though drugs had been found at Smithy's gaff. Every day at work he sensed eyes on him, but hopefully, since Trigger had told him to steer clear of any King work for six months, whoever was watching him would get bored and he'd be home and dry.

"Smells bloody lush in here," Warren said.

Peter brought his attention back to the job and smiled at Bruce Cribbins, who'd insisted they enjoy a tour of the factory first. Why hadn't he retired yet? Was he a control freak who couldn't stand to pass over the reins? The man had no idea Peter ran with the Kings, his grandson wouldn't have told him — or, if he *did* know, he'd chosen not to make it obvious in front of Warren.

Joshua, known as Parole because of his many stints in prison, had told Bruce he'd left the gang, but he hadn't. As a bribe to keep Parole on the straight and narrow, Bruce had bought him a posh apartment in Westgate next to Jubilee Lake and showered him with money and a nice red Porsche. Parole's antics with the Kings would look bad for business, and if he didn't toe the line he wouldn't be inheriting anything. So he did his dealings for the gang quietly, determined not to get caught.

The old man would have a heart attack if he found out Parole had been lying through his teeth this whole time. Peter shrugged, deciding he didn't give much of a shit, to be honest. What he *did* care about was keeping his own nose clean. He'd told Trigger he wanted to leave the Kings, knowing that, when you took the pledge to join them, you were in it for life whether you liked it or not. It had all been getting too much, straddling the two camps, and he'd realised he preferred belonging to the police over the gang. Still, Trigger had spoken, and rather than suffer an "accident" Peter had chosen to enjoy the six months' reprieve.

Not that he could enjoy it when he thought he was being followed.

Once again, he snapped himself out of his head and got back into work mode. Warren and Bruce must have been talking while Peter had zoned out, as a decision had been made to move on from the dressing area to the factory floor. He endured the lesson on how the chocolate was created, and by the time they got to the packing bay he was fit to burst. Anna would wonder why they'd taken so long, leaving only Sally behind to look into Toby Potter and Albert Frost.

Why didn't I say no to the bloody tour?

Because Warren wanted one. Thinks his name's Charlie and he's got a golden ticket, the twat.

At last, Bruce took them to his office. He sat behind his big mahogany desk and gestured for them to take the wing-back chairs opposite. Peter's sore back appreciated the comfort. He'd tweaked it playing squash with Warren.

So his mind didn't go off on another wander, Peter took charge. "Thank you for the tour, but we need to ask a few questions regarding an investigation. I realise you've seen many people come and go here over the years and—"

"Are you suggesting we have a high staff turnover because of the working conditions? Because I can assure you that's not the case. Who's been talking? Or lying, should I say."

Stunned by Bruce's brusque outburst, Peter blinked a few times to digest it. To think of an appropriate answer instead of sniping back. "Um, no, what I meant was just that, people leave their jobs for whatever reason, and what I was *going* to say was that you might not remember them all." *Now he'll think I'm having a dig at his age.*

"I remember every single person who's worked here." Bruce sat up straight and rolled his shoulders. "Who do you need to ask about?"

"Maureen and Albert Frost. Toby Potter."

"Ah, yes."

A flicker of something Peter couldn't determine swept over Bruce's face, then it was gone.

Bruce adopted a poker face. "I found it harder when I first took over from my father to admonish people around the same age as me, and I recall a to-do between Albert and Toby that meant I had to read them the riot act. No fights at work. There's the machinery to consider, accidents should one of them have slipped, not to mention discord between staff. They come here to work, not settle scores with one another. Whatever happens outside here must be left at the door."

"What was it about?"

"Maureen had ended her relationship with Toby and went off with Albert instead. A bad decision, in my opinion. Put it this way, Albert isn't the easiest person to get along with. Let me just access the files. I had the paperwork typed up on the computer when we entered the digital age." He clicked his mouse and peered at his monitor. "Ah yes, here we are. Toby came in that particular morning and had it out with Albert — I heard second-hand from one of the line managers who'd seen and heard the altercation, plus several witnesses. There was the usual posturing about one's penis being larger than the other's — a verbal retaliation after Toby accused Albert of thieving from the factory. Albert threw a punch, Toby dived out of the way, and that was the end of the spat."

"Did it continue after that, though?" Peter asked. "A grudge?"

"Oh yes, but, like I said, discord isn't tolerated. They threw dark looks at each other from time to time, Maureen included, but as that didn't affect their work, I left it at that."

"You said you had to read the riot act. How did that go down?"

Peter had the last murder case in mind. One by one, Matthew Brignell had been bumping off people who'd upset him, and who was to say Toby or Albert wouldn't do the same? Bruce could be next on the list. Peter had done a quick check on the database before they'd come to the factory, but he hadn't met either of the other men and, only knowing they were getting on in age, he couldn't say whether they'd be strong enough to batter someone to death; but you never knew.

Bruce folded his arms and leaned back. "I told them off for arguing, said I wouldn't stand for it, then I kept Albert back to have a word about the theft accusation. It's true, some of our product *had* been stolen after he'd started work here, but it wasn't him. I'd been keeping my eye on someone else and eventually caught her in the act. Do you need to know who she is?"

Not really, but Peter sensed he should go with the flow. Bruce didn't appear the type to not get his own way.

"That might be handy, yes."

"Elizabeth Kettering. She left here with no one knowing it was her. I promised to keep it quiet, and even paid her wages. She'd been selling the goods on so she could feed her two small children. Her husband had died, and she was struggling. I'm not the ogre some people would have you believe."

Is he referring to Parole? "So with Toby accusing Albert in front of witnesses, and you keeping it quiet that it was Kettering, were the witnesses left to believe it was Albert?"

"I suppose they might have done."

Peter frowned. Was Kettering even relevant? Not unless Maureen knew she was the thief, had kept the secret for years and then recently spilled the beans. Would Kettering batter another woman with a pole?

Was it worth looking into this? Paying her a visit?

Peter glanced at Warren, who didn't seem to get the gist that he wanted him to message Anna and tell her about Kettering. God, he'd have do it himself in a minute.

"Why all these questions about something that happened years ago?" Bruce asked.

"Unfortunately, Maureen's been murdered."

Bruce slumped forward, his hands smacking onto the desk, his chin to his chest. Warren shot up, likely thinking the man was having a heart attack, but Bruce eased back, one hand on his chest, and waved him away.

"Good God, what a shock." He breathed deeply a couple of times. "Well, that changes things."

"What does?" Warren loitered close to Bruce.

"Sit down, man," Bruce barked. "I'm not about to keel over." He looked at Peter. "When did this happen? With Maureen?"

"Last night, as far as we're aware."

"And where was she killed?"

"In a lay-by just outside Upton-cum-Studley. She was on her way to see her sister."

"That's where you're wrong," Bruce sighed. "She was coming to see me."

CHAPTER EIGHT

Once a year, on the anniversary of when their affair had begun forty-five years ago, Maureen had met up with Bruce. Her sister had kept the subterfuge to herself all this time, and Albert never found out. So Maureen could, for one night, enjoy the company of a man who loved her.

Bruce couldn't have kept that hidden, not now. The knowledge that she was dead burned a great big hole in his psyche, and his chest ached for what could have been if they'd only gone with their hearts, left their respective partners and set up home together. They'd kept their affair a secret, obviously, because Albert might have harmed her more than he usually did, and Bruce's wife had been a frail thing when she'd been alive and he hadn't wanted to upset her or their children. Besides, Bruce had loved Dulcie, he'd just been unable to stay away from Maureen, that's all. So a yearly dalliance it had been, the one indulgence they allowed themselves. All other times, while Maureen had still been working at the factory, they'd remained as boss and employee, and no one was any the wiser.

At least, that's what he'd thought.

But what if Albert had finally found out — or worse, Maureen had blurted it to him last night? She'd told Bruce about what she'd had to put up with during her marriage, although "had to" didn't sit right with him. She could have left Albert. Bruce had even offered her money to get away, to create a new identity so she could hide, but she'd declined.

What if Albert had turned on her, killed her in that lay-by?

"Coming to see *you*?" Peter asked.

Bruce wished that other man, Warren, would stop staring at him like that. Yes, the news had shocked Bruce, broken him, and perhaps Warren had thought he needed assistance, but surely he could see he was all right now. On the outside. Inside was another matter. It was like losing Dulcie all over again. The second love of his life was gone. How would he get through this?

He cleared his throat. "Um, we stayed at a hotel once a year."

"Why?"

Bruce's cheeks warmed. "Do I need to spell it out?"

"Oh, for sex?"

"That, and just to be together for a few hours." Bruce explained about their affair. "I didn't want to jeopardise Maureen's safety. Albert can be aggressive. My wife's dead now, so it won't hurt her, but I suppose it will lower the rest of my family's estimation of me if this has to become public knowledge. I had to say something, given the circumstances, otherwise I'd never have breathed a word. I promised Maureen I wouldn't."

"What did you think when she didn't arrive?"

"I assumed Albert had come up with some reason as to why she couldn't go. I'm surprised he let her stay overnight every year anyway. I couldn't phone her to check in, and he might've seen any messages. She couldn't trust herself to remember to delete them, and if they came in while he was there he'd want to know who they were from. He ruled her, every aspect of her life. The only thing she had for herself was her supposed visit to the Christmas market with her sister, Gloria, when she was, in fact, staying with me at the Spencer hotel in York."

"Did you stay there last night?"

"Yes, I waited up for her until past midnight. I left early this morning, around seven, and came straight here, so yes, I have an alibi. I ate dinner in their restaurant, spent some time in the bar afterwards. Obviously, check if you need to."

Peter smiled. "We will. Is there anyone you know who may have wanted to kill Maureen? We're trying to establish whether it was a random attack to steal her car — it had been stolen and was found burnt out earlier this morning — or if it was someone she knew."

"Only Albert. She never told me of anyone else."

"What about Toby?"

Bruce laughed. "Err, no. He wouldn't harm a hair on her head." *Wouldn't bloody dare.* "He's been in love with her for years. She loved him, too, once. He was good to her when they were together. Then Albert came along, the big brash type some women prefer, and she fell for him."

"And then you."

"Yes, but it didn't start off like that. She'd been weepy at work — she was in a different section to Albert, so he wouldn't have seen her crying — and I was concerned for her welfare. Being a boss, you have to look after the staff. We chatted, and it all came tumbling out, how she'd made a mistake with Albert but she was stuck with him."

He wasn't about to go into great detail. The burden of Maureen's story had always weighed heavy on him, but he didn't have it in him to bring it out into the open now, even if it *would* get Albert into trouble. He didn't want her memory ruined, although it might be if news of their affair came out.

He continued. "I suggested she wasn't stuck with him, she could leave, but she said could *never* leave. She said Albert would try to find her, punish her when he did. There were several chats in my office over a period of weeks, and one day

59

she cried so much I got up to cuddle her. We kissed, and it went from there. Nothing sordid, it was a genuine connection between two people who happened to be married. I shall miss her dearly."

"So you'd point the finger at Albert, then?"

"He's the only one I can imagine losing his temper enough for her death to be the outcome. Of course, if her car was stolen, it *could* be kids. They killed her by accident when they tried to get the keys off her." The scenario played out in Bruce's mind and he winced. "Just dreadful."

After a few more questions, the officers rose to leave. Bruce showed them to a staffroom where they could take their protective clothing off, gave them boxes of complimentary chocolates, as he always did with guests, and then ushered them out of the building, relieved to see them go.

As a last parting shot, Peter had mentioned DI Anna James may want to question him further. He grimaced at having to speak about the affair as though it had been a dirty thing, something to stay buried. Perhaps it was finally the right time to dig up the past and bring it all out into the open air.

CHAPTER NINE

"You stupid fucking cow! What did you think, I wouldn't notice your gut getting bigger? Did you reckon you could get right to the end and have the kid and by then I wouldn't have a choice in the matter? Well, let me tell you, I'd have killed the little fucker, made it look like an accident, even if it took me months."

Maureen cringed away from Albert. When he was like this, it only meant one thing, and, as she'd **really** deceived him this time, breaking the biggest rule, God knew what he'd do to her.

She'd committed a mortal sin. Getting pregnant.

"I didn't know what to do," she said.

"Do? You go down to that woman in Marlford who gets rid of them, that's what you do. What's her name? Needle Nelly. You get it done as soon as you miss your monthlies, you don't carry on as if it isn't happening. Jesus wept, I told you I didn't want babies when we first started seeing each other, and you said it was fine, but as soon as we got married, what did I hear? 'Please let me have one, please.' There's no negotiating here. I said no and I mean no."

"But I'm too far along now."

"You're not."

The swift punch to the stomach shouldn't have been a surprise, he regularly beat her, and she — perhaps insanely — wanted to be the one

61

to fix whatever demons lived inside his mind, to change him, make him love her properly, so she took whatever he dished out. It had been a hard couple of years since they'd married, and she wanted him to go back to being the man he'd been when she'd met him. If she'd just behave herself, follow his rules, he might return to his old ways.

But something inside **told** her to disobey him. The thrill of it was a disease she didn't understand but gladly carried around with her.

I'm broken. Not right.

Pain lanced her tummy, and he hit her again until she went down to her knees, her arms over her bump to protect it. He kicked her, and she fell onto her side, trying to roll away from him so the strikes would land on her back. He bent and wrenched her towards him, kicking some more, one harsh wallop to her lower abdomen creating an agony she'd never felt before.

He backed off for a moment, breathing heavily, then gripped her wrist. Hauled her to her feet. Pulled her in close. "Let this be yet another lesson to you."

Wetness seeped between her legs. Oh God. He'd hurt the baby. A gush gave way, trickling down her legs, and she knew. It was over. Her plan to get him to love a baby once he saw it had failed. She stared down. Blood and her waters mixed together on the floor, soaking into the carpet. A sharp slice of pain wrapped around her middle, griping, squeezing.

"There, I've sorted it. And don't even think about pulling this stunt again, because the same thing will happen."

And despite that, Maureen knew she'd ignore him.

Again.

CHAPTER TEN

In the village, while talking to Tom Quant, the scene sergeant, Anna had received an enlightening call from Peter. So Bruce Cribbins had been having a decades-long affair with Maureen, had he? Anna had given Peter the go-ahead to contact the Spencer hotel to check Bruce had, in fact, been there, but a tiny *what-if* niggled at her.

Bruce supposedly didn't know what Parole was up to with the Kings, but what if he knew more than he was letting on? Could he have ordered Parole to kill Maureen? Bruce was fanatical about his reputation. Perhaps she'd threatened to expose their affair and he'd arranged it to look like she'd been killed in a carjacking. That would need an accomplice, though, if the thief had come by in their own vehicle. Someone else would have had to drive hers away.

Really?

Anna was always looking for the unexpected before it had a chance to smack her in the face. Her favourite TV show as a child was *Scooby-Doo*, and she'd be the first to admit she perhaps modelled herself, just a little, on the character Velma, who always thought things through to the nth degree and discovered snippets the others missed.

Sadly, she had to concede that this particular theory didn't fit. Bruce had freely admitted to the affair despite the potential fallout, and he wouldn't have done that if he wanted it to remain hidden.

Unless he knew it would come out at some point, so had no alternative but to tell Peter and Warren about it.

Anna struggled with the familiar annoying feeling that she was tying herself in knots — tying the *case* in knots, muddying the waters when she didn't need to.

As she was already in the village, it wouldn't hurt to nip over and see Elizabeth Kettering, then they'd pop to Hawthorn Farm and question Robert and Diana. Uniforms had already been there to check if they'd seen or heard anything, but Anna wanted to ask them herself. She liked to look beyond first impressions, to poke further. Things usually lurked beneath the surface. These people were all in the same age bracket, and the older you got the more secrets you had to keep.

Was that what had happened? Were Bruce, Elizabeth, Maureen, Albert, Robert and Diana close friends? Had they *all* worked at the chocolate factory? Were they hiding something, and had Maureen threatened to expose them? Was that why Bruce had let Elizabeth leave the factory without involving the police — because he *owed* her for something?

Tom sighed. "No one in the village owns a black car, can you believe that?"

"I'd have thought it would be a popular colour," Lenny said.

"Not here. It's all silvers and whites, a few reds. Karen scanned for any dark blues and greys just in case, but nothing. She's also cross-checked residents' ages against all vehicles, and the only people in their fifties are two couples who live next door to each other in the same row of cottages as Albert Frost — sisters and their husbands."

Lenny frowned. "But Toby said he couldn't gauge ages under fifty, so she could have been forty, thirty, twenty, even."

64

"And she might only have been passing through, going into the city," Anna said. "There's the Christmas market, remember. It's a big draw, and people come from all around. Lenny, can you message Sally to get on with narrowing down dark cars and women drivers below fifty in the area."

"The results will be in the thousands," Lenny said. "Aren't we better off appealing for the driver to come forward?"

Anna nodded. "Good shout. I'll ring Placket now."

She wandered off and selected the DCI in her contact list. It rang twice, then his deep tones filled her ear. "Good morning," he said, as if it wasn't at all.

"Sorry to do this over the phone, sir," she said, "but we're out in the field and will be for a while. Upton-cum-Studley. I haven't been able to get back yet to update you — I assume you already know what's going on."

"Sally came to me not long ago."

Anna went on to explain everything, even her Velma-type theories.

Placket grunted. "That sounds like a giant can of worms. You've got several threads to follow there, but you need to be careful you don't get tangled up. Which one tugs at you the hardest?"

"I'm leaning more towards Toby Potter, but maybe that will change once I've been to see Robert and Diana Jobs." *And Parole. He might know something about this.*

"But they may never have worked at the factory, in which case your 'big secret' theory doesn't hold water. If Vernon asked them to mind his farm — which isn't a big deal since he only has pigs and chickens — then surely they'd need *some* experience of keeping animals. Maybe they're former farmers."

"I'll soon find out. I want to keep an open mind."

Placket chuckled. "I should have known."

"What?" she asked, smiling.

"No stone left unturned when it comes to you. Okay, was there anything else?"

"What I originally rang for is to ask if you can get an appeal going. You wouldn't have to show your face on the telly, just send a line or two to the TV, newspapers, radio, and stick something up on social media. Sally's going to have her work cut out for her trying to find the driver of that car."

"You know not everyone will see or hear the appeal."

"Yes, but it's worth a shot."

"I'll see what I can do. Right, I'll let you get on."

His way of telling her he was busy. Anna said her good-byes, and slipped her phone into her pocket on the way back to Tom and Lenny.

Tom raised his eyebrows. "Sorted?"

"Yes, thankfully. Okay, me and Lenny are going to speak to Elizabeth Kettering, then Robert and Diana Jobs." She held a hand up. "I know uniform have already spoken to them, but indulge me."

Tom nodded. "You'll have your reasons, as usual. See you when I see you." He wandered off towards two PCs.

In the car, Anna clipped her seat belt in and twisted to Lenny. "So we're on the same page . . ." She let him in on her thoughts as they drove.

"I get you, and it's better to cross all of your theories off the list than get bitten on the arse later down the line. Let's get it done so we can go back to the station and hash things out with the others."

Elizabeth Kettering was a terribly skinny woman, Anna thought. She stood in all her blue-haired glory talking to her next-door neighbour over the dividing hedge in her front garden. Beige cardigan over a white blouse. Navy trousers. Pink slippers.

Elizabeth's shoulders sagged when Anna and Lenny got out of the car. Was she worried they'd bring up the theft? Did she think that Anna wouldn't hear about it?

She'll soon understand that skeletons have a habit of falling out of closets just when you think the doors are firmly shut.

"Can we have a chat indoors?" Anna asked her.

Elizabeth nodded and turned to her front door, which stood ajar. "I'll speak to you later, Joyce."

The neighbour turned to her own house. Going by the swift look Joyce sent Elizabeth's way, Anna got the distinct sense the women were good friends. They appeared to be around the same age, although Joyce had settled for natural grey hair.

In Elizabeth's warm but dated-looking kitchen, the woman turned to the Aga to put an old-fashioned kettle on to boil, a brass effort with a swan-neck spout and a large whistle on the end. The handle looked fancy. It reminded her of the carving on the front of Toby's cane stand — it was the same pattern.

"Toby's work?" Anna sat at the scar-topped pine table.

Elizabeth pointed to the handle but still faced away from them. "That? Yes. The kettle was my mother's, and it still works fine. The old handle split, so Toby fixed it for me."

"Do you know him well?"

"I used to work at the factory with him, back in the day."

No one around here needed to ask if she'd meant Cribbins — it was the only factory for a fair few miles.

Elizabeth took cups off a wooden mug tree. The cups may also have belonged to her mother, as they were bone china if Anna was any judge, and the painted pink roses on the sides spoke of days gone by, as did the pile of six matching saucers to the side. "I left there a long time ago, but we still kept in touch. He only lives over the road, so . . . Anyway, what can I help you with?"

The woman kept her back to them, and Anna grew increasingly annoyed. The coffees she'd drunk so far had only shaved off the edge of her irritation; she hadn't had her usual strong shot from Brunch, the café in Marlford. With no kids to pay out for, she could afford to indulge, yet she always felt bad for those who couldn't.

"Come and sit down," she said.

Elizabeth stiffened for a second, but turned and sat. She folded her hands in her lap, her cheeks pinkening in the middle.

The woman may be worrying about her past being dragged up, but sometimes parts of people's lives, parts they'd thought long buried, got the devil in them and popped up in their futures. Like now.

"Could you just humour me a second?" Anna said, aware the question she was about to ask might be way off base, but if she didn't ask it now she'd drive herself mad with supposition. "You, Bruce, Maureen, Albert, Robert and Diana. Have you all been close over the years?"

Elizabeth flushed. "Bruce was my boss and nothing more. I used to be friends with Maureen until Albert came along and put a stop to that. Well, a little while after they married. As for Robert and Diana, yes, I know them pretty well. They were at the factory all their working lives. I made friends with them as a child because they lived down the road. We all went to school together."

So they're not farmers. "And they're good friends with Vernon Brignell, I assume, if they're looking after his farm."

"I would think so." Elizabeth shuddered.

Was she recalling the fact that Vernon's first wife, Wilma, had been buried in the corner of his potato field? The recent discovery had been all over the news.

"Is that why Vernon chose them to run the farm? Because they're friends?"

"Probably. He must trust them."

Anna got back to the main point. "So, all of you, you weren't friends?"

"No."

That put her theory firmly to bed, then.

"What about Toby?"

"Toby I chat to if we're both out the front or in the Jubilee, and, like I said, he fixed the kettle handle."

"Were you aware of the situation between him and Albert and Maureen? Back in the seventies?"

Elizabeth's eyes lit up. "Of course."

"You said you were friends with Maureen. Did she ever confide in you regarding Toby and Albert?"

Elizabeth nodded. "She was quieter back then. Albert changed her into . . . well, into a spiteful woman, although maybe it wasn't him per se but her situation. I had a feeling she'd turned bitter because of what she'd got herself into. From what I could see, Albert ruled her."

The kettle whistled, and Lenny got up to move it off the burner. Elizabeth didn't appear to be in any rush to make them a brew, so Anna ploughed on.

"What was her relationship like with Toby, before she left him?"

"They were a perfect match. My husband died when I was young, I was on my own with two kids and only one wage, and I would have given my eye teeth for a man like Toby. He worshipped the ground she walked on, yet she threw it all away. I told her she was making a mistake, that to be with a man like him was her best bet — you know, steady, dependable. But she snapped at me and said she was bored. Toby was *too* steady, *too* dependable, she wanted some excitement. I suppose with Albert being confident and whatever, she thought he'd give her a more eventful life. Instead, she got beaten up, I'm sure of it. She had bruises on her face sometimes, *and* on her wrists in the shape of fingertips. I asked her if she was being abused, but she barked at me to mind my own business."

"So you didn't try to get her any help?"

"You didn't do that in those days. You did whatever your husband said, and anyone who had a feeling something was going on tended to stay out of it." Elizabeth closed her eyes for a moment.

Anna couldn't imagine it, everyone following that road, putting up with your lot even when it was clear you shouldn't, and outsiders choosing not to get involved because that was what society dictated. That said, there were plenty of people even today who'd turn a blind eye if their neighbour was being assaulted.

"Do you know of anyone who'd want to hurt Maureen?"

"Hurt, yes. Plenty. As I said, she turned spiteful. She was nasty to so many people, always after Albert gave her a nudge. I swear he was telling her to say things on purpose, like he got enjoyment out of it."

"Do any names spring to mind?"

Elizabeth seemed to struggle with her answer. Maybe she'd include herself on that list. "Oh, it's just villagers. Loads of people will have a story to tell about how Maureen spoke to them. You'll find she wasn't well liked."

Anna would have to check in with Tom on that as he hadn't mentioned anything of the sort. Maybe the residents didn't want to speak ill of the dead. It wouldn't help the investigation if they were holding back.

"And Albert, of course," Elizabeth said. "I told Maureen a year or so after she married him, just before she cut our friendship off for good, that he'd do something to her he couldn't undo, but she wouldn't have it. Said I didn't know what I was talking about. But I do. My dad used to beat my mother, and he went too far one day. She died as a result of her injuries."

"Did he serve time in prison for it?"

"No, he was a coward and hanged himself." Elizabeth shifted her gaze away and twiddled her fingers.

Did something dodgy go on there, or was it just a painful time?

It never failed to surprise Anna how almost everyone she spoke to had some trauma, no matter how small, which they hid from public view years down the line, going about their lives with a brave face. Anna's childhood had been close to perfect, she didn't have any skeletons to speak of, so when people revealed theirs it fascinated her how she'd escaped such things.

"I'm sorry to hear that. Did you ever confide any big secrets to Maureen when you were good friends?"

Elizabeth looked alarmed. "What do you mean?"

Why so jumpy? "Was there anything she kept secret for you?"

"No."

"So there's no chance of her telling anyone and you found out?"

The cogs in Elizabeth's mind visibly turned, and her eyes widened. "If you're suggesting she blurted something out and I killed her, you're wrong. I was here all night, nowhere near that lay-by. Joyce will tell you because we spent the evening together playing cards."

Talking of playing cards, Anna revealed her ace, although it might not mean she won the game. "Did Maureen know about the thefts at Cribbins?"

Elizabeth's whole face coloured. "*That* was a long time ago and a mistake. I was desperate. Who told you? Bruce? He promised he'd never let on."

"Just answer the question. *Did* Maureen know it was you? I ask because everyone was left to assume it was her husband, and if she recently found out he'd taken the blame and the suspicious looks, when in fact it had been you . . ."

Going by Elizabeth's face, Anna was barking up the wrong tree.

"Maureen would have come to me direct, I can assure you. And she'd have done it in the Jubilee, in front of everyone to get maximum attention. She didn't, so I can only assume no one knew I'd nicked a few boxes of chocolates."

But there's something else, isn't there, Mrs Kettering? Whether it's linked to this case or not, you've got something to hide.

Anna switched subjects. "Did you see Toby go out for his walk last night?"

"I told you, I was playing cards with Joyce."

"You were out the front when we arrived." Anna knew Elizabeth was the village gossip, everyone in Upton-cum-Studley avoided revealing anything about themselves to her for that reason, and she was probably nattering to Joyce about

Maureen's murder. "Did you see Toby leaving his house after we were there earlier?"

"No." Elizabeth looked at Lenny. "But I saw you taking things from his place and those policemen coming to collect it. Is it Toby? If it is, why are you trying to say it was me?"

Anna had heard enough. Satisfied Elizabeth hadn't attacked Maureen, she stood and thanked her for her time.

Elizabeth gaped at her. "So, are you going to go round saying I did it? Bring up the thefts? Like I said, that was years ago, and it was dealt with between me and Bruce. No one needs to know about it. I don't want people poking into my life."

Why not? Sod it . . . "I suspect being on the other end of gossip isn't as satisfying as being the one to spread it."

Lenny coughed to warn her she'd gone far enough, and looked at the kettle, sighing. He'd probably wanted another coffee. He stood and nudged Anna subtly with his elbow.

"We'll see ourselves out." Anna removed herself from the kitchen and went into the short hallway.

"I can't believe you just said that to me," Elizabeth ranted, her voice betraying a hint of panic.

Anna glanced over her shoulder. The woman scuttled after her, rage contorting her features.

What are you hiding, lady?

"People only get offended when the arrow hits the mark," Anna said. "And to answer your question, no, I don't think it was you who killed Maureen, and no, I'm not going to tell anyone about you nicking chocolates. That information will remain confidential — unless it's linked to Maureen's death and it comes out in trial."

"There you go again, accusing me. Stop it. Just *stop* it."

Anna opened the front door and stepped onto the path. "I didn't accuse you. I'm sorry if you think I did. Maybe that's your guilty conscience talking." *I shouldn't have said that last bit.*

Annoyed at herself for winding the woman up, Anna sat in the car and waited for Lenny.

He got in and glanced at her. "What was *that* all about?"

"There's something she's not telling us."

"I doubt very much she killed Maureen, though."

"I agree with you there."

"So why poke at her?"

Anna didn't answer. She took her phone out and messaged Sally to ask her to see how Elizabeth's husband had died. Just in case. At least if it wasn't a suspicious death, Anna could strike that off her list. But Elizabeth's reaction, her blustery anger at being accused of something, it didn't sit right.

Slipping a few boxes of chocolates into her handbag at the end of a shift wasn't all that woman had done, Anna was sure of it.

CHAPTER ELEVEN

At Hawthorn Farm, Robert and Diana sat on the opposite side of the kitchen table to Anna and Lenny and stared at them blankly. Had they adopted those faces in order to hide something or were they as perplexed by her question as they appeared?

Or am I being Velma again?

Anna repeated what she'd said. "Did you see anyone walking round the field last night?"

Robert blinked, his ruddy complexion possibly from the weather, or maybe too much booze. He was palpably irritated, and clearly didn't want coppers in the farmhouse. "But those policemen have already asked us that."

Anna smiled. "I know, but I'm asking you again."

He glanced at his wife. "We didn't see anything, did we, Diana?"

"No." Diana shook her head. A little too vigorously? "We're good people. We didn't do anything."

Why say that? "I'm sure you are. What were you doing last night?"

Diana lifted a hand to her neck and pinched the baggy, wrinkled skin there. Was it a nervous tic, or did she need to do that as a trigger to remind her not to reveal anything? "We were watching the telly."

"What did you watch?"

Diana shifted her eyes to Robert. Surely she didn't need his help with that. She'd *know* what they'd watched.

"*You* tell me, Diana," Anna said.

"Um, we'd recorded that thing with the policeman in it, the one who played that man who killed all those men."

"*Des*, that was called," Robert said.

"So you watched *Des*," Anna confirmed.

"No, but it was the man who played him," Diana said. "The one we watched, he's a poorly person in it. Something to do with rat poison."

Robert rolled his eyes. "It was *Litvinenko*, and it wasn't rat poison."

"Still poison," Diana mumbled.

Robert folded his arms. "He was ill from polonium-210-induced acute radiation syndrome, as a matter of fact."

Bloody hell, he's a bit of a particular sort, or does he like having one up on his wife? Imagine having to live with someone like that.

Anna gritted her teeth. She needed a wee, and her bladder, along with these two, was becoming a pain.

She recalled her time here questioning Vernon and calculated in her head that the living room faced the wrong way for them to have caught a glimpse of headlights going past or spotting anyone in the field, and that, if they'd had the curtains closed, they'd have been oblivious.

"Did you hear anything? Screaming maybe?" she asked.

"No." Robert shuddered.

"We don't like screaming." His wife shivered. "No, we don't like that at all."

Robert glared at her, and Diana dipped her head.

What the hell is going on here? "How come Vernon asked you to take over Hawthorn? As far as we're aware, you're not farmers."

"Anyone can feed pigs and chickens, muck them out," Robert said. "Vernon explained everything. And the potato crop will be dealt with by some fella who has a farm a few miles away."

"I can't remember his name," Diana said absently. "Do I need to remember it? Is that one of the things on the list?"

"What list?" Anna asked.

"It doesn't matter!" her husband barked. "All we were told to do was deal with the animals and put the eggs on the table, then collect the money." He stared at Anna. "If I'd known we'd be interrogated, I'd have never agreed to do it."

"I wasn't aware I was interrogating," Anna replied.

Diana pinched her neck harder. "But it saves us money, being here. You said it was best all round that we left our cottage and got some tenants in."

Robert bristled. "Anna doesn't need to know the ins and outs. What we're doing in that regard is no one else's business."

"And we didn't like our house after—" Diana stopped at a sharp jab in the ribs from Robert.

"After what?" Anna asked.

"Nothing," Robert said. "She talks gibberish."

Rather than spend any more time with this strange couple, Anna decided the team could look into them instead and see if anything cropped up. But like Elizabeth, they were clearly hiding something.

She rose. "Thank you for speaking to us."

They left the farmhouse, and Lenny went off to wait by the car while Anna walked around the other side of the building to look at the field. The top windows afforded a good view of the crime scene, though, if the couple's claim was the truth, they'd have been downstairs in the living room.

Don't assume. She returned to the front door and banged on it.

Diana answered. "What is it now?"

"Where did you watch telly?"

"In bed."

"Did you get up at any point and glance outside?"

Diana pinched her wrist several times. Another tic? She whispered something that sounded like, *It wasn't us. We didn't do it.*

Robert appeared behind her. "No, she didn't. Please can you go? We need to feed the pigs. Get your wellies on, Diana."

The woman retreated, and Robert shut the door.

Anna went over to Lenny at the car. "Is it just me or . . . ?"

"Nope. They're weird."

"Thought so."

Anna got in the driver's seat and messaged Sally, apologising for sending more work her way but explaining that the team needed to look into Robert and Diana Jobs as well as Elizabeth Kettering.

Lenny got in the passenger seat. "Where to next?"

"Back to Tom."

Anna drove into the village proper and found him in Elizabeth's street along with an ambulance, blue lights flashing. He was talking to Joyce in her front garden.

"What the hell's gone on here?" Lenny muttered.

"Elizabeth's door's open, look."

"Christ, I wonder if *she's* been offed an' all."

"Don't say that! No need to get out. Stay put. Saves you getting cold." Anna met with Tom on the pavement.

He led her away from Joyce and said quietly, "Elizabeth's had a suspected angina attack."

Immediate guilt poked at Anna. "Oh shit. I had a feeling she was hiding something so I let her know, in a roundabout way, that I was on to her. Seems I was right if she got stressed enough to set off her angina. I feel bad now."

"Don't. Gut instincts, we rely on them in this job. And if *you* feel there's something going on, there likely is. You're usually correct. This is on her."

Tom was right, but it still didn't make Anna feel any better.

"I should have taken her age into account." She glanced over at Elizabeth's house as the paramedics were leaving. "Two secs while I see what's going on." She strode over to them. "Are you not taking her to hospital?"

The dark-haired one shook his head. "Turns out it was a panic attack. She's fine now, and she doesn't want to be taken in. We did a quick ECG. Her ticker's working normally."

"We were here questioning her earlier about the murder — have you heard about it?"

"Ollie told us when we stopped at the cordon on the road into the village. Elizabeth mentioned something about someone being dead. Said about a noose, but Ollie told us the woman had been battered. You might want to go back in and question her, although I'd advise you go gently."

"It's okay, I know what the noose relates to."

He nodded.

"Thanks anyway." Anna went over to Joyce, who lingered at her garden gate. "Did you phone for the ambulance?"

Joyce shook her head. "Elizabeth must have. I came out when I saw it arrive. I should go in there, sit with her for a bit."

Anna left her to it and returned to Tom. "Panic attack, not angina. I originally came here to ask you whether any residents gave your officers an insight into how they felt about Maureen. Elizabeth said quite a few people didn't like her."

"No one's reported anything to me, but I'll get the PCs to push more if you like. See whether anyone owns up to disliking her. Some might not, seeing as it'll make us think they're in the frame."

"Okay, cheers." Anna got in the car.

"What's the score?" Lenny asked.

"Panic attack. Brought on by being questioned, I think. I should have been more careful."

"Don't beat yourself up about it. What's on the agenda?"

"We'll go back to the station and chat to Sally. Peter and Warren should be there by now, too. We'll have a natter, see what we come up with between us, then we need to visit Parole."

Lenny's eyebrows rose. "Why?"

78

"Call me paranoid, but for all we know Bruce could have asked his grandson to murder Maureen."

"I doubt it. Parole told us himself he has to behave. Bruce is worried about Parole's shit with the Kings affecting the chocolate factory, so why would he then go and ask him to kill someone?"

"Do you think it's a dead end, then?"

"I do, but if it puts your mind at rest then we may as well go on our way back to the station. If he's even in."

Anna quietly conceded her imagination was in overdrive, and she might only want to visit Parole because, well, it was an excuse to see the magnetic man.

You're playing with fire.

She sighed and drove away.

CHAPTER TWELVE

Toby had been watching the goings-on in his street with alarm. What had happened after Anna and Lenny left the first time? Why did Elizabeth need an ambulance?

His memories from years ago reared their ugly heads again. Toby and Elizabeth had lived in these houses their whole lives. Robert and Diana had also lived here before they'd rented theirs out and moved to the farm. Some young couple were at theirs now — nice enough, kept to themselves.

Back when they'd been teenagers and Elizabeth's mum had died, something hadn't been right. Robert and Diana had gone in there on the day Elizabeth's dad, Jack, had snuffed it, apparently to listen to music in her bedroom. They supposedly hadn't known Jack had hanged himself from the light fitting in the living room while they'd been there, hadn't heard the fitting being wrenched from the ceiling after it had given up bearing the weight of his lifeless body.

The music was too loud, according to them.

Toby had thought it was a likely story at the time, and he'd been proved right in the end. Elizabeth had confided in him as to what had really happened. Had information come to light about it and that was why the police had paid her a visit twice in one day?

Did that mean the investigation into Maureen's death would be overshadowed by something from the past? He hoped so. If Anna wasn't solely focused on Maureen, that could go in his favour.

Anna, Lenny, the ambulance and a copper in uniform had all been and gone now, but Joyce had nipped into Elizabeth's. Whatever was up with the woman couldn't be too bad, else she'd have been taken to hospital. Still, it was intriguing, if annoying — what if Elizabeth had to phone for an ambulance again, say, when Toby was on his way out to dump the suitcase?

Mr Baggins came and sat at his feet, glaring up in attack mode. Toby sighed, wishing he'd never taken the cat in — he was far too much trouble — but did as he'd silently been told and ambled into the kitchen to fetch a pouch of food for his bowl.

He threw the empty packet in the bin, Maureen's crime scene on his mind. Had she been driven away yet? Was she in a fridge by now, waiting for a post-mortem? The not knowing was doing a number on him. If it wasn't for the ambulance, he'd have gone over to Elizabeth's to ask her, she'd be bound to know. All he was left with was the pub, but Anna had warned him not to go there.

Toby didn't like being confined to his home as if under house arrest, and why *should* he hide away from that man? He'd put up with Albert's rubbish for years, so what would one more tirade matter? He might accuse him of killing Maureen, but Toby could brush that off if he chose to. Or he could hurt the man one last time; put his plan in place early.

Getting up-to-date information was more important than cowering at home, so sod it, he was going out.

He brought the suitcase indoors and stowed it in his workshop. Shut Mr Baggins in the kitchen. He put on his outdoor gear and left via the side door, feeling tempted to wander down to the lay-by but steering himself the other way instead. He passed Yvonne and the scraggly Florence, who walked in the opposite direction to their street. He nodded as a greeting and a minute later entered the Jubilee, taking a deep breath and steeling himself for the imminent onslaught from Albert.

The ornery man sat at a table with Wilf, coffee cups and an open copy of *Marlford Views* in front of them. Toby made out he hadn't seen them and approached the bar. He ordered a latte and a bacon sandwich, then cringed at the shout from behind him.

"Of all the things you've done to me, Toby fucking Potter, I'd say murdering my wife is top of the list, wouldn't you?"

Albert's booming voice would have been heard by everyone, just as the prick intended. Toby ignored him and tapped his bank card against the reader as the barmaid gave him a small smile of support. So at least *one* person here didn't think he'd done it.

"Don't act like I'm not talking to you," Albert shouted. "Face me like a man. Oh, I forgot, you're not one. You're a worm."

"Pack it in," Wilf said. "If it was him, they'd have arrested him."

"Not until they've got proof off that stuff they took from his house."

Toby sat on a bar stool and glanced side to side at the other customers in his peripheral. They all stared his way, likely to see when he'd bite. He thought about how he'd respond. In an ideal world, it shouldn't be with anger; he should behave calm and considered, to make Albert look bad, a ranting bully who'd hounded Toby for years. On the other hand, there was satisfaction to be had by spilling a secret he'd kept for too long.

"Got nothing to say?" Albert called. "You can't even look at me, so you must be guilty."

82

Toby turned and made eye contact. "I loved Maureen!"

"Loved her? She wasn't yours to love!"

"I can love whoever I want. Just because she chose you over me, it doesn't mean I can't still care. That's one thing you *don't* have control over — people's emotions. I'm sorry you lost her, but I didn't do it." The devil sat on his shoulder, urging him to drop the bomb. People would expect that of him as he and Albert had been spatting for fifty years. Yes, best to stick to the usual routine. "Some might say it was you. Did you finally find out she was seeing Bruce Cribbins? Lose the plot, did you?"

"*What* did you say?" Albert rose, fists clenched.

"She never went to see Gloria for the Christmas market — ever."

Albert's clenched his jaw, his cheeks red. "How the fuck would *you* know?"

"Because I followed her once." That had come out sounding creepy. "I was going to York and saw her car ahead. I got curious. She went to the Spencer hotel, and Bruce met her outside. They were *kissing*. She was seeing him behind your back." *Feel the pain of that like I did, you bastard.*

"You're lying." Toby's verbal bullet had hit him right where it hurt. Albert's face screwed up in pain. "She'd never do that to me."

Toby shrugged. To be spiteful, he added a lie. "It was common knowledge, apparently. Seems like you were the last to know. You're a cliché."

"I'll fucking kill him."

Wilf gripped Albert's arm. "Calm down, he's just winding you up."

"No, I'm ringing Gloria. I need to tell her Maureen's dead anyway."

He hasn't even had the decency to phone her sister yet?

Albert stormed towards the door, glaring at Toby on his way past, then the door thudded behind him, and conversations erupted, everyone dissecting what had been said.

Wilf picked up his cup and strode over. "Did you have to say that? The man's grieving."

Toby snorted. "He's only mourning the loss of his skivvy and punchbag."

"Is it really true?" Wilf asked quietly. "I mean, Maureen with Bruce? I can't see it myself. Bruce was devoted to Dulcie."

"Yes, it's true. I confronted them about it that night. Promised to keep it a secret. Can you believe it, she'd dumped me for someone else, then expected me to cover for her when she was doing it to her husband? But I did. I loved her. I'd have done anything she asked."

Except that was another lie. He'd been *forced* into keeping the secret.

Or so he liked to tell himself.

CHAPTER THIRTEEN

Toby stood in the shadows outside the Spencer, contemplating whether to approach Maureen and Bruce. Anger burned bright, souring his gut and infecting his mind with thoughts of murder. She was a cheater to her core, had to be. Why was she taking the risk of Albert finding out? Or did she want him to? Had she and Bruce concocted some plan where he'd leave Dulcie and they'd run away together? No, he wouldn't give up the factory. It was his life.

Toby stepped out of the darkness onto the path. "Fancy seeing you two here." The power that surged through him, he'd never felt anything like it.

Bruce and Maureen sprang apart, their expressions clear in the lit doorway. Maureen smirked, as if she enjoyed being caught; then she must have realised it was Toby and thought of the damage he could do, and her face dropped.

"It isn't what you think," she said.

"No? What is it, then? Does your old man know you're here with our boss? What did you tell him, that this is a business meeting?" Toby glanced down at the overnight bag beside her feet. "Ah, a romantic sleepover?"

"Now, now." Bruce tugged at the lapels of his expensive suit jacket, the navy-blue one he swanned around in when he wanted to impress

clients. Was he hoping to impress Maureen? Or had he already done that several times over? "No need to bring Albert into it."

"Why not? He's being cheated on. Like I was. I know how it feels to have your heart ripped out. Are you prepared for that? Because you can bet you're not the only one she's got on the go." That was spiteful, but Toby was hurt. Disgusted.

Maureen's cheeks flared red. So he'd hit the mark, then. Who else was she seeing? This was showing her in a poor light. Despite everything, he'd put her on a pedestal, and he wasn't sure he could cope with her falling off it. That would mean he'd have to face up to her bad side, and he didn't want to. He preferred to keep his memory of her the same as when they'd first started dating.

"What I do is none of your business," Bruce said.

"Same here," Maureen added.

Toby glared at her. "It is when you and your husband keep pecking at me, waiting for me to rise to the bait. I reckon he'd leave me alone if I told him what was going on." He looked at Bruce. "And you. Think about the scandal in the papers if Marlford's great industrialist was caught red-handed having an affair. Dulcie would take you to the cleaners."

"Listen to me, you," Bruce snarled. "Back off and shut up if you want to keep your job."

Toby hadn't expected that, but he countered with, "I want money or I'll talk."

"What?" Bruce's mouth formed a tight line. "It's like that, is it?"

"How much is she worth?" Toby asked. "How much is your reputation worth? What would you pay me so your wife never finds out you're a filthy, stinking adulterer?"

"One hundred pounds."

Toby laughed. "Are you taking the piss?"

Although, he calculated, it would be enough to pay off a chunk of his parents' mortgage. They'd recently bought it off the council for nine thousand pounds, and the repayments were higher than the rent they used to pay. Now, if Bruce would up the offer to seven hundred, he might consider it.

"Higher."

Bruce snorted. "Three hundred."

"Higher."

"Look, enough of this messing about. How much do you want?"

Toby was going to chance his arm, ask for enough so he had a fair few quid for himself an' all. "Eight hundred. Actually, make it a round thousand." He'd have roughly three hundred for himself, then it wouldn't matter if Bruce sacked him. He could live off the cash until he found another job. But he wanted to twist the knife further. "And you can never sack me."

Bruce blew air out, and his cheeks puffed up. "Okay. But that's a lot for me to withdraw if you want cash. The accountant will ask questions."

"I don't care. Deal with it." Toby gave Maureen a scathing glare. "Count yourself lucky, considering what you've done to me." He aimed his stare back at Bruce. "And there's another stipulation. She stops being a bitch to me."

Bruce smiled, a predator. "The deal's with me, not Maureen. Take it or leave it."

It was useless bargaining further. He knew his boss well enough to accept there was no more persuading him.

"I want the money by tomorrow at work," Toby said. "If you go against our agreement, I'll go and see Dulcie first, then Albert, then the papers. Have an unpleasant evening."

He strutted away, thinking of the money and how his parents were going to love him forever when he paid off the house. He'd safeguarded his future on the back of catching two people kissing. Mum and Dad would leave the house to him when they died.

His euphoria at coming out on top for once soon faded, though, the old hurts crashing back in. Maureen was a user, a nasty piece of work, yet he still loved her, probably always would. But over the coming years, if she upset him enough with her jibes, he'd whisper a few things to her, reminding her of this night.

And that he had all the power here, not her.

CHAPTER FOURTEEN

Anna and Lenny stood in the kitchen area of Parole's swanky apartment. Anna had asked to use his toilet as soon as she'd stepped inside as his infiltrating gaze had sent her skew-whiff, her stomach rioting with butterflies that had no right to be there. She'd composed herself while washing her hands, and switched into work mode, and had avoided any eye contact with him since she'd emerged. Whether she'd be able to keep that up would soon be revealed.

"What can I do you for?" Parole asked.

Anna stared at the crown tattoo nestled among the many others on his toned, muscular arm. "Where were you last night?"

He laughed. "Oh, fuck me. What do you want to pin on me this time?"

"Please just answer." Anna made the mistake of looking at his face. Her tummy rolled over.

We shouldn't have come here.

"I was in the Kite from six until midnight. Why? Is this about the old dear who copped it in Upton?"

88

Anna shouldn't have been surprised. "Did you hear about it because one of the Kings stole her car and killed her in the process?"

Parole winked at her. "I'd never say if they did, but I *would* say if they didn't. And they didn't. Her car's got nothing to do with us, I already checked that with Trigger earlier. Now, why would you think we'd do that to an old lady? Or is it me you're targeting?"

"For your grandfather."

Parole seemed genuinely perplexed. "What the fuck? Nah, he's too strait-laced. He wouldn't ask me to do anything that could make his precious factory hit the news in the wrong way. And why the hell would he want some old dear topped?"

Anna wasn't about to divulge that. "Thanks for speaking to us." She turned to walk away, wanting to get out of there fast, but she stopped just as her palm met with the door handle.

"Can I use your loo an' all?" Lenny asked.

For God's sake. "I'll wait on the landing."

Anna stepped out and moved towards the lift opposite, her back to Parole's front door. She glanced to the side where Vernon Brignell's son, Matthew, had thrown himself out of the window, committing suicide rather than face time in prison for murder. Parole had witnessed it, as had his next-door neighbour, Jane, and Anna suspected Parole had had a hand in encouraging Matthew to jump. But she had no proof; he insisted the camera above his front door was a dummy, and Jane had seemed genuine in her statement. She hadn't behaved as if Parole had threatened her to cover for him.

One of those things I'll never know the truth of.

Unless she did what Placket had recently suggested and let Parole take her out, got close to him in order to extract information about the Kings. Specifically Peter Dove. Lenny had opened his mouth to Placket and said he reckoned Parole fancied her, and the DCI's eyes had lit up, spotting an opportunity to once and for all discover if Peter was a mole. Anna had declined to go that far, but only because of how magnetic

Parole was. If she went ahead with it, she'd soon find herself wrapped up in him more than she should be, and her professionalism might be compromised. She hadn't admitted as much to Placket, but there was something between her and Parole she couldn't explain. Unspoken. A draw. Chemistry.

She shelved those thoughts, and stiffened at his reflection in the steel doors of the lift. Why did he have to be so fit?

"Nice to see you again," he said right behind her, his breath on the back of her neck.

She held off a shiver. "Sorry to have asked you what I did, but we have to cover everything."

"I get it, so don't worry. I'm curious as to why my grandad might be involved, though."

"I can't tell you that. It's his story." Her phone rang. Karen. Anna pressed the phone to her ear and moved to the window, leaving Parole where he stood.

Now his reflection tormented her in the glass, so she concentrated on the covered row of hot tubs in the communal area below.

"I've just had a call from Toby Potter," Karen said.

"Oh, right."

"There's been a row in the Jubilee."

"Bloody hell, I *told* him not to go there."

"Hmm. Albert accused him of killing Maureen, so Toby told him something he's been keeping a secret. He wants to tell you what it is, wouldn't let on to me. I've got his phone number here if you want it."

"Send it to my phone. I'll only forget it otherwise."

"Righty-ho. Wonder what he's been hiding?"

"I'll find out in a minute. Thanks for passing that on."

"Have fun!"

"You always say that."

Karen laughed and ended the call.

Anna caught sight of Lenny in the glass and spun round, her emotions coming under control now he was around. She'd yet to confess to him how she felt about Parole — or, more particularly, how he made her feel — and she knew damn well how he'd take it. He'd tell her to steer clear. Which she should.

"We need to get going," she said. "Something's come in."

Lenny walked to the lift and pressed the down button. Anna joined him, not daring to look at Parole's shape in the doors. Thankfully, the lift arrived, so she got in and kept her back to him. Lenny stood beside her, facing the other way. Once the doors had closed, Anna turned around.

"What's up with you?" Lenny asked.

Anna shrugged. "He unnerves me."

"You shouldn't let him know it, though. You keeping your back to him will tell him all he needs to know, that he intimidates you."

That isn't it at all. "Sorry, he just . . . I prefer to avoid eye contact with him."

"Yeah, his stare is a bit much, I'll give you that. So, what came in?"

"Toby went to the Jubilee."

"Oh, for God's sake."

"And there was a spat. He told Albert a secret regarding Maureen, although I don't know what that is. I need to ring him."

In the car, she opened Karen's message, added Toby's number to her contact list, and gave him a bell, putting it on speaker so she didn't have to repeat it to Lenny afterwards.

"Hello, Toby, it's Anna. What did you need to talk to me about?"

"I shouldn't have said it. Now everyone will know."

"Said what?"

The sounds of footsteps filtered down the line, and a gust of wind whistled past the mouthpiece. "I'm walking home now. I should have listened to you and stayed there instead of going to the pub."

Anna gritted her teeth. "If you can just get on and tell me what the issue is, that would be great."

"Maureen's been having an affair with Bruce Cribbins."

How does he know? "And you're aware of this how?"

Toby told her his story about seeing the couple at the Spencer hotel.

Anna seethed at him for withholding information. Yes, she knew about it via Peter, but that wasn't the point. "Why didn't you mention this when we questioned you earlier? It could be extremely relevant to the investigation."

"I promised I wouldn't."

"So why blurt it to the whole pub *now*?"

"Bruce said I'd lose my job if I said anything, and I don't work there anymore, so . . . And Albert goaded me, like he always does. He outright accused me of killing Maureen!"

Anna sighed. "Okay, thanks for *finally* letting us know. What was his reaction?"

"I hate sticking up for that man, but it looked like the affair was news to him. Unless he's a bloody good actor, I'd say he had no idea. And one other thing . . ."

Anna rolled her eyes. "What?"

"He said he'd kill Bruce."

Did she detect a note of smugness in his voice? "That could just be something lots of people say. An expression. I'll warn Bruce so he's aware of the situation."

"Oh God, will you tell him it was me who let it slip?"

"I expect someone else will anyway, seeing as you announced it to a pub full of customers. We'll be in touch." She cut the call and twisted towards Lenny. "Ever get the feeling that some cases grow tentacles and we're being pulled away from the main thing — the murder?"

"Yep, but your theory about Bruce getting Parole to kill her doesn't sound so out there now. And it may not be Toby but *Albert* we should be looking at."

"We're going to have to nip to the factory and see Bruce. I'd rather tell him the cat's out of the bag to his face than on the phone."

Lenny groaned. "But we'll smell chocolate and I'll want it."

"Then restrain yourself from asking for a sample."

"A sample. Which means it's free . . ."

Anna laughed and drove away. "You don't have to take every freebie that comes your way."

Lenny nudged her. "Oh, I think I do when it comes to a box of Cribbins Deluxe."

CHAPTER FIFTEEN

Anna smiled at Lenny sniffing the air and had to admit the aroma of chocolate had her mouth watering. She'd refused a tour of the factory — she didn't need Bruce posturing about his products and how they were made — and they now sat in his office. Her phone had bleeped not long ago, but she'd ignored it.

"What can I do for you?" Bruce asked. "I rather thought I'd given Peter and Warren enough information for you to be going on with. Have you questioned Albert about last night? I've been worrying he found out about our affair and killed Maureen. I assume your officers passed that on to you."

"From what a witness has just told us, until earlier today he didn't have any idea what you and Maureen got up to."

Bruce frowned. "Witness?"

"Unfortunately, Toby Potter told him not long ago."

Bruce rubbed his temples. "I should have known he'd slip up eventually. He hasn't got any reason to keep it quiet since he doesn't work here anymore. I had a word with him one night; he caught us at the Spencer in York. I panicked and said his job was on the line if he spoke about it."

"We're aware of that." Anna interlaced her fingers on her lap. "I need you to be up front with us, and I'm going to say it outright. Did you arrange for your grandson to kill Maureen?"

"What? That's ludicrous."

"You know his history, so it isn't a stretch."

"He's out of that bloody gang now. And even if Maureen *had* blurted about our affair, it wouldn't matter to me, not anymore. My wife is dead, and I've already decided to tell my children about it, so I have nothing to lose but their respect. Did you check that I stayed at the Spencer last night?"

Anna thought of the message she hadn't read and accessed it on her phone. Warren had sent her confirmation of Bruce's alibi. "Ah, yes, you're clear on that." *But you could still have paid someone to murder her.*

"I loved Maureen, I would never have organised for her to be killed. Can you imagine the uproar if I got caught? This factory is my legacy, it'll belong to my children and grandchildren one day. Times have changed, people openly have affairs and they're more accepted now, which is why I'm going to tell my kids. Me seeing Maureen once a year isn't the scandal it would be if it had come out years ago. A man's reputation was everything back then. Let the chips fall where they may. I'm tired of carrying the secret."

"Are there any other secrets?"

Again, he frowned. "What do you mean?"

"Have you had, or do you still have, any relationship with Robert and Diana Jobs and Elizabeth Kettering?"

"No. They were employees, nothing more. Look, what's this about?"

Anna wasn't going to admit her mind went off on tangents and she was determined to find out why those three people had acted so weirdly. "It's not important."

"Would it satisfy you if I said I'm willing to let you look into my finances to see if I paid out a lump sum to some random person, a hitman? Actually, I'd welcome it. Me being suspected of killing Maureen *would* affect the business."

"We can do that, yes. I'll arrange for someone to contact you."

Bruce eyed her. "You'll find that I don't withdraw money, haven't for years. I only use my cards, so any cash I'd need to pay someone, well, where would it have come from?"

Anna stopped herself from mentioning a secret bank account somewhere. "I see your point," she said instead. Investigators would follow any leads to hidden accounts as a matter of course, plus check any credit cards. "Apparently, Albert said he'd kill you for this, so I needed you to be aware."

Bruce's face stiffened. "Right, well, that's not something I wanted to hear, but I can imagine him saying it. Brash as he is, though, I can't for the life of me see him going through with it. He only hits women."

"And you know this from Maureen?"

"I've seen the evidence. Bruised ribs, the lot."

Anna winced. "Thank you for speaking with us."

"I appreciate you telling me what you have. I think I'll call it a day and go and break the news to my children before it hits social media. Someone's bound to mention the row at the Jubilee online."

They parted ways at the reception doorway, Lenny clutching two boxes of Cribbins Deluxe that Bruce had given him along the way. Anna had jokingly mentioned that taking bribes was frowned upon — *me and my big mouth* — and Bruce had laughed, thankfully, seeming not to take offence.

Once again in the car, Lenny tucking into a strawberry truffle, Anna got on the road, heading towards the station. The rest of the team would soon rein her in if they felt she was off the mark regarding Elizabeth, Robert and Diana, but it would still bug her all the same. The question was, were they hiding something together or were there separate secrets?

CHAPTER SIXTEEN

The answer became clear a short while later. Anna's instinct had been spot on, and Diana's words came back to haunt her.

We're good people. We didn't do anything.

We don't like screaming. No, we don't like that at all.

And we didn't like our house after—

It wasn't us. We didn't do it.

Placket had joined them for the debrief, leaning in the doorway, his arms folded. Anna stood at the front of the room. Everyone else was sitting at desks.

She pinched the bridge of her nose. "So, what you're saying, Sally, is that Elizabeth's father's death might be murder? How did you come to that conclusion when the SIO at the time didn't?"

Sally nodded, her blonde hair swaying. "Things just seem weird. Bits don't add up. The SIO back then is now dead, so we can't ask him for his take on it, which would likely be what's in the file anyway, but some of the other officers on the team are still around. Retired, but I can go and speak to them if you like."

Anna wasn't sure about that. "This is kind of a distraction, though. It'll take you away from helping out on Maureen's case."

"Not if Maureen knew what went on," Placket said. "I've looked at the file, and it just seems off that Elizabeth, Robert and Diana didn't hear the ceiling give way — that their excuse of having the music on loud is convenient, because the lounge where he supposedly hanged himself was below Elizabeth's bedroom, which was where they were. Come on, you can't tell me a racket like that wouldn't have made the floor shake or something."

Anna nodded. "Sounds like you and Sally are more suspicious than the SIO was. It would depend on *how* loud the music was."

Sally pointed to the papers she'd printed out. "Other neighbours said they heard music coming from the house. My immediate reaction when reading the report was: did they put the music on loud for a reason? Other neighbours have stated that it was unusual to hear it in their own homes, even though their windows were open because it was summer, so it stood out. People heard it through the walls, even across the street."

"Yes, that's definitely something we'd have picked up on," Anna said. "Not dissing the SIO or anything, but it seems obvious the music was turned up loud for a reason."

Sally continued. "It was thought that Jack Hudson killed himself because his wife died. But that was as a result of him beating her up. He was out on bail for assaulting her, awaiting a post-mortem to determine the cause of death, so the assumption was he didn't want to face a trial or prison. Sorry, but that bit had my alarm bells ringing, plus he didn't leave a note."

Anna's mind zipped back to the farmhouse. "Did anyone hear screams? Diana told us they don't like screaming, which I found off. Why even say that?"

"Nothing like that reported. Again, the music might have covered it."

"How old were those three at the time?" Anna asked.

"All eighteen, which was why Elizabeth was allowed to live there by herself afterwards. The house was left to her in her parents' will. Robert and Diana also lived in the same street. They all went to school together. What if they planned to kill Elizabeth's father and that's why she had a panic attack? She's worried the truth will come out. What if she received a phone call from Robert and Diana after you left the farm today and that set her off?"

"Robert mentioned they had to feed the pigs," Anna said.

"But that could have been a lie." Warren leaned back and stretched his legs out. "This is like the Brignell case, a can of worms."

"I thought the same," Anna mused. "Weird how that's happened. So, we know Robert and Diana have rented their house to someone while they tend to the farm. Diana said they didn't like it 'after', but she didn't specify what that meant. Who lived in their place at the time Jack died?"

"Diana and her parents." Sally drew a finger down one of the pieces of paper from the sheaf on her desk. "It says here that her mum and dad moved away to Cornwall a year after Jack died — they're now dead, so we can't ask them anything. Robert moved in with Diana after they'd got married and the deeds were transferred to them. Before that, Robert lived in the same street with his parents. After his father died and Robert moved out, his mum relocated to Marlford to be closer to her brother. Jack's death happened close to their marriage, so maybe they don't like the house because of the memories associated with it."

"How so?" Anna asked.

"They went there after they'd listened to music at Elizabeth's. They ate dinner with Diana's parents, then the police showed up."

Lenny scoffed. "Why stay if you don't like it? Why remain close to the scene of a crime if you were involved in it?"

Warren shrugged. "Who knows, they might have felt they couldn't leave it because they had a pact with Elizabeth. Or if they moved away, it would make them look guilty."

"We won't know unless we outright question them about it," Anna said. "I'm wary of that, given Elizabeth's panic attack earlier."

Placket butted in. "But we have a duty to if it's linked to Maureen's death. One of them may have told her what happened, and she might have passed it on to someone else."

Anna took her ponytail out and ran a hand through her hair. It needed washing. "Albert? What if Maureen threatened to reveal their secret and one of them killed her? Robert and Diana live next to that field, and, if Maureen supposedly went to stay with her sister once a year on the same date, that could have been common knowledge. Her car being stolen may well just be some little scrotes taking advantage of it being there, not linked to her murder at all. Maybe she'd left the keys in the ignition."

"This is doing my head in," Peter said. "Can we recap, please? My mind's scrambled."

Anna, who preferred whiteboards over the wall-mounted interactive screens that were filtering into stations, picked up a marker. She went to the middle whiteboard. "Okay, we have four scenarios." She wrote them down.

1. *Elizabeth, Diana and Robert had something to do with Jack's death, and Maureen kept it a secret until recently. One or all of them are complicit in killing Maureen to shut her up*

2. *Albert found out about Maureen's affair with Bruce and he killed her.*

3. *Bruce found out Maureen was going to tell Albert about the affair and he arranged for someone to murder her.*

4. *Toby never got over her leaving him and attacked her on his walk.*

"There you go, Peter." Anna stepped to the side so everyone could read the list. "This is one tangled mess. So where do we go from here?"

Peter raised a finger. "My take on Bruce was that he was telling the truth."

"Yeah, same," Warren agreed.

Anna was glad Warren had spoken up because her initial thought was that, if Peter was still with the Kings, he *would* have tried to steer the focus away from Bruce for Parole.

Anna put her hair back into a ponytail. "Right, so we'll put the Bruce theory to the bottom of the list of priorities. His alibi came back clean, so it's just his bank accounts and credit cards to sort through."

"I'll get someone else on that," Placket said, "so it frees the team up to concentrate on the other scenarios."

"Thanks." Anna smiled at him, then turned to the others. "Okay, so it appears, according to Toby, that news of Maureen's affair came as a shock to Albert. Do we agree that he can also go down the list in order of importance?"

Placket pushed off the door and took a seat. "No, keep him near the top. What's he like these days?"

"I doubt he'd want us two hounding him again," Lenny said.

Placket smirked. "I can go and speak to him. He might be more receptive to my charms."

Again, Anna thanked him. "Right, so the rest of us will concentrate on the trio theory and Toby Potter. Me and Lenny will go back to see Toby and find out exactly what happened in the Jubilee." She gestured to Sally, Peter and Warren. "You three poke more into Jack's death from here and see if you can find anything that links to Maureen's death."

Placket got up. "I'll go and sort someone to look at Bruce's bank accounts," he said on his way out.

Anna made eye contact with Lenny. "Come on, pal. Let's go see Toby."

CHAPTER SEVENTEEN

The phone calls this afternoon had been doing Peter's head in. Calls he shouldn't be getting. Why the hell wasn't Trigger sticking to the plan? He was supposed to leave Peter alone for six months, yet . . .

The problem was, Trigger had him by the short and curlies. The number of things Peter had done for the Kings could all be traced back to when he'd accessed the police database. So many years of watching his PC colleagues' keystrokes when they'd logged in had given him numerous passwords he could use, but Trigger knew that and could tip the police off. Every crime, every person Peter had looked up, he'd married it with a PC who'd worked that particular crime, but it was still a worry that someone inquisitive like Sally or Anna would suss what had gone on.

Peter had been letting the calls ring out. They'd come in on his Kings phone, which he'd forgotten to silence — years of having it ingrained in him that he should carry it with him at all times had stuck, despite him being on a break. He'd argued years ago that if he ever got hurt in the line of duty and needed to be taken to hospital, say he was unconscious, that phone would be found on him, but Trigger had assured him nothing would come of it, all the burners were safe, couldn't be traced to the Kings.

But any messages Peter may have forgotten to delete, which had happened a time or two when he'd been busy, would immediately look suspicious.

Peter was paranoid that Sally or Warren had clocked that it wasn't his personal or work phone ringing. Neither of them had seemed to pay him any mind, though, except for a filthy look from Sally after the third unanswered call, but that wasn't unusual because she liked quiet when she was researching. Anyway, loads of things got on her nerves. He'd swear she was going through early menopause.

He'd gone to the loo and messaged Trigger back each time, stating that he couldn't be called while he was at work. Trigger's reply churned Peter's guts.

T: *Time for a loyalty test.*

P: *What the fuck? You know I'm solid.*

T: *And you know the rules. There's a job for you later. Go to the back of the nick in one hour.*

Peter switched off the sound alerts, leaving it on vibrate, and tried to work out what the hell he could do. If he left the incident room for more than the time it would take for a quick visit to the canteen, it'd be noticed. *Whatever* he did might be noticed — he was in a station full of coppers, for fuck's sake. And Trigger expected him to meet him out the back? Where people went for their cigarette breaks?

Christ.

Peter returned to his desk shaking. Annoyed at the loss of control. And a bit scared, if he were honest. Those men who'd been smoking outside the Hoof that time. *Had* they been watching him? He'd been so careful since he'd taken a break from the Kings, hadn't seen anyone following him,

103

but with the snarls of traffic in Marlford it would be easy for surveillance officers to tail him without it being obvious.

He dug into one of the files to try to keep his mind busy. Glanced at Sally and Warren from time to time, worried they'd catch him doing it. It had been one thing to be a mole for the Kings before he'd come under suspicion, it had been hairy enough then, but now it would be career suicide for him to go out on a job with the gang.

Why was Trigger insisting he prove his loyalty when they'd already agreed he should keep his head down? Yes, he knew the rules, that if you were called by a King, you answered, you did what they wanted, but this situation was different. Wasn't it?

Obviously not, you twat.

Peter had known Trigger since they were kids, and he'd thought they were friends first and Kings second. And that was another thing. Someone else in the police must be in with them if Trigger wasn't asking him to poke into the database. The Kings couldn't run properly without a copper's input. There were times they'd planned a job and the police were scheduled to be in the vicinity on a completely different matter — a house raid, a dawn arrest. Peter used to tell them those sorts of things so the plans could be changed. But until now he hadn't thought about who might be doing it when he wasn't on shift.

I've had my head up my arse. Got above myself by thinking I'm the only one.

Why did that sting?

Because he'd thought he was indispensable. Important. Integral to the gang.

What a bloody joke.

The burner vibrated in his pocket, and he wanted to scream. Too much pressure. The walls closing in. He shot up and headed for the door.

"Have you got the shits or something?" Warren muttered.

Peter ignored him. Locked himself in the toilet and opened the message.

T: *Don't think you can bottle it just because we're mates.*

Peter shivered. Trigger knew him too well. Knew he'd be thinking of ways to get out of it.

Back at his desk, for the first time since he'd been little, Peter wanted to cry. He couldn't do anything about this. Trigger would do whatever it took if he disobeyed him. No matter that they had a shared past, shared secrets, and loved each other like brothers, Trigger wouldn't think twice about killing him if he thought his precious gang was under threat.

Peter had no choice but to go out the back of the station when the clock hit the appointed time and see what the hell Trigger expected him to do.

CHAPTER EIGHTEEN

DCI Ron Placket had worked on a case in Upton-cum-Studley before. As a DI at the time, he'd been involved in trying to discover how Evelyn Brignell from Hawthorn Farm had wound up being eaten by pigs. He'd never forget the lesson Vernon had given him on why the animals attacked. Territorial sods. It got him thinking about Robert and Diana Jobs. If they'd killed Maureen, had they forgone feeding her body to the pigs because that would be the first thing Anna would have suspected, seeing as Evelyn's son Matthew had so recently fed his victims to the animals, minus their heads?

Placket knew Albert from a separate case that had occurred before Evelyn's, where someone had reported him for punching Maureen, hence the reason for coming out here to speak to him today. They'd had a rapport of sorts, and the man might confide in him like before.

Back then, as it had been the second call accusing Albert of abuse, Placket, a DC, had gone to Upton with a PC to see what was going on — they'd been on another job when the call had come through the radio, otherwise Placket wouldn't have gone out for a domestic. He tried to recall when that had been. Maureen and Albert had already been married for years, he knew that much.

During that visit, Albert had admitted to Placket that he had, indeed, hit his wife, with a promise that it wouldn't happen again. No further incidents were reported, so Placket assumed Albert had learned to control himself.

The calls had been made by Elizabeth Kettering, which was interesting now her name had cropped up again. Placket recalled speaking to her about it. The woman was convinced something was going on but, as it had turned out, she had no proof other than bruises to Maureen's face and wrists, which are easily explained away.

Placket drew up in the Jubilee car park, entered the pub, and spotted Albert right away. He hadn't aged well, and it was a bit of a shock to see him all these years later, when Placket still thought of him as a dark-haired fella. The same could be true the other way around, as, when Placket approached him, Albert didn't appear to know who he was.

ID out and held low so the other customers didn't get an eyeful, Placket introduced himself, adding, "I came to your house once years ago."

Light dawned in Albert's eyes. "Ah, I remember you now. Have you come with news about Maureen?"

"It's related. Can we go to your cottage?"

Albert tutted. "I've only just come from there. That fucking Toby Potter ran me out of here with his lies. I waited until he'd gone, then came back."

"It's better we chat in private." Placket smiled.

Albert sighed and got up. "Bloody hell."

Placket followed him over the road, and they entered the cottage, where Albert took him to the kitchen. The old man stuck a kettle on to boil without adding any water.

"I assume you could do with a cuppa," he said, sorting cups and instant coffee. "Shouldn't take long because I've not long had one. Water's still hot."

"Thanks. Can I sit?"

Albert nodded. "Yep. I'm that angry about Toby. What's he done, reported me and they've sent the big guns out to have a word? You must have gone up in the world if you're in a suit."

"DCI."

"Why aren't Anna and that Lenny fella here?"

"They're busy elsewhere."

The kettle clicked off, and Albert poured water into the cups. "Milk's in the fridge. Get it out, will you?"

Used to Albert's gruff ways from years ago, Placket did as he'd been ordered and added the milk to the drinks while the man stirred.

"No sugar for me." Placket took his coffee back to the table.

Albert added three spoonfuls to his, stirred again, and strutted over to sit opposite. "Let's be having it, then. What's he said?"

"He phoned up and mentioned what he'd done, and I'm here to see how you feel about it."

Albert's brash demeanour disappeared and his shoulders sagged, a replica of the last time Placket had been here. He anticipated Albert opening up to him and wondered why, when he'd clammed up with the other PC. Maybe he imagined they were kindred spirits, as if Placket was the sort to agree with a man hitting his wife.

Albert scraped a hand down his cheek over white whiskers that were just coming in. "I don't know if I believe him or not. Maureen knew the score if she ever cheated on me."

"You giving her a bunch of fives?"

Albert grinned. "Something like that." He sobered. Stared at the table. "I still hit her after you came."

"I thought you might."

"Punched her where the bruises wouldn't show."

As Albert had admitted such a big thing, Placket was inclined to believe that the affair *had* been a shock to him, but he'd test the waters further anyway. "What was your reaction when Toby told you about Maureen and Bruce?"

"I covered up the shame of it by giving him a bit of verbal, but inside I was raging. How the fuck did she hide that from me for all those years? She got pregnant half a dozen times or so and lost the babies. No skin off my nose, I didn't want any kids, but now I'm wondering if they were Bruce's."

"How far along was she when she lost them?"

"A few months."

"So that doesn't ring true."

Albert squinted. "What do you mean?"

"She'd have known way before a few months and would have got rid of them sooner if she thought they were Bruce's. She'd have been too afraid of you to cuckold you like that."

Albert nodded. "True. I said I'd kill him. I'm telling you that now because you'll find out anyway. I wouldn't. I mean, I feel like it, but I wouldn't."

"If you're willing to take my advice and you *didn't* murder your wife, keep your nose clean. Anything you do now will be scrutinised. Saying you'll kill Bruce — not the smartest move, is it?"

"I didn't kill her. I thought she was going to Gloria's — that's her sister — and all along she'd been at a hotel with that man."

"Have you spoken to Gloria?"

"Yeah. When I stormed out of the pub, I came home and got hold of her on the phone. She made out she didn't know what I was talking about, but it was obvious."

"Do you think she knew you hit Maureen, too?"

"Maureen wouldn't dare tell her."

"You didn't think she'd have an affair but she did."

"Fucking bitch."

Placket had heard enough. He had to try to make this bloke see sense. "Have you listened to yourself?"

Albert's cheeks coloured. "Yeah, all these new rules now. You can't clout the wife to get her in line. But it's ingrained in me, I couldn't stop if I tried, and she was always messing things up, forgetting what I taught her — or she was disobeying me on purpose. It pissed me off, and the only way to get her to behave for a bit was by giving her a wallop."

It sounds like a blessing she's out of it now. "Do you not think you two weren't suited? That it would have been kinder on her to part ways?"

"No. She was mine, and I wasn't giving her up so she could go running back to Toby."

"She ran to someone else instead."

Albert shook his head. "I swear to God, that was the last thing I thought she'd do. Now everyone in the pub knows, I'll be a laughing stock."

Placket moved on. "Other than Elizabeth Kettering, did Maureen have any friends?"

"Nah, friends give them ideas. You've got to nip that in the bud."

"If I remember rightly, a woman accused you of strangling her before you moved to Marlford. I mentioned it to you on the night I came here to question you about the assault accusations. Is that the sort of thing you were trying to 'nip in the bud'?"

"Yeah, it was her friend who encouraged her to dob me in. I soon sorted that. Threatened her so she withdrew her statement. Paid her a few quid then left town."

Placket couldn't get over how some people discussed these things as if they were in the right, that what they'd *done* was right, and everyone else was wrong. And to say such things to a police officer, well . . . "Did you cut Maureen off from her friends?"

"Yep. She had to stop speaking to Elizabeth and anyone else she was mates with at the factory or in the village. Things were much better after that."

"You do realise that's not normal behaviour, don't you?"

"So some would say." Albert sniffed. "But I didn't kill her. I was in the Jubilee all night. I'd tell you if I'd done it."

It sounded as if Albert would be proud to pass on the news.

This man's not right up top. "Okay, well, keep your head down, like I said. Do you think you'd benefit from some counselling?" Placket felt Albert needed psychological help, but he couldn't force it on him.

"Nah. That's all a load of bollocks. I don't want anyone poking into my life, thanks."

I bet you don't.

Placket drank his coffee while Albert raved on about how much he hated Toby. The man was clueless as to how to hide his feelings when it came to people he disliked.

I don't think he did it.

Placket finished his drink and brought Toby's rant to an end. "Another bit of advice. Going on about Toby killing her is going to look bad on you. As if you're protesting too much. Anna may wonder whether you keep pointing the finger at him so it isn't pointed at you."

"Ah, I get you." Albert tapped the side of his nose. "I'll keep my gob shut for now, then." He chuckled. "Never thought I'd have a copper telling me how to stay under the radar."

Alarmed, Placket rushed to make his advice clear. "No, what I'm concerned about is my team following leads they don't need to. And we both want to find who killed Maureen, don't we? Let us do our jobs without you muddying the waters."

"I suppose I can do that, but I can't promise anything. If he riles me up in the pub again, I might end up clocking him one."

"Why are you so upset about him anyway? *You* were the one Maureen married."

Albert leaned back. "Because he kissed her first. He did every first with her apart from sex."

Really? You've let him bug you for fifty years because of that?
Placket shook his head.

He'd never understand some people, especially not Albert Frost.

* * *

Placket walked into the heart of the village and arrived outside Elizabeth's house, telling himself he was only going to speak to her to see if she could withstand more rigorous questioning, should it be agreed that they needed to speak to the trio later down the line in relation to Jack's death.

He knocked on the door and it opened, revealing a grey-haired woman he was sure wasn't Elizabeth; but the passage of time could have once again skewed his mind.

"Is Elizabeth in?" he asked.

"Yes. Who are you?"

"DCI Ron Placket."

"Oh. Um, can I see some ID?"

Placket took it out and held it up.

She scrutinised it and must have deemed him legitimate, as she stepped back. "She's in the living room."

Placket followed her halfway down the hallway. Elizabeth sat in an ancient recliner, a fluffy blanket over her lower legs, the colour matching her pale-blue hair. He remained standing, as no offer to take a seat had been forthcoming, and the woman who'd opened the door lingered beside him.

"It's okay, you can go, Joyce," Elizabeth told her.

Joyce's eyes darted between her friend and Placket. "Are you sure? Only, the last time the police were here—"

"It's fine." Elizabeth sounded a little testy.

Joyce scuttled out, and Elizabeth closed her eyes until the sound of the front door shutting filtered in. She opened them and flicked a hand towards the sofa. Placket sat on the edge and smiled.

"We meet again," he said to put her at ease — would she even remember him?

Elizabeth sagged. "What now?"

"I came to check on you since I heard you called an ambulance."

She scoffed. "That's not the only reason you're here. I wasn't born yesterday."

"No, I wanted to ask you something."

"Like what?"

How could he say this without accusing her of being a gossip and knowing everyone's business? There was no point in beating around the bush regarding the subject matter, though, as she'd hear it for herself soon enough. "There was a row in the Jubilee earlier. Toby Potter told Albert Frost that Maureen had been having an affair with Bruce Cribbins. Were you aware of that?"

She shut her eyes again then opened them a crack, as though the lids were too heavy to keep up, or perhaps this was her version of a filthy look. "Yes, and I was glad she got happiness somewhere. God knows she didn't get it from Albert."

"How long have you known?"

"Since a little while after it started." She flushed.

"Did Maureen tell you?"

"No, she'd cut me off way before then." A stubborn pout of her lips, then she softened her features.

"So how did you find out?"

"Toby told me." She appeared to mentally kick herself for revealing that.

"Right. Why didn't you mention this to Anna and Lenny this morning?"

"I didn't think it was relevant."

"But of *course* it is."

She nodded. "I see that now. Albert could have found out and . . . and hurt her. Or Bruce could have, although I don't think he would."

"Exactly. But why don't you think Bruce would have harmed her?"

"He isn't the type. He's calm and collected. Didn't even get angry when I . . . Oh God."

"When you what?"

"When I stole from the factory. I was only young. He was understanding as to why I'd done it and even paid my wages until the end of the week after he let me go. A man who does that wouldn't go round killing anyone. Look, I'm sorry I didn't mention the affair, all right? I can tell you're annoyed about that."

Placket opted to continue prodding her to see how she reacted. "People who don't tell the whole truth when questioned risk sending the police in the wrong direction." *Like you might have done with your father's case.*

She jolted. In alarm? "I . . . I really didn't think, did I? Toby made me promise not to tell anyone. I know everyone says I'm a busybody because I've got nothing better to do, but I do know how to keep *some* things to myself."

Do you now? "I suppose that's best if it means getting into trouble."

She narrowed her eyes at him. "Yes, well . . ."

"Is there anything else you'd like to tell me? Anything at all that may be useful in this case or any other?"

"Any other? No."

"Like you may have perhaps still been friends with Maureen but you both pretended you weren't so Albert wasn't aware?"

"I told you, she cut me off. I tried to help her years later, you know I did. I rang the police about what he was doing, and nothing was done about it. All that happened was he stopped hitting her where people could see the bruises."

"How do you know this if you weren't friends?"

"I had a feeling, that's all."

"Feelings aren't facts, though."

"I know the signs. I watched my mother, how she behaved. My dad used to beat her all the time."

"How did you feel about that?"

"How do you *think* I bloody felt?"

114

"Did you want to prevent Maureen from ending up like her? Is that why you phoned in about her?"

"Are we done here?"

He stood, accepting that he wasn't going to get anything more out of her. "Yes. Thanks for speaking to me. I'll see myself out."

He walked outside, only to catch sight of an arm flapping in his peripheral. Joyce stood at her front door, beckoning him over. He strode up her garden path and into her house.

She closed the door. "Is she okay? She says she is, but all these police visits can't be good for her. I'm worried she's going to make herself ill with anxiety."

"Why would she get anxiety if she hasn't done anything wrong?"

"It'll be a reminder of what went on with her parents."

Placket feigned ignorance. "What was that, then?"

"Jack, that's her dad, he used to beat her mum up. She died because of it. He'd hit her one too many times in the head. The next day, he hanged himself. Elizabeth was a wreck with all the police here, asking questions."

"Did you live here at the time?"

"Yes, but I was out when it happened. In Marlford with my friend. I came home to see all the police cars and everything. My dad was at work, so he couldn't help, but my mum was home. She said the music coming from that house was so loud the walls buzzed with it. Well, it would, wouldn't it, being right next door."

"I see. So you feel Elizabeth might be remembering the past because of the police presence today?"

"Yes."

"Did she ever talk to you about what happened?"

"No, we weren't really friends back then. It's only been the last ten years or so that we've become close. Since my husband died."

That reminded Placket to send a message to the team to ask them to look into the death of Elizabeth's husband. Who knew, if Elizabeth had helped kill her father, she may have gone on to help her husband on his way, too.

I'm getting as suspicious as Anna.

"I'm sure she'll be fine now," he said. "I must get on."

He headed towards the Jubilee to collect his car. Elizabeth was fine to be questioned in the future, she'd certainly recovered from her panic attack, although, if they had cause to speak to her again about her father and what had gone on that day, she might well panic again.

For now, she was safe.

Unless Sally and the team discovered something that would give them the green light to bring Elizabeth, Robert and Diana in.

CHAPTER NINETEEN

Anna had made a detour to Brunch and picked up a couple of ham and tomato baguettes for her and Lenny to eat on the way to Upton — and a proper shot of coffee each. Now invigorated at last, she felt a bit more human.

"We'll go in the Jubilee first to get other people's take on what happened," she said, parking outside.

"Placket's here," Lenny noted.

Anna glanced at the DCI's car, then across the road. "No spaces outside the cottages, maybe that's why he parked here. Or he could be having a cheeky spot of lunch."

They entered the pub, and Anna checked around for the boss, but Placket wasn't there. At the bar, she smiled at the server and jerked her thumb to the end where no one stood. The young woman met them down there.

"Have you got a minute to chat?" Anna asked.

"What, about Toby and Albert arguing?"

"Please. What's your name?"

"Laura. Hang on, I'll get Ian to cover the bar."

Laura went back to the other end, and the landlord nodded, spoke to a customer he'd been chatting to, then lifted the hatch and got on with serving. Laura dipped through the hatch, too, and joined Anna and Lenny. She led the way through a door marked "Private" and into a room with a table and chairs in the middle, a little kitchenette to the side. Everyone sat, and Anna smiled.

"Okay, Laura, what went on?"

Laura related the event as she'd seen it. "Albert was shocked, I can tell you. He had no idea. I didn't either. I mean, Maureen's not exactly at the top of my Christmas card list, she's such a cow all the time, but I can see why she'd be shagging someone else. Albert's an arsehole to her. The times I've heard him telling her off in here."

"What kind of things did he say?"

"He moaned about how she sat, stood, talked, loads of things. Like, he nagged her. If it had been him attacked in the lay-by, I'd have said it was her, but I can honestly say I don't think he killed her."

"How come?"

"He relied on her to keep their cottage running. Everyone knows she's his skivvy. There was a row about it once, where Elizabeth went up to him and said he treated Maureen like shit."

"Elizabeth Kettering?"

"Yeah, Mrs Gossip. If you want to know anything, go and see her."

"I didn't think Maureen and Elizabeth were friends."

"They're not, but Elizabeth talks to loads of people and finds things out. Someone must have mentioned Maureen being a skivvy, else how would Elizabeth have known about it?"

So Maureen had confided in someone who'd then passed it on to Elizabeth?

Thank God I don't get involved with this lot.

While Anna lived in the village, she kept to herself. Her instincts had proved correct. Some places were toxic, and it seemed this one was more infected with small-town mentality than she'd realised.

"Albert said he'd kill that Bruce fella," Laura says. "You know, the man who runs the factory."

"Do you think he would?" Lenny asked.

"Nah, he's all mouth. Think about it. My grandad said Albert and Toby have been arguing for years, and, apart from one time when Albert went to punch Toby at the factory, they've never hit each other. Makes me think Albert isn't into hitting men, only his wife."

A coward. "Would you mind asking Ian to come in here so we can get his opinion on it all?"

Laura nodded, got up and left the room.

Lenny groaned. "Are we going to speak to all the customers?"

"No, I'll get hold of Tom after, he can send some PCs down here. I just want Ian's perspective, see if it matches Laura's, then, if Placket lets us know he doesn't think Albert knew about the affair beforehand, we'll have a near enough solid answer."

Ian came in and sat, propping his elbows on the table. "Before you ask, the row is nothing new. I haven't been running this place for long, but even I could see they didn't get on as soon as I took over. You get to sense these things. Those two blow up from time to time, so what happened earlier isn't unusual. Toby doesn't normally go for the jugular like that, though. I mean, Maureen and old Cribbins . . . blimey, he kept that one under his hat."

"Do you think it came as a shock to Albert?"

"God, yes. The bloke was stunned, I'd say. He couldn't even hide it after the initial blow hit home."

"Do you mean they fought?"

"Nah, figure of speech, sorry."

"Okay, thanks. I'll have to send some PCs this way to speak to the other customers."

"Why, is Albert in the frame for killing Maureen?"

"I can't discuss that."

119

"Because he wouldn't have done it. I'm telling you, he was in here all night, and he relied on her more than he'd like to admit. I can't say there's much love lost between them, they didn't appear to have that kind of marriage, but she was the one who ran the household. He wouldn't know how to boil an egg or anything. Why kill your maid?"

Anna thanked Ian and they left the pub. Outside, she phoned Tom to arrange for statements to be taken. Better to have it all on file in case something came back to bite them on the arse later.

Placket, walking from the direction of the heart of the village, drew Anna's attention. She waited for him to reach them and cocked her head.

"Did you get a lead from Albert?" she asked.

"Sort of." Placket explained how he'd had to talk to the man years ago. "Elizabeth was the one to make the accusations. I went round to see her after I'd spoken to Albert. I wanted to see how she'd hold up if we have to question her later down the line."

"Do you think he knew about the affair?"

"No. But Elizabeth did. Toby told her years ago."

"Yet she never said a word to us about it." Anna shoved her hands in her pockets to warm them up. "Bloody people, holding things back. Did you ask her why she hadn't informed us?"

"Yes, she said she'd promised not to say anything to anyone. Toby asked her to keep it to herself."

"Yet Elizabeth is the village gossip," Anna muttered. "I wonder how she managed to keep a lid on *that*?"

Placket shrugged. "She said she's sorry, she didn't think it was relevant."

"Oh, so the idea that it could have been Albert or Bruce never entered her head?"

"Not everyone thinks like a copper, but she twigged what I was getting at in the end." Placket took his car keys out of his pocket. "I also spoke to her neighbour, Joyce, who brought up Jack's hanging."

120

Hope blossomed in Anna's chest. "Oh, did you get anything juicy?"

"Afraid not. Her version of events is the same as the others in the file. Loud music, that sort of thing. She said Elizabeth has never talked to her about what went on."

"Do you believe her?"

"Yes. From what I've gleaned today, it's looking more likely that it's Toby who killed Maureen."

"How did you come to that conclusion?"

"Because despite Maureen cutting off her friendships, Elizabeth still cares about her even now. I didn't get the sense she'd have had reason to kill her. She said she was glad Maureen had found happiness elsewhere with Bruce."

Anna hated the fact that she hadn't seen Albert's or Elizabeth's faces when Placket had spoken to them. She trusted her boss, but he might not have picked up on things like she did. Or maybe Anna liked being in control too much.

Placket swung his keys around his finger. "I messaged the team to look into Elizabeth's husband's death, a gentle reminder."

"Ah, Sally might not have got around to that, what with finding out about Jack."

"I thought the same. Have you spoken to Toby yet?"

"No, we nipped into the pub to see what went on, to check if it matches what Toby said."

"And does it?"

"Yes, but I've asked Tom Quant to send officers here to take statements."

"Good, we don't want to ignore anything that might be crucial later. I don't fancy a rap on the knuckles, which I'd have to pass down to you."

Anna smiled. "Okay, we'll go now, then meet you at the station."

Placket strolled over to his car. Anna got into hers and Lenny joined her.

She drove them towards Toby's street. "So if Albert and Elizabeth didn't kill Maureen, and it wasn't Robert or Diana, we might well be back to my initial thought that it's Toby. We just had a little detour along the way."

"Don't count your chickens until that stuff with the trio is cleared up."

Anna pulled up outside Toby's and glanced over at Elizabeth's. "I'm dying to question her again."

"I know what you mean, but leave it."

They approached Toby's door, and Anna knocked. Toby opened it, and his face dropped. "Oh. Am I in trouble for the argy-bargy at the pub?"

"We just want to pick your brains about a few things."

The ginger cat shot past Toby and legged it across the garden. Toby stared after it, shook his head and walked down the hallway. Anna and Lenny followed, and, instead of staying in the kitchen like before, he went through another doorway in there. Anna found herself in a workshop. Shelves, lined with tools, filled the right-hand wall. A wooden bench with some contraption or other on top stood in the centre. A piece of wood with the same carving at one end, like Elizabeth's kettle handle and the cane stand, lay rigid within a clamp.

And a suitcase sat to one side, looking distinctly out of context. "Going somewhere?"

Toby frowned, then glanced to where she stared. "Oh no, I use that to deliver some of my pieces. It has wheels, so I can walk it round to the customers' houses."

It seemed a reasonable explanation, except he had a car. "You don't drive?"

"I told you, I love walking." He picked up a chisel and continued the carving.

The *tap-tap-tap* got on Anna's nerves. "If you could just stop that while we talk." She smiled. "Thanks. Okay, a couple of things. You told Elizabeth Kettering about Maureen's affair with Bruce."

Toby flushed. "I had to talk to *someone*. And I thought, seeing as she used to be a good friend of Maureen's, that she could warn her not to keep seeing him."

"Why would you do that? Because you used to date her?"

"Maybe. I was jealous she didn't pick me to have an affair with."

"What Maureen did after she finished with you isn't your concern." Anna stopped herself from going on a rant on Maureen's behalf. "Why did you choose to tell Albert about the affair now, of all times, when he's just lost his wife?"

"I couldn't help myself. He accused me of killing her, so I had to get him back."

"Don't you think all this is childish? Fifty years. Surely you should have moved on."

"I told you before, I couldn't. She was my life."

"She wasn't, she made hers elsewhere with someone else. Did you know anything about Elizabeth phoning the police regarding Albert abusing Maureen?"

"I might have had a chat with her about it when she told me her suspicions."

"Did you encourage her to phone the police?"

"Yes, I wanted Maureen to be safe. For Albert to get arrested."

"I recall Elizabeth saying she didn't have much to do with you, just said hello from time to time. From your point of view, it seems you knew each other well enough to trade secrets."

"We do, I don't know why she'd say otherwise."

"Because of that, did she ever confide in you regarding her father's death?"

Toby paled and clutched the chisel harder. "No."

I don't believe you. "You lived here when he hanged himself, yet your name didn't come up in the file. Were you out when the residents were questioned?"

"I was here. My mother spoke to them at the door."

"And what did she have to say?"

"That the music was loud enough for us to hear it through the open window."

"Did Elizabeth ever tell you why it was so loud?"

Toby flinched. "Ask her. Or Robert and Diana. This has nothing to do with me."

"Why mention Robert and Diana?"

"Just ask them, all right?"

I've riled him. So he has a temper. Did he lose it with Maureen in that lay-by? "If you know something that you've failed to mention, that could be classed as perverting the course of justice, so think carefully before you decide whether to keep any secrets from us."

"I can't say anything. I promised."

Anna laughed. "Like you promised to keep quiet about the affair? You told Elizabeth! Are you sure you can hold another secret inside you for years to come, eating away at you?"

Toby remained tight-lipped.

Anna sighed. "Fair enough, but don't say I didn't warn you. I'll ask you one more thing. Whatever it is you're keeping to yourself about Jack, Elizabeth, Robert and Diana, does it have anything to do with Maureen?"

"No, absolutely not."

Anna believed him this time.

She walked through the house and took a deep breath in the front garden. Tried to centre herself. If Toby was telling the truth, the trio scenario was a sideshow, but what if he wasn't?

"Fuck it," she muttered.

"What's the matter?" Lenny came out and closed the door.

Anna explained her thoughts. "I don't know what to do for the best."

"Keep it as it is. We now know for sure something's up with Elizabeth, Robert and Diana. Toby is covering his back by not saying what the issue is. If he wasn't, he wouldn't have told us to ask them about it. Maybe he doesn't want us poking around in his life because he killed Maureen and he can't handle too much at once."

"You have a point there." Anna let out a stream of air, her breath clouding. "I'll ask Placket what he wants to do regarding those three. He did say they needed to be spoken to if the team finds anything concrete. Maybe the interviews had better be done by either Sally, Warren or Peter at the station while me and you concentrate on Maureen."

She drove towards Marlford, her brain firing all over the place. Some cases seemed to have a life of their own. Why couldn't things be simple?

CHAPTER TWENTY

Peter took a packet of cigarettes and a lighter out of his pocket as he walked out of the back door. He'd swiped them off someone's desk on his way here. He didn't smoke, he'd given up, but if anyone asked he'd say he'd taken up the habit again. There was no way he could come out here and not light up if someone else was around. They'd think it was odd.

Two detectives from another team stood talking and smoking over the way, hashing something out in muted tones. Peter took a ciggie out and sparked the lighter, hating himself because he knew he'd love that first hit of nicotine after a period of abstinence.

He did. Too much.

He casually wandered to the tall metal-runged gate at the end of the smoking area, and leaned on the wall next to it. You had to have a key to get out, and he didn't have one. The best he could do — and to prove that Trigger couldn't control *everything* like he seemed to think he could — was to stand here and show him he'd done as he was told.

He studied the cars parked on both sides of the road beyond the gate. The houses opposite, a scraggly row of run-down terraces with sash windows and manky net curtains. A kid came by on a bike, must be about ten, and the thought that he should be in school skated through Peter's head, then he chuffed out a derisive laugh, swallowing smoke and choking on it. His coughing fit drew the attention of the other detectives.

"You all right there, Pete?"

"Yeah."

"Go down the wrong hole, did it?"

"Yeah."

They returned to their conversation.

He should have known Trigger would use a kid to deliver the message. He wouldn't have turned up here himself. The lad had stopped across the road, his position such that he could see the two detectives. His face, partially hidden by the overhang of his black hood, gave no indication as to his thoughts. No clamped mouth. No scrunched nose. He pedalled to the left, then stopped, shielded from the officers by the high brick wall that enclosed the smoking area. He came over, parked his bike against it, and nonchalantly sauntered close to the edge of it where the gate started. He dipped a hand in his pocket, bringing out a folded piece of paper. He placed it on the ground.

"Read it," he whispered.

Peter glanced at the coppers, his heartbeat ramping up. He shifted his head to tell the lad to bugger off, but he'd already gone.

Peter dropped his half-smoked cigarette as an excuse to collect the note. He bent over to pick it up with one hand and the paper with the other. Stuffed the note in his pocket. Pretended to take a puff, then walked over to the ashtray on the wall and stubbed the ciggie out.

He returned inside, the nicotine bringing on nausea, though maybe the note had something to do with that, too. He checked the open-plan area he'd strolled through. The desk he'd stolen the cigarettes from was now occupied, so he placed them on another on his way past. Whoever worked there would probably be accused of nicking them, but he was past caring.

He rushed upstairs and entered the toilets. Locked himself in a cubicle and pulled the paper out of his pocket. Stared at it.

In childlike writing, probably that lad's, were the words *SEE YOU TONIGHT*.

This was more than Peter knowing the rules. Trigger wanted him to know that, if Peter ever tried to leave the Kings again, they could get to him at any time, even if it meant sending a young kid to deliver his messages.

Even if it meant being as bold as to approach him at the station.

I'm so fucked.

CHAPTER TWENTY-ONE

Toby couldn't risk going to see Elizabeth — the police might come back any minute — but he had to speak to the woman. He lifted the landline phone in the hallway and prodded in her number from memory. His hand shook and he closed his eyes, wishing, once again, that he hadn't killed Maureen. None of this would be happening if he'd controlled himself.

"Hello?" she said.

He jumped. "It's Toby. I think they know what went on."

She actually growled. "What do you mean?"

"With your dad."

"What gave you that idea?"

"Anna's just left. She knows you lied about us not being that friendly. And she mentioned your dad and asked if I'd kept a secret for you."

"Oh God. Why has this come out after all these years?"

"Isn't it obvious? With Maureen dead and you being her old friend, I don't know, maybe they looked into you and the case came up. You should never have told me what happened. I really can't be doing with it all." *More than you'll ever know.*

"I had to speak to someone, you *know* that. Robert and Diana wouldn't. I had no one."

"Hmm. But that's not all."

"What have you done?"

"I told her to ask you, Robert and Diana about it."

"You stupid bastard!"

"I don't want to be involved in your dad's business. I was home with my mother, it was nothing to do with me. Anna mentioned perverting the course of justice. Do you *know* I can get in trouble for not reporting it?" Ironic, since he hadn't reported himself for Maureen's, but he couldn't think about that in depth right now.

"Go to the farm."

"Why?"

"So we can all talk about it."

"But the police will see us. I bet they're still in the field, collecting evidence or whatever."

"Not if we go down the alleys and scoot across to the farmhouse."

"The coppers will see us from the lay-by."

"Then we'll say we're going there for a cuppa if anyone asks. That's not a crime or any of their business. Do it. Now."

"Don't order me about! Christ, this is *your* mess, not mine."

"You know why I had to do it. Why I needed help. Why I couldn't let him live."

"You should have just let him go to prison. Then there was Lionel after that."

"Do *not* talk to me about my husband. We promised we never would."

"Do Robert and Diana know about that?"

"No, just you, so don't go bringing it up in front of them."

Toby cursed himself for ever getting involved with the Lionel episode. "Okay, I'm going now, but I don't see what good it will do if the police have already started poking into the past."

"We'll make a plan; go over our stories again to make sure they're straight."

"Right, I'll see you soon."

Toby put the phone down and stuffed his feet into his wellies. He slipped his coat on and took his large umbrella from the stand. It reminded him that the police had his canes. Had they tested any of them yet? Would they let him know when they were going to bring them back or just turn up with them?

He left the house, annoyed with himself that he hadn't checked out of the living room window first. Wilf ambled by and stopped at Toby's gate.

"Off out?" he asked.

"Well, I'd have thought that was obvious, seeing as I have my coat and wellies on."

"No need to be sarky. No cane?"

"If you're fishing as to why I'm using an umbrella, the police took all my canes to eliminate me from the inquiry. They also took the shoes I was wearing last night in the field. There, you can go and tell Albert all about it, you bloody arse-licker."

"I wasn't licking his arse! I was trying to be a friend because his wife's died."

"Yes, well, sorry if I don't believe you."

Toby marched down his path and yanked the gate open. "Your wife isn't back yet with Florence. You might want to check where she is in case *she's* been murdered an' all."

Pleased with his snipe but wishing he hadn't engaged in quite such a nasty manner, Toby huffed off down the alley. He sifted through everything that had been said during Anna's last visit, and his cheeks flushed hot at remembering she'd spotted the suitcase. He'd been so intent on finishing the carving, he hadn't factored it in. Carving took him away from all of his troubles, and it would have kept him calm while he was questioned if she hadn't insisted he stop it. Had his response sounded plausible?

Usually, he didn't dwell on things much beyond talking himself into believing everything would be all right. But this was murder, and every nuance, every look, every bloody thing had to be scrutinised. And now, here he was, going off to the farm to talk about a murder that was sod all to do with him.

But you know all about what happened to Lionel, so that's got something to do with you.

Oh God.

Maybe I should grass them all up about Jack and be done with it. Take my punishment for keeping it a secret.

But Elizabeth will bring Lionel up. She'll drop you right in it.

He tromped to the left at the end of the second alley and sidled towards the farmhouse. The spiked metal end of his umbrella dug into the earth, and he worried the police might come and take *that* and test it, too.

It would mean more questions.

Why did you go to the farmhouse? What are you hiding?

Rapping on the door, he caught sight of Elizabeth in his peripheral, trotting with purpose towards him. Well, *she'd* certainly got over whatever had gone on earlier. She looked full of beans. Or was it anger?

She reached him and glared. "Robert is going to be livid."

"*I'm* livid," Toby snapped back. "I didn't even do anything, yet I've been dragged into it."

"If you didn't open your mouth to Anna, we wouldn't *have* to be here, would we?" She stared at the door.

"Does he know you told me?"

"No."

"So why am I here?"

"I wasn't thinking straight, but he'll have to know now because of Anna snooping around."

Robert opened the door and stood in the frame, a frown bunching his features. "For all that is holy, what the hell are you two doing here?"

"Blame big-mouth here." Elizabeth barged in past Robert.

He stepped back. "I suppose you'd better come in an' all."

Toby sighed heavily. "I wish I never knew."

"About what?"

"Jack!" Toby walked by him and propped his umbrella against the wall.

Robert shut the door and leaned on it. "What about Jack? Which Jack?"

"Don't make out you're thick. You know which Jack."

"Jesus Christ, she *told* you?"

Toby jerked his head towards the room opposite. "I've known for years. Ask her."

Robert flew into the room, and Toby trailed after him. Elizabeth sat beside a flustered Diana on the sofa. Everyone stared at each other in turn.

"Look," Toby said, holding his hands up, "I haven't said anything for years, and I didn't today either. But Anna's got wind of Jack's case, she asked me about it. All I did was say she had to speak to you lot. Elizabeth's panicking now, when really she doesn't need to. Of *course* Anna would need to speak to you, because you were in the house when it happened. What good would talking to me do when I wasn't prepared to tell her anything?"

"Why tell her to speak to us when you know what's at stake?" Robert barked.

"No shouting," Diana said. "We don't like shouting."

"Shut up, you stupid, insane old cow," Robert yelled.

The silence that followed, broken only by the crackling flames in the fireplace, seemed to last forever. They all knew Diana wasn't well, that she'd gone a bit strange after Jack's death, but there was no need to bawl at her like that.

She rocked, hugging herself.

Elizabeth wrapped an arm around the woman's shoulders. "Don't speak to her like that. She doesn't deserve it."

"This is all your fault, Liz." Robert paced in front of the fire. "*You* wanted him dead, and I told you we'd get found out one day, but did you listen? No. Every time I watch one of those fucking shows where cold cases are revisited, I shit myself. There was *blood*, Elizabeth, blood we cleaned up, but it will still be there. These days, they'll find it."

Blood? Toby hadn't known about that. He raised his hands again. "I'm not staying here for this. I don't need to hear all the bits that were left out. I won't be saying anything to Anna, all right? If they come here, you stick to the original story, just leave me out of it." He stared hard at Elizabeth. "And if you know what's good for you, stick to what we said about the other thing, too."

"Other thing?" Robert asked.

Elizabeth nodded.

Toby stormed out, snatching his umbrella, and marched to the alley. The draw to turn around and look at the field was so strong he gave in. A tent stood where he'd left Maureen, and people in white outfits dotted the grass. They'd be searching every blade of it. And there was still the suitcase to dump, which weighed heavy on his mind.

Angry about all of it, but especially at himself for losing his rag with the one woman he'd promised to love forever, his Maureen, he thundered home, once again encountering Yvonne, with Florence. Yvonne opened her mouth to say something, but he cut her short.

"Just fuck off, woman. Fuck. Off."

He ignored her expression of surprise and went indoors, kicking off his wellies. He stripped off his coat, put it in the cupboard, and took the wellies and his umbrella upstairs to give them a soak in the bath. Fuck the police. It was time to change tack.

Albert wouldn't know what had hit him.

CHAPTER TWENTY-TWO

Elizabeth had hated her father for as long as she could remember. She'd often dreamed about a dad who swung her round by the waist instead of her hair, and bought her sweets as a treat. He was handy with his fists, too eager to let them fly, and her mother was usually on the receiving end. Elizabeth had taken a fair few whacks in her time, too, but he favoured slapping the backs of her bare legs, even now when she was older. It was humiliating. Soul-destroying. And now Mum was dead.

Crying hadn't done anything but make Elizabeth feel worse. It wasn't going to bring her back, no amount of grief would, and ever since she'd died Elizabeth had thought about killing him. She'd dreamed about it often enough, usually when she was sulking in her room after he'd smacked her, quietly calling him all the names under the sun — ones he'd spat at Mum when his belly had been full of booze and often when it wasn't. Nice words rarely came out of his mouth. Mum had said he loved alcohol more than them. Booze was the love of his life. And gambling. He placed bets in the city, staying away overnight. Elizabeth thought he had another woman on the go, especially since she'd spied lipstick on his collar that time. Mum had scrubbed it off without a word.

Living here with him now would become impossible if he was let out. There would be a post-mortem to decide what killed her, a nice policewoman had told her — as if it might not be her dad's punches and kicks — and this morning Robert's father had said he might be released on bail until the cause of death had been determined. He'd popped round to make sure she was okay. Mr and Mrs Jobs were lovely.

The police had been called out only once before, going by Elizabeth's memory. She'd been five, something like that. For years the neighbours had looked the other way when Mum had screamed for help, and there were the mutterings that it was a man's place to keep his missus in line, as if her being knocked about was okay. This time, though, Elizabeth had called it in. She'd come home from a long day at the factory yesterday to find Mum on the floor, her breathing raspy, and God, she'd been in such a mess. Blood, bruises, split lips, two front teeth missing. Bloated face. An arm skewed at an unnatural angle.

Dad had gone to the Jubilee.

An ambulance had arrived, as well as two policemen, and Elizabeth had finally got Mum to admit that Dad had done this to her. She'd been taken away, Elizabeth riding in the ambulance with her, and the police drove round to the pub to question Dad.

Mum had died an hour after their arrival, her final words, "Get away from him, my darling. Please. Please."

How could she? The wages at the factory weren't much cop unless you were a supervisor or line manager. And she had nowhere to go with both sets of grandparents living so far away, one in Spain, the other in Scotland. Elizabeth didn't want to live in either place. She loved Yorkshire, didn't want to be anywhere else.

To calm her mind, she wandered around the house, looking at all the things Mum had sewn. Touching them. Remembering the feel of the cloth when her mother had brought the bolts home, saying she was dead happy at finding them on the market. The curtains, the cushion covers on the three-piece suite, the quilted bedspreads, the clothes, even Elizabeth's pink dressing gown, she vowed never to part with. She'd never let go of any of it. Those things were too precious.

As it was Saturday, she'd have to wait until Monday to tell her boss, Bruce, about what had happened to Mum. Although she might have to have the day off. She could be in a cell at the police station. But not if she could help it.

It was the best option, getting rid of him, and her plan was now solid in her mind. It would be easy for people to believe he'd killed himself, considering what had happened, whether it was out of grief for losing his wife or guilt for killing her.

And it depended on whether the police let him go.

But she'd need help, and the only two people she trusted other than Toby were Robert and Diana, who'd been boyfriend and girlfriend since they were fourteen. Elizabeth envied their easy relationship, how they'd grown through their teens together and would finish each other's sentences. She wanted a man she could do that with, and she had her eye on Lionel Kettering, a right dishy fella who worked at Dobsons, the pottery place. He lived with his mum and dad in a cottage opposite the Jubilee, and she always walked into the pub on a Friday night hoping he'd be there.

Not last night, though. She'd been too busy crying in bed.

The front door slammed and, with her heart thumping, she rushed out of her parents' bedroom where she'd been absently stroking Mum's fur coat, another market find.

She stood at the top of the stairs, Dad staring up at her, a grin splitting his ugly face.

"They let me out," he said.

He was smiling? When Mum was dead?

Her hatred of him grew, something she didn't think was possible, and she made her mind up to definitely go through with it. Kill him. Get rid of the bastard.

He strode away towards the kitchen, and she went downstairs, slipped her shoes on and left the house. The key dangled on a string inside, easily pulled through the letterbox, so she didn't need to take it with her. But maybe she should in case Dad took it off so she couldn't get back in. He'd done that before, said it was a joke.

She decided not to bother and wandered along the pavement to Robert's and knocked on the door. Mrs Jobs answered and her face immediately showed her sadness.

"I'm that sorry, love. Come in. Do you need something to eat and drink? I just took some scones out of the oven, and there's a brew in the pot."

"Yes please, Mrs Jobs."

She followed the wide brunette woman into the kitchen, swallowing down emotion. The curtains at the window were the same as Mum had made for their house. Mrs Jobs had liked them so much she'd paid Mum to whip her a pair up, too. They had pictures of kettles and saucepans on them.

"Sit yourself down, lass. Is it Robert you're wanting? Of course it is."

Elizabeth nodded and sat. "I wasn't sure if he'd be out with Diana."

"Oh, they're upstairs in his room. Door open, you know."

Elizabeth couldn't imagine Dad letting her take a boy upstairs, door open or not. Well, that wouldn't be a problem once he wasn't around.

Mrs Jobs twittered on about anything except Mum, maybe thinking that was too painful at the minute. Elizabeth appreciated her thoughtfulness and accepted the tray of tea and scones.

"Take them up," Mrs Jobs said. "I daresay our Robert and Diana will be peckish. You can shut the door when it's the three of you."

Elizabeth thanked her and climbed the stairs, her tummy rumbling at the smell of the scones. They were still warm from the oven, and the butter had melted perfectly. Mrs Jobs made her own butter, and as a kid Elizabeth had sometimes watched her churning.

She shuffled into Robert's room, and her friends looked like they didn't know what to say. Elizabeth smiled, trying to be brave, because what she planned to ask them could go two ways: they say no and grass on her, or they say yes.

Time would tell.

* * *

They stood in Elizabeth's living room, Dad staring at them belligerently.

"Get out of the fucking way," he shouted. "I can't see the telly. I can't hear it either with all the racket going on upstairs. Go and turn it down before I give you a ruddy great clout."

Elizabeth's music blared, filling the whole house.

"No," she said.

"Pardon me, young lady?" Dad stood, fists bunched.

Robert punched Dad in the stomach. He was a big lad, strong from stacking the factory storeroom all day, used to lugging heavy boxes of chocolates about. The evil bastard went down onto the sofa, clutching his gut with both hands. Robert dragged him to the floor and sat on his stomach. Diana was squealing that she'd changed her mind and wanted to go home.

"Get off me!" Dad roared.

Elizabeth clutched the kitchen knife by her side, her leather gloves squeaking, and knelt next to the man she hated more than anyone. She attempted to slit his wrists, but each time she dragged the knife against his thin skin she drew the blade away, gasping. She tried five times on one, three on the other, but she hadn't gone deep enough, didn't have the courage after all. The cuts would soon scab and heal.

"There's rope in the shed," Robert said. "A great big coil of it." He struggled to pin Dad's hands down to the floor, but he managed it in the end, kneeling on his hands.

Dad laughed. Why wasn't he bothered that she'd cut him? Why did he think this was all a big joke?

"I'll get it." Diana stared at her gloved hands and left the room, probably so she wouldn't have to see any more cutting. She'd been the least up for doing this, worrying they'd get caught, nattering on in the way she usually did when she was flustered.

"Can you hold him down until I get back?" Elizabeth asked Robert. "We're going to hang him. We'll need a stool and the stepladder."

Dad bucked then, trying to get Robert off him, but he was too big, too heavy. Six foot, if Elizabeth was any judge.

"Pack it in now," Dad barked. "This has gone far enough."

"No, it hasn't," Elizabeth sneered, her courage returning because he looked so pitiful, so useless down there.

"What the fuck are you playing at?"

She bent over and stared him in the eye. "A life for a life, isn't that what they say? You took Mum's, I'll take yours, and I'll love every second of it."

"Will you heck as like," he fumed, and tried to raise his back off the floor to throw Robert off.

Robert remained steady.

139

Elizabeth dashed out to collect the stool from the kitchen. Mum had used it because she was short and couldn't reach the top shelves of the wall cupboards or the larder. Elizabeth put it in the living room, then found Diana in the shed.

She turned wet eyes Elizabeth's way. Some tears spilled over, rolling down her cheeks. "I can't find the rope."

"Because it's in Robert's shed, you stupid cow! Bloody hell." Elizabeth went inside. She checked the back windows of all the houses she could see, then closed the door. In the semi-darkness, she whispered, "Did anyone clock you coming in here?"

"I didn't look."

"Diana! We went through all this."

"S-sorry. I shouldn't be here. I'm not good for something like this. I'm frightened."

Elizabeth felt a bit sorry for her. Diana hadn't been brought up with violence, she didn't know what it looked like, smelled like, sounded like. She'd been coddled, and something like murder, well, it would scare anyone, wouldn't it?

Even me.

Elizabeth sighed. "I know, but you can see why this has to be done, can't you? He'll kill me next, you watch."

"But if they find out your mum died because of him, they'll put him in prison, then you won't have to be anywhere near him."

"But he could escape. Break in. Murder me in my bed. Then you'll feel really bad." Diana was the type to believe anything.

"Oh my God! Don't say that."

"So we have to get rid of him. You don't have to do anything except lie afterwards, all right?"

"All right."

They'd agreed to get rid of the knife and their outfits for good at some point, but Robert would stash them in the outhouse Diana's parents used as storage for now. If their mums and dads asked, Robert and Diana were going to say a bottle of lemonade had splashed all over them because Elizabeth had shaken the bottle, to explain their change of clothes.

140

Elizabeth checked to see the coast was clear, then said, "Go to Robert's shed, quick!"

Diana dashed out and across the grass. Elizabeth turned her attention to the stepladder, yanked it from behind the lawn mower and carried it out. She shut the shed, hoping they could pull this off.

Because if they didn't, she wasn't sure what she'd do.

CHAPTER TWENTY-THREE

In the incident room, everyone present, Anna sat on the edge of Sally's desk. "So, have you had a chance to look into Elizabeth's husband's death?"

Sally nodded. "Wayne and Peter dug into her dad's case a bit more while I did that."

She stared at Anna as if to try to convey something. What, that either Warren or Peter hadn't really done much in that regard? Sally shifted her gaze to Peter quickly, and Anna got the gist. Maybe he was being lazy today.

Sally returned her attention to some papers on her desk. "Right, so, given we're all in agreement that Jack's death *might* be suspicious, I'm naturally suspicious about this one, too." Again, she glanced at Peter.

She's been watching him. Has he done something? If he has, why hasn't she told me before now?

Sally cleared her throat. "Do you want to write this on the board as I speak?"

Anna got up and collected a marker pen. "Go on."

"Okay, his name's Lionel. Died in his car. But it wasn't your usual crash. It was on fire when someone spotted it in the parking area behind the factory. Elizabeth was at work at the time. Now, according to the file, she was on her lunch break prior to the incident. No one recalls seeing her eating except Toby. She claimed to have been around the side of the factory tucked away by the rubbish bin enclosure."

"Oh, Toby's name crops up again," Anna said.

"Who the hell wants to eat their food by the bins?" Peter asked.

Sally pointedly ignored his comment. "So of course my radar pinged, like it usually does when something's iffy." She paused and nodded at Anna's querying gaze. "I skimmed every statement, plus the final reports, to see what the outcome was. Toby said he'd also eaten there with her, and the officers accepted their story."

Anna jotted that down. "I'm already annoyed with her for saying she didn't really have much to do with him when it's clear she did." She went on to explain what Toby had said about Jack's death. "Yet it's obvious, if he's willing to give her an alibi for her husband's death, *if* we're assuming she killed him, then they know one another pretty well. You don't lie for someone unless you care for them or you're scared of the consequences, do you? Especially with murder."

"The coroner put it down to Lionel killing himself," Sally said. "Accelerant was used, petrol, and the seat of the fire was in the driver's footwell."

"Did he leave a note?"

Peter jolted. He quickly covered the involuntary movement up by rubbing his arms and exaggeratedly shuddering.

"Someone walk over your grave?" Anna asked. "Or did mention of a note bother you?"

"The grave thing," Peter said.

Hmm. Whatever. "So, did he?" Anna asked Sally.

"He did, actually. On the mantel at home."

"What did it say?"

Sally held up a piece of paper. "*Dear Liz, I can't do this anymore. Goodbye.* He'd signed it. She found it when she went home and phoned the police as soon as she'd read it. It was

Lionel's handwriting, apparently distinctive. But what if he wasn't saying goodbye because he was going to kill himself, but because he was leaving her to make a life elsewhere, and she killed him before he could drive off into the sunset?"

"That's possible," Anna said. "But say he did commit suicide. Why do it in the car park behind the factory? Did he want her to see the car in flames? Was he punishing her? Did he work there?"

"No, he didn't," Sally said.

Placket grunted. "Let's suppose she murdered her father and husband. It's plausible to think she killed Maureen, too. Maybe Elizabeth has a temper that flares when people upset her. Her face hardened when she spoke to me about Maureen cutting her off, but she quickly smoothed it out when she saw I'd noticed. What if she's held a grudge all this time, bumped into her at the lay-by and attacked her? Which means Joyce agreed to give her a false alibi, and brought up Jack to deflect the spotlight from her."

"What if Elizabeth got Toby to kill Maureen?" Warren suggested. "He helped her before by giving her an alibi for Lionel. We know he was in that field. He owns canes. He supposedly didn't hear Maureen screaming. All a bit suss, if you ask me. And you said, Anna, that the mud on those shoes was bone dry."

"Or he killed Lionel for her," Lenny said. "Maybe Maureen wasn't the only woman he was fixated on."

Anna sighed. "We're all just playing *Scooby-Doo*. We may well suspect more has happened, but unless we find something concrete we can't just bring them in to question them on old cases for no good reason. Let's take a breather for a second."

She retreated to her office to check her emails, hoping Sally would follow if she had something to say about Peter. She browsed her screen. Nothing from Herman yet, which wasn't surprising, and the lab understandably hadn't got back to her about Toby's shoes and canes. At the earliest they were talking a couple of days.

144

Which route should she and Lenny go down next? The swerve into the past had led them astray. Who else might Maureen have upset over the years? Tom hadn't rung her with an update on the witness statements from the Jubilee, and, with many keeping their mouths zipped about Maureen, they couldn't proceed.

She checked the time. Where had the day gone? She powered down her computer and, back in the incident room, they discussed Maureen's case some more to see if they'd missed anything. An hour passed, then, when it became clear they were going round in circles, she called it a day. Placket agreed.

Anna sidled over to Lenny. "Do you fancy dinner at the Jubilee tonight? Hopefully pick up some gossip?"

"Can do."

With that sorted, everyone went their separate ways apart from Peter, who said he'd stay and do some overtime. Sally left before Anna could have a private word with her. Whatever the issue was couldn't be that important.

In the car, Anna started the engine and put the heating on high. "We should nip to the factory first to speak to Bruce about Lionel's death."

"He said he was leaving to tell his children about the affair," Lenny reminded her.

"Bugger, I forgot about that. I'll ring him instead." She'd put everyone's numbers in her phone before the debrief in case she needed them. Pressing Bruce's icon, she put him on speaker and waited while the call rang.

"Who is this?" Bruce asked.

"It's Detective Inspector James."

"I don't want to be rude, but what do you want? My children have just left, they've been here for a while, and I'm feeling a little emotionally bruised."

"Didn't they take it well?"

"Not at first, and a few choice words were thrown my way, but they seemed to accept my reasons in the end."

"Good. What I wanted to ask was whether you remember the death of Lionel Kettering."

"Of course I do. It was suicide."

"So no one gossiped about it being anything else?"

"What, murder? Probably, you know what people are like, although I never heard them speaking about it in my earshot. Everyone had been told to be respectful and not mention it in front of Elizabeth. She was in quite a state."

"Toby was with her while she ate her lunch?"

"He was."

"Did people regularly eat food by the bins?"

"Err, no. But it's an enclosed area, brick walls around it. Perhaps they wanted to be alone."

"What are you suggesting?"

"Nothing."

"It's just we'd been given the impression Elizabeth and Toby weren't close, so my mind boggles as to why they'd eat lunch together."

"I have no idea."

"Okay, thanks anyway. Bye now." She ended the call and looked at Lenny. "Do you think they *were* friends but cooled it off because of what went on with Lionel?"

"God knows. Come on, I want my dinner."

A short queue greeted them on the way into Upton-cum-Studley. The side of the road closest to the lay-by was still cordoned off, but the other allowed for single-file traffic.

They entered the pub to a few sighs and grumbles.

"Not here for work," she said loudly. "Even coppers have time off."

Albert sat in his usual spot, the chair next to him conspicuously empty. Anna still couldn't get over him carrying on as normal, although the plate in front of him was perhaps evidence that he really couldn't cook and, with no wife to make his dinner, he was having it here.

It was Anna's turn to pay for their meal, so she put the order in at the bar. She chose Cokes for their drinks in case they were called out to work again. Ian placed them on the bar and held the card reader towards her. She tapped it, and he leaned closer.

"There's been a lot of chat about the police taking things from Toby's house, just so you know. Everyone thinks he did it. You know, *Maureen*."

As people seemed to know the ins and outs, what she'd say next wasn't going to compromise anything. "Maybe you can put them straight, then. We've taken some items so we can eliminate him from our enquiries, that's all. We could really do without the speculation."

Says me, when we're speculating about those old cases.

Ian nodded. "Right. I'll subtly filter that to them, then."

She returned to the table, draped her coat on the back of her chair, and sat so she could see the whole pub. Laura, clearly no longer working, lounged in the corner by the front window. She nodded to Anna, then pointed to the ladies'. Anna resisted rolling her eyes at her for being so obvious, but nevertheless she followed the woman into the toilets.

"I spoke to Albert when my shift ended," Laura said, after checking the cubicles were empty.

"Oh right."

"I don't think he did it. He was crying, and he never does that."

Murder can change people. "I see."

"He said something that really bothered me, though."

"What was it?"

"That Maureen would finally get to have her babies."

Anna frowned. "I don't get what you mean."

"I don't understand it either but I thought I'd pass it on in case it's relevant."

"Thanks. Anything else?"

"No." Laura dipped into a cubicle and locked the door.

Anna left, rejoined Lenny at the table and told him what had gone on.

"It's a riddle," he said, "and I hate those."

"It's going to bug me an' all."

Anna pondered the comment about the babies for a while, then swept it out of her head when their food arrived. A little respite from the case would do her good. They'd opted for pie and mash, Lenny loved that, and ate while talking about anything but the case — too many ears listening in.

The reprieve didn't last long. Once their plates were clean, she couldn't resist asking Albert what he'd meant. She got up and went over to him, avoiding Maureen's chair out of respect and choosing another.

"Laura's just told me what you said earlier, about the babies." At his dark look, she jumped back in. "Don't go getting angry with her, she did the right thing. She's trying to help the investigation."

Albert sighed. "I didn't kill her, you know. I told Placket that. I've wanted to many a time, but I never even got close."

"The babies. What did you mean?"

"She was pregnant a few times but lost them. At least now, if there's a heaven, she's with them. She'll be loving that, knowing I can't stop her from being with them."

Anna swallowed. "How far along was she when they died?"

"I don't know, but they looked like babies when they came out."

Anna closed her eyes. Those poor little things. It sounded like Maureen had to give birth to them as she'd been too far along for the other options. And he'd seen them when they'd come out. It struck her as odd that Albert would be so caring as to have been there with her when she was induced. He didn't strike her as the considerate sort.

She opened her eyes again, to find him smiling. "Something funny?"

"Yeah. If I *had* killed her, at least I'd get my cooking and washing done when I was inside. I've got to pay someone to do it all now. Maureen's left me in a right bind."

Anna stared at him. She shook her head — no words — and went back to Lenny to relay the conversation.

"I swear he's an A-grade arsehole," she whispered.

"Sounds like he's stuck in the past, hasn't moved with the times. Misogynistic."

Anna grimaced. "And then some."

Her phone rang. It was Placket's name on the notification bar.

Anna showed Lenny, then got up to answer the call outside. She'd forgotten to put her coat on, and the cold air quickly seeped through her clothes.

She swiped her screen. "Everything all right, sir?"

"I'm still at the station, had a few bits of paperwork to get done. A call came in from the driver, the woman Toby saw. She just caught the appeal on Facebook. She's in Marlford."

"If you give me her name and address, we'll pop to see her."

"I'll do it. It'll save you coming back into town."

"Okay, cheers."

Anna rushed back in and a welcome wall of warmth hit her. She sat and brought up her notes app, typing in what Placket had said, letting Lenny read it. She didn't need any earwiggers hearing anything. At the end, she added, *Watch what you say in here.*

"Good," he said. "She might have seen something."

"But if she had, wouldn't she have phoned it in at the time?"

"Maybe it didn't register as important until she saw the appeal."

Anna checked no one was listening. "Anyway, the boss is dealing with it."

"Thank God for that. I didn't fancy going back out there tonight."

"Me neither. Let's hope she gives us something we can work with, hopefully in the morning. I'm ready for my bed."

"You've got to drop me home first."

"Ugh. Why do you have to live in Marlford? Can't you kip at mine? You conveniently left a bag of your clothes in my spare room last time, as if I wouldn't notice. Cheeky sod."

Lenny smiled. "All right, you've twisted my arm. Your spare bed's more comfy than mine."

CHAPTER TWENTY-FOUR

Zara Gaines welcomed DCI Placket and PC Jacobs into her large new-build house, saying her husband was upstairs in his office. Thankful she hadn't expected them to stand in the cold on the doorstep, Placket sat at her kitchen table with a coffee and a plate of biscuits in front of him. Jacobs used his electronic device to record the interview.

"Would you prefer to have your husband here?" Placket asked.

"No, it's fine. I don't get weird vibes off either of you."

Placket held off a frown. "Tell me about your journey from when you left work last night."

Placket had looked the woman up before they'd set off from the station. A thirty-year-old beautician, specialising in hair and make-up. She worked in an upmarket salon — or rather, she owned it. Her husband was an architect. Nothing untoward had come up for either of them.

She fiddled with her wavy blonde hair. "I left work late because we had a couple of clients who needed a last-minute up-do."

"Up-do?"

"Yes, where we pin their hair up in a fancy style for weddings and things."

I need to get more with the times. "Right."

"The salon's on the other side of Upton-cum-Studley, so I needed to drive past to get to Marlford. I saw a man, he was old, and he had a walking stick. He was on the pavement, heading towards the lay-by with the egg table. I had planned to stop and buy some, but it was dark and I didn't fancy doing that when he was around."

"Because he frightened you?"

"Because I'm a woman and he gave me bad vibes."

Is she one of those psychics or just trusts her gut? Placket nodded. "I'm sorry you have to live like that. Sorry for all women."

She gave him a pointed look. "It's part of our lives, we're used to it. You couldn't possibly understand."

"You shouldn't have to be 'used to it'."

"No, but that's the way it is, and even though he was an old man I got one of my warning feelings. So I drove past. I did glance at him to see his face, and he was staring at me. I felt better about my decision not to stop."

"Why? Did he look angry?"

"No, it gave me the creeps. Can't explain it. Anyway, I neared the lay-by and saw a car parked there. I think it was a Ford Focus, but I can't be sure on the Focus bit. Definitely a Ford because I clocked the badge at the back. It was either grey or silver. A woman was at the table, putting eggs into a carton. She was old, too. I wanted to stop, to park and make sure she got into her car safely before the man got there, but something told me not to. This is going to sound horrible, but I'm glad I didn't. It could have been me who was killed."

"It's a natural and understandable reaction." *Although it would have been kind to have waited in your locked car.* Placket checked himself. Maybe he *didn't* understand how women felt. To have to choose between helping someone else and saving your own skin must be difficult. "Go on."

"I kept going, glanced in my rear-view, but couldn't see the lay-by at that point because of the trees, and the man was gone."

That's in keeping with what Toby said; he dipped through the first opening in the hedge.

Placket visualised the road, going from memory. He wouldn't be able to judge properly unless he went there to have a look or he had photos to go by, but was it possible Toby could have made it to the lay-by by then? Had he sped up in that short time in order to get there?

"How far ahead were you when you checked behind?" he asked.

"A good few metres, could be more. I don't know exactly. Then I went round the bend and carried on to Marlford."

Such a slim timeframe, yet it was so important.

"Did you happen to see what kind of walking stick he used?"

"Yes. It stood out because it was so pretty."

Pretty? The images Placket had seen were of plain canes with hooked handles, like an old-fashioned shepherd's crook.

"Did the handle curve?" he asked.

"Not that I saw. I assumed it was one of those ones with a ball on the end because his whole hand covered it."

"That's pretty specific. I'm wondering how you picked up so much detail in a matter of seconds."

"I'd looked at him for a while when I was behind him."

"What did you mean when you said the cane was pretty?"

"Oh, it was carved, all of it. It really stood out in my headlights."

Carved. He's bloody got rid of the one he used or he's hidden it.

Placket's stomach rolled over. "What was he wearing?" He brought to mind the clothes they had at the lab.

"Dark trousers."

The ones we have are beige.

"A black coat, like a Barbour. I remember the diamond pattern in the stitching."

We have a brown tweed jacket.

"Gloves, a dark bobble hat."

We don't have those.

"And walking boots. He had his trousers tucked into the tops of them, which is why they stood out."

We have shoes.

"You're very observant," Placket said, his heart racing. "And I'm grateful for it, believe me. Okay, we'll have to leave it there. What you've said has been extremely useful. We'll get your statement typed up, and someone will be round for you to sign it, unless you'd prefer to pop to the station."

"I'd prefer the station. My hours are erratic because it's coming up to Christmas. Everyone wants their hair and make-up done for work parties."

"Okay, I'll make sure someone rings you to let you know it's ready. Sorry I didn't drink the coffee, but we have to get on."

Zara showed them out, and Placket all but jumped in the car, Jacobs scrabbling to get in too, obviously sensing the urgency.

"Something going on, sir?" he asked.

"You could say that." Placket rang Anna. "Get yourself round Toby's. I'm on my way there with Jacobs."

"What's going on?"

"He's given you the wrong bloody clothes, and he had boots on, not shoes. The cane he used was carved — pretty, the woman said. We don't *have* any carved canes."

"Shit. His cane stand is carved, and he was making something in his workshop earlier with the same pattern on it."

"We're also missing gloves and a bobble hat. He's lying, and we need to bring him in."

"Okay, we'll go now."

Placket tossed his phone into the cup holder and gunned the engine. He drove off, adrenaline flushing his system, and smiled.

Anna's gut feeling had been right from the off.

Brilliant woman.

154

CHAPTER TWENTY-FIVE

Peter had been putting off the inevitable by staying at work, and, when the last message had vibrated in his pocket and he'd seen what it said, he couldn't put it off any longer. The problem with loyalty jobs was they tended to get a bit messy. People got stabbed or shot at best and killed at worst. You did whatever you were told as proof you belonged to the Kings.

What had set Trigger off? Was it because Peter had said he wanted out — for good?

Stupid of me to have said that.

He slid the key into the lock of his front door and stepped inside. At some point tonight he'd be contacted again, told where to go and what to do. The biggest test yet, because Peter could be followed by those men or whoever else was after him. Or was that Trigger's game? Did he *want* Peter to get caught? Or were those men King members?

He slung his keys onto the little table in the hallway and walked to the kitchen at the end in the dark. He put the light on, found a ready meal in the fridge and popped the plastic top, getting an unusual amount of satisfaction each time he jabbed the fork into it as he imagined it was Trigger's face.

He stuck it in the microwave, and, instead of his usual coffee when he got home from work, he went straight to the booze cupboard. Then stopped.

He might need to drive. He couldn't risk getting pulled over.

That meant he was definitely going to go through with it. *Like I have a choice.*

"Fuck's sake."

He took out a Coke and downed half the can. Stared at nothing while his thoughts raced and his food warmed. He should never have agreed to join the police for the Kings. Should have changed his name and moved away. Distanced himself from Marlford and everything in it.

The microwave pinged, and he slung his dinner in its plastic container onto a wooden tray, adding the Coke and the fork. He carried it to the living room, using his elbow to jab at the switch on the wall, missing it completely.

A lamp snapped on in the corner, Trigger's arm stretched out, his hand beneath the glass shade. He withdrew it and smiled. Wheels sat beside him on the sofa as if they had every right to be there. They were both in black. "Job" clothes. Hats on, the hems rolled up, so that meant balaclavas. Peter didn't need to ask how they'd got in. Trigger had a back-door key from years ago.

Peter sat in the armchair and ignored them, digging the fork into his macaroni cheese, cursing as the steam came off it. If he ate it now, he'd burn his tongue.

"Steady," Trigger said. "That looks like it's the temperature of the sun."

Peter dropped the fork into the food. "What do you want me to do?"

"There's a King, new recruit, and he's fucked up."

That meant death.

"Right." Peter swallowed. "How old?"

"Sixteen."

Aww, fuck. "Do I know him?"

156

"No, he started after your little breather began. You're going to take him out while we observe."

"I've told you already, I think I'm being watched."

"Yeah, two men drew up not long after you. They're parked on the other side of the road. But it's okay, they didn't see me looking out, and I doubt they'd put more than those two on you at one time. There'll be no one round the back. At least there wasn't when we turned up."

Wheels crossed his ankles. "The thing is, *why* are they following you? What gave them the idea you need to be watched, eh?"

"No fucking clue," Peter said. "Look, can I eat my dinner before we go?"

"Not advisable," Trigger said. "You know how you get when you've killed someone. Sometimes you go all silly and throw up. The less you've got in your stomach the better. You of all people know how clever that forensic lot are these days. They can get all sorts out of a pile of sick."

Peter put the tray on the side table next to his chair. "I need to go and get changed."

"Clothes are in the bag on your bed," Trigger said.

Peter traipsed upstairs. He'd have the unenviable task of seeing the comings and goings of the coppers who'd be dealing with the traitor's death by tomorrow, the street crime team dedicated to gang-related incidents, although none of the murders of youngsters had been put down to the Kings. Two other gangs operated in the area, kids mainly, who fought for prominence and regularly fell out. Stabbings, drive-by shootings, all the criteria of standard rivals. Nothing that would make its way to Anna's desk, thank God. He couldn't imagine investigating his own crime.

He stripped out of his work suit, then showered to remove any trace of the station off him, including washing his hair. He took out the stuff in the bag on the bed, dreading it if the transparent clothes packages had already been opened.

That would mean Trigger had tampered with them, planted something that would likely drop off at the scene and incriminate Peter. He'd done it before to others.

The packages were intact, but Peter no longer trusted Trigger, so he checked for signs of them being shut with one of those handheld sealing gadgets.

It all looked okay. So this was just a lesson, then. For Peter to understand he would never get out of King life. He put on the boxers, socks, black T-shirt, jogging bottoms, hoody and gloves. Looked at himself in the mirror on the wardrobe door and hated who stared back at him. A bent copper. He slid on the brand-name trainers he'd never wear again after tonight, the soles the same as many a gangster kid would wear. Nothing distinctive that would stand out from the crowd, but it would point to them belonging to a teenager if Peter left any footprints. The trainers cost well over a hundred quid. No self-respecting gang member would be seen dead in a pair less than that.

He found two hundred pounds inside the bag in a ziplock. They'd be fake notes, and it meant Peter had to hand them over, probably for drugs. He folded them and slipped them in his pocket. Next, a flick-knife sealed in a plastic packet and a pair of scissors for cutting it open. He extracted the knife, hating that it would slide through some kid's thigh, slice that crucial artery, and he'd be the one to do it. He tested that the mechanism worked and how quickly the blade shot out. Retracted it. Stuck it in his pocket.

Ready, he went downstairs and met Trigger and Wheels in the hallway. They left via the back door, and as they walked over the grass Peter scuffed his soles over it to dislodge any fibres that might have attached from the carpet on his stairs. Wheels nipped through the back gate and took a quick look across the road to yet another kid on a bike, who nodded that it was safe to proceed. They slipped into a black car with tinted windows, Peter in the back, Trigger in the passenger seat, and Wheels drove away.

"One stab if you can manage to keep it at that," Trigger warned.

"I know."

One stab was the usual for the youth gangs — a fast punch with the blade, then the attacker fled, either hoping for death if that had been the plan, or for the victim to be found alive so it sent a message: fuck us about again, and next time it'll be worse.

"What did he do?" Peter asked.

"Fumbled a job. Could have got us caught."

"*What*, though? What exactly did he do?"

"Wanting to work out if he deserves it, are you?"

Fuck off with reading my mind. "Just answer, will you?"

"No."

So I could be killing someone for no reason, so Trigger can make a point with me. "Where is he?"

"Manning his corner, like usual."

"So you want me to approach as a buyer."

"Yep. Get him behind the wheelie bins. Do it there."

Peter had to check. "You've put fake plates on this car, yes?"

"Don't even ask such a stupid question."

The car would be dumped, burned out.

"Don't go near Upton to torch it," Peter warned.

"Yeah, Parole said your lot are over there, some old dear copped it."

"What's the target's name so I can listen out for any chatter at the station after?"

"Goes by the tag name Puppet."

Wheels parked opposite a lad standing on a corner. A moped leaned against a wall behind him, and to the left was a snake of wheelie bins where residents had put them out for collection in the morning. Peter assessed the scene, working out what he'd do and when.

"On you go, then," Trigger said.

"Are you going to film it?"

159

"Of course I fucking am."

Then I'll keep my face away from the car. "Any CCTV here?"

Trigger nudged Wheels. "Hark at him, getting into copper mode." He twisted to look between the seats at Peter. "Fuck me, pal, do you really think I'd have one of our lot selling if there were cameras? Use your loaf."

Peter got out of the car and checked both ways before crossing, scoping out the immediate vicinity. Lights on in the houses. Some curtains open, some closed. He approached the kid, who wore a black face mask patterned with neon skulls.

"Whassup?" Puppet said.

"What have you got?"

"Show me the pound signs first, bruv."

"Behind the bins. I don't want any feds copping a look." Peter hunched his shoulders. "Fucking paranoid, know what I mean?"

Puppet tutted and walked behind the first bin, unfazed by a man covering his features and acting oddly. Maybe people did this all the time.

Peter followed him and took the money out of his pocket. Showed it to him. "Keep the exchange low, man, so no one sees."

"Jesus, you're trippin'. What do you want?"

"Coke."

"How much you got?"

"Two hundred."

Puppet took the cash, flicked through it and stuffed it in a bumbag on his right hip. As he reached into the one on his left, Peter withdrew the knife. He clicked the button, gripped the front of Puppet's hoody and spun him round so his back was against the bin. It moved a tad, then held steady. Probably full.

"I'm sorry," Peter whispered. "Blame Trigger."

"What the hell, man?"

Peter stuck the knife into the inside of his thigh, where he knew Puppet had no chance of survival. He stepped back,

160

the blade coming with him, and dropped it on the ground like Trigger would expect. The bin trundled away from Puppet's sagging weight and clattered into the road on his side. The top popped open and a black bag slid out.

The noise!

Puppet landed on his arse in a sitting position, stunned. He stared down at his leg, then up at Peter. "What did I do?"

"I don't know. I don't fucking *know*."

Puppet sank slowly onto his side, crying for his mum, blood seeping onto the pavement in a dark pool. There was already so much, the poor bastard wouldn't pull through even if someone came out to help.

Peter sped away and jumped in the car, his stomach clenching, bile rising. Wheels drove off, glancing the bin as the car left the kerb. He took the roads he already knew didn't have cameras, laughing and saying he hadn't had such a rush in a long time.

Peter thought of that boy, bleeding out on the street. Puppet would have thought of himself as a big man for being accepted into the Kings, someone important. Yet, like Peter had, he'd also have known he was out of his depth, and he'd have been scared at times, wishing he'd never chosen that path, knowing there was no way off it.

Anger came, directed towards Trigger. "Happy now?"

"If he's dead, I will be."

Peter stared to the side at the passing scenery, images springing into his head.

The first person to find Puppet — that memory would stay with them forever, scar them, haunt them.

The police turning up and cursing the wayward youths of Marlford for yet another senseless murder.

The mother being told her baby was gone, her wail the loudest she'd ever released.

All because of me.

Peter glared at the headrest in front of him.

And you, Trigger, you utter bastard.

CHAPTER TWENTY-SIX

Toby went in the opposite direction to the lay-by. He drove a few metres and panicked. Two policemen held their hands up for him to stop. Shit, he'd thought he was being clever by choosing this route, but of *course* they'd be stopping people both ways to ask if they'd seen anything last night.

The suitcase on the back seat . . .

His father's shotgun in the boot . . .

Oh God.

He opened his window and smiled, thinking up an excuse as to why he'd turned right out of the village instead of left. Yes, he'd planned to tell anyone who asked that he'd gone to the Christmas market, but why would he be going *this* way to get there?

"Hello, sir," one of the PCs said.

"I've already spoken to the police about Maureen," Toby blurted. "They know what I saw and what I didn't. I live in the village."

"Can I have your name, please?"

"Toby Potter."

The PC tapped on an electronic pad, then retreated to the front of Toby's car. He must have been taking down the number plate, as he prodded the screen again. He used a phone, spoke for a moment, then came back to the window.

Toby felt sick.

"That's fine, your name's been ticked off," the officer said. "Where are you going now?"

"The Christmas market in Marlford."

"But that's the other way."

"I didn't want to drive past where it happened. Maureen was special to me. It's very upsetting."

"I understand." The PC tapped the roof of the car and moved away, probably to speak to the person whose headlights currently blinded Toby in the rear-view mirror.

He drove off, his heartbeat painful. It took him a good five minutes to calm down enough to think a little more rationally. By the time he arrived in Westgate, he had his thoughts in order. He parked in front of the Premier Inn and hauled his suitcase out, glad of his gloves because of the biting cold. He walked away with it rumbling on its wheels behind him — just any other man leaving the hotel, should anyone be watching. He made his way towards Jubilee Lake feeling thankful the Christmas market was on. If those officers saw him coming back in a couple of hours' time, it wouldn't look suspicious.

Maybe they'll have buggered off home by then.

Toby approached the treeline around the lake and stooped amid a clump of bushes. Waiting. Observing. Despite the weather, a few people stood around the water's edge, feeding the ducks and swans, their bleeding hearts on full display. Lamp posts lit the scene, which he hadn't anticipated; nor had he factored in the apartment block that had been built a few years ago. Toby hadn't been here for a long time, so how he remembered it wasn't how it was today.

Again, he hadn't thought things through.

Even if he hung around until the duck-feeders had gone, residents might see him dropping the case into the water. It was blatantly suspicious — there was something on the news about a body found in a suitcase in London not long ago, so they would report it. He swallowed, chilled to the bone now, wishing Maureen had been kind to him last night rather than basically accusing him of stealing, then she'd still be alive.

An hour passed, people leaving, others arriving with their near-mouldy loaves of bread, and, at last, no one stood around the lake. He'd spotted a darker area to take the case —the bulb in one of the lamp posts was out — so he lugged it over the grass, shielded by the trees, the wheels dipping into the uneven ground and bumping back out.

He ducked behind a tree and checked out the building. Some curtains had been closed, but other windows showed the furniture within, and higher up the ceilings bathed in cones of light. He couldn't see anyone staring out, but that didn't mean they weren't. He regularly nosed into his street through a small gap in the curtains.

He pulled the hem of his woolly hat down low, drew up the hood of his padded black coat and lifted the suitcase to the edge of the lake, panting; it was heavy. One last sweep of the windows, and he dropped the evidence into the water. Unbelievably, despite its weight, the case bobbed, then lay on its back, floating for what felt like an inordinate amount of time, just *staying there*. Time felt skewed, his perception of events slowing down, a second seeming like an hour. Water must have seeped in, as the case quickly descended, and time snapped back to normal. He reversed into the treeline as bubbles burst on the lake's surface, then a big balloon of air pressed against it, letting off a glugging noise as it popped.

He watched for a while, flicking his attention from the lake to the windows, and then, satisfied the case wasn't coming back up — *it'll be all right, there's all those pebbles* — he walked away, only for a shout to stop him momentarily.

"Oi, what the fuck do you think you're doing?"

With no suitcase to use as a walking aid, Toby had trouble hobbling off. His chest tightened at the *shush* of footsteps scuffing the ground behind him, likely old leaves from autumn that had turned into mulch. Wasn't that an inane thing to think when someone was coming after him?

He shot behind a wide tree trunk and held his breath.

More footsteps.

Toby dipped his mouth under the front part of his coat to release air — he didn't want a white cloud giving him away.

The footsteps stopped. "Fuck it. Where's he gone?"

The *shush* came again, except it grew fainter the more the sound continued. Were they walking away? Toby closed his eyes, tears leaking. This was finally becoming too much, all of it. His usual confidence faded fast, and he clung to the last vestiges of it, pressing onwards, praying he could get to his car without any hassle. He risked a glance behind him, but whoever it had been had gone. Relieved, he struggled back to his car and spied a security camera on the front of the Premier Inn.

Shit.

He really wasn't any good at this.

* * *

Toby drove into the village from the other entrance at the back so he'd avoid seeing the police. Why he hadn't done that on his way to the lake, he didn't know. He blamed it on his mind not processing things properly. He had murder on the brain — his beating Maureen to death, his knowledge of what had really happened to Jack, and his involvement in Lionel's death. He'd known what Elizabeth was going to do and had let her do it, covering for her afterwards. There was too much information swirling, so was it any wonder he hadn't planned things just so?

He turned into his street and gawped at the scene ahead. He had the wherewithal to douse his headlights before anyone turned his way, but Anna, Lenny and some other man in a suit and coat stood in his front garden with two policemen in uniform. He reversed and drove around the back of Elizabeth's, panicking about where to leave his car. If so many officers were at his, it meant bad news.

He had Albert to see yet. He needed to speak to him before he went to prison, and he'd accepted that was where he was going. Dealing with Albert was more important than staying a free man. If they'd come to arrest him, he wasn't going down for only one murder. He'd rather blast Albert's head off and be put away for two. Out with a bang an' all that. But they might not be there because of Maureen. It could be to do with Jack or Lionel.

Or maybe that woman driver came forward.

Bloody hell.

He carried on until he reached the street behind Albert's, then took a turning to park beside a set of council-owned garages in their own area. With his car tucked away beneath the overhanging branches of a tree, he got out and collected the shotgun from the boot.

This feud was going to end tonight — no matter the consequences.

* * *

Toby sat at Albert's kitchen table for ages in the dark. He'd planned his escape route, although where would he go when he left here? He'd need a breather after this, some time to come to terms with being sent to prison. Would the police still be at his house, waiting? Then there was the shotgun. The noise it would create. The neighbours would hear it and phone the police. He had limited time in which to get away.

The glowing digital clock on the microwave showed a green 11.15, so the scrape of a key in the lock of the front door shouldn't have come as a surprise, yet he still jumped. It kick-started his adrenaline and he shot up, the chair legs scraping against the floor.

Shit.

"Who's there?" Albert said.

The long pause stretched out so much Toby felt sick again.

"Bloody hearing things," Albert grumbled, and his footsteps tapped down the hallway.

Toby took aim with the gun, pointing it towards the open kitchen door, and quietly moved to the back wall opposite the cupboards and the cooker.

The light flicked on and he blinked, startled by the illumination. He'd expected Albert to go straight up to bed. The stupid prat ambled over to the kettle, then turned to the sink, didn't even see Toby to his right.

Until he did.

Albert's eyes widened, but only for a moment. Then they narrowed on the shotgun, and the cheeky fucker laughed. "Oh, I've seen it all now. Jesus wept." He filled the kettle and put it on the base, his back to Toby, prodding the switch. "I suppose I'm next, am I?"

This nonchalance, Toby couldn't get over it. For once, couldn't Albert be afraid of him? How could a man be so sure of himself? So unbothered by having a gun pointed his way? Or was he so mocking because it was Toby who held it?

"I know you killed Maureen." Albert swung round. Folded his arms and leaned against the edge of the worktop to look Toby in the eye. "I had a feeling you'd show up here, which is likely why my instincts told me to stay at the pub all day, like usual. But then I told myself you didn't have the balls to confront me one on one, you only ever do it in front of an audience so you're safe. Come on then, get it off your chest. *Again*." He rolled his eyes as if bored with Toby's fifty-year narrative.

"You need to be scared of me," Toby said. "I killed Jack *and* Lionel. Bet you didn't know *that*, did you?" He hadn't done that at all, but he needed this man to fear him, and he was desperate to feel the power of having one up on Albert, like he had by knowing about the affair. His revelation about it earlier had given him such a thrill.

"Oh, *right*." Albert chuckled. "You're a liar. For one, your mother said you were home all day when Jack hanged himself, and two, you were at the bin store with Elizabeth when Lionel burned to a crisp."

"That's what we *wanted* people to think. You're lucky I didn't kill Maureen years ago. Elizabeth wanted me to, your bloody wife upset her when she cut her off, but I couldn't do it at the time." How many more lies would he tell?

"Yet you killed her last night."

Toby could admit that now, if he chose. Albert was going to have his head blown off, so did it matter *what* Toby told him?

"It was an accident." There, he'd said it. An odd sense of relief filled him.

"You *accidently* battered her to death? It was with your cane, wasn't it?"

"She was spiteful to me again. I lost it."

"She was bitter towards you right until the end. Just like I wanted."

"What?"

"There's a reason I taught her how to behave. So no other man would want her. So I got to keep her. No one would be interested in a cow like her."

"Bruce was."

Albert's face darkened. "There's no proof she did that. I'm going to see him tomorrow, hash it all out."

"You won't be here tomorrow."

Albert laughed. "What, you reckon you've got the guts to shoot me? Fuck off, have you!"

Toby tightened his gloved finger on the trigger. "You've underestimated me, always have. To you I'm just this stupid arsehole you like to pick on. But I'm not. I've wanted to do this for years. Then take Maureen back. Give her a better life than the one you handed to her."

"Except, true to form, you fucked it up and killed her first. What a dick." Albert shook his head as though he pitied him. "She had kids with me, you know. Something you were never able to give her."

Toby frowned. *That's an outright lie.* "What?"

"Babies. Tried to hide it from me, didn't she? Thought I wouldn't notice when her guts got big. Daft bitch. I soon sorted it."

A terrible sense of dread replaced the relief from Toby's confession. "Oh God. What did you do to her?"

"The usual. Punched her. Kicked her in the stomach a few times until she went into labour. No skin off my nose, I didn't bloody want kids."

The kettle clicked off, and the sound echoed along with the noise of the bubbling water.

"You murdered your own *babies*?" Toby's breathing grew ragged.

"No, *she* did. If she'd been more careful, she wouldn't have got pregnant, would she? I wouldn't have had to do it."

This man was more of a monster than Toby had thought. What the hell kind of life had Maureen lived? Why had she stayed with him? What hold did Albert have over her?

"*You* should have been more careful," Toby said, his voice quiet while he tried to rein in his temper.

"She was meant to be on the pill."

"If you didn't want kids, you should have had a vasectomy."

"Piss off! It's the woman's job to take care of stuff like that." Albert sniffed. "They're buried in the garden. Every single one of them. By her. So *she's* the criminal here. Nasty little rats, that's all they are, and I needed to get rid."

Revolted, Toby remembered someone else had done that. It had been on the news about a baby being buried in a garden. On the north-east coast. Scudderton, wasn't it, that place near Robin Hood's Bay?

"You're sick," he said.

Albert sneered. "And *you're* a coward. You'd never shoot me. All mouth and no trousers, that's what you are."

Albert turned to the kettle and took a cup off the draining board. He made a coffee as if he didn't care whether Toby was there or not. He didn't care what he'd done to Maureen. That poor woman, having to bury her babies. No wonder she'd become bitter. Had she been horrible to Toby, not only because Albert had told her to, not only because Toby had caught her with Bruce, but because she resented Toby for not fighting for her, for not taking her away from the cruel life she'd led?

Things could have been so different.

Toby would have let her have babies.

He pulled the trigger.

CHAPTER TWENTY-SEVEN

In the car outside Toby's, where they'd been waiting for ages, Anna jumped at the sound of her phone ringing. It was the station, so she swiped to answer. "DI James."

"It's me, Wilson."

God, what had happened *now* for one of the evening sergeants to get hold of her?

"Have you located his car? Toby Potter's?" she asked.

"No. It was last logged leaving the village about eight. This is a different matter entirely. A gunshot coming from Albert Frost's cottage. Armed response and about twenty uniforms are on the way."

"Oh, fuck me."

"A witness saw someone coming out of Albert's cottage and walking down his back garden, didn't seem to be in any rush. Control pulled officers off road duty outside the village. There's a fatality. An older gentleman."

"Oh no. Albert. Who reported the shot?"

"The next-door neighbour, a Paul Shepherd. He said he'd get all the neighbours along the row out of their cottages. They'll all be in the Jubilee. Ian opened up to let them in. The PCs at the scene have cordoned the front and back gardens off."

"Okay. Cheers. We'll go there now." She ended the call and glanced at Lenny. "Gunshot at Albert's. He's likely dead, unless it's another older man who copped it."

"Shit."

"Hang on while I let the PCs know we're leaving."

Anna got out of the car. Placket had gone home, leaving her, Lenny and two PCs sitting outside Toby's, the consensus being that he'd return home at some point. One of the officers on road duty had logged Toby's car leaving the village, with the excuse that he was going to the Christmas market. At the time it hadn't been any cause for concern, as Placket hadn't alerted control that Toby needed apprehending.

As the market was on until late, the plan was to stay here until he came back. Anna had considered going home about midnight, and the PCs would remain, giving her a ring when Toby appeared. Placket had told the two uniforms to ignore any shouts that came through the radio, but why hadn't one of them come to tell Anna about the gunshot? Had they taken Placket's directive literally?

"Fuck's sake," she muttered and approached their car, tapping on the driver-side window. It glided down, revealing Jacobs. "Fatality at Albert Frost's. Gunshot. I gather you've heard about it?"

"Yes, but Placket said—"

"I know." She wasn't going to argue the toss with him. "We're going over there now. You stay put, but move your car so it's less likely to be seen. A witness saw someone leaving the scene, so if you see Toby don't approach him as he may be armed. Get hold of me straight away if and when he shows up."

PC Jacobs nodded.

She returned to her car and drove towards the Jubilee. "This is a nightmare."

Lenny rested his head on the side window. "Maybe he was the driver of the car we saw earlier, the one that backed out of the street."

"Bloody shame it disappeared before the PCs could catch up with it." Anna gritted her teeth. "Sod's law."

One old man, wreaking havoc. Because it *had* to be Toby, didn't it?

"I said from the start it was him," she said.

"You did, but we have to follow the rules. We can't just arrest someone because of your gut feeling, so don't beat yourself up. Don't deny that's what you're doing, I can tell by your face."

"Yeah, well, it annoys me because all this could have been prevented if that woman driver had come forward sooner. What's the betting Herman finds carving imprints on Maureen's wounds once he's cleaned them up?"

"I thought the same."

She drew up to the Jubilee car park and stopped next to one of the police cars already there. Two PCs stood in Albert's front garden. Anna found packets of protective clothing in the boot, and they dressed up. Lenny followed her over the road. They dipped beneath the cordon strung across the gate and signed the log. Anna signalled that she was going round the back.

The rear door stood open, light spilling out, another PC standing nearby.

"Was it like this when you arrived?" Anna eyed the jagged glass close to the handle so someone could stretch inside and turn the key.

"Yes. Fair warning, it's not pretty in there."

"How so?"

"Looks like a shotgun to me."

"Ah, that much mess, then?"

"Yep."

Anna stepped inside, skirting around the glass fragments on the lino. Normally she wouldn't have gone in until photos had been taken as it would have disturbed the scene, but the PCs had already done that in their rush to see if the victim could be saved. She stopped by the table and turned to stare ahead, the garden to her right. Skull fragments and brain matter marred the cupboard above the kettle and the walls either side, and some had found its way to the white cooker top. The victim had fallen backwards, what remained of his head pointing towards Anna and away from the kettle, his feet towards the floor cabinets.

Going by the mess and the height of it, he'd been standing at the kettle when shot. The force of the blast would have shunted him forward, which would explain the patch of thicker blood and a smear from his body hitting the top, then he'd slumped down onto his back.

Facial identification was impossible as there was hardly any face left. But the hair and clothing gave it away. Definitely Albert. Whoever had done this maybe couldn't look him in the eye when they'd shot him. Or had Albert turned away at the last second, unable to stand seeing someone pull the trigger?

Lenny came to stand beside her. "Oh. Nasty."

"It's not nice, is it? No signs of a struggle."

"Do you really think he'd have let Toby in, though?"

Anna glanced at the back door. "He was already in here, by the looks of it."

Lenny nodded. "He must have come straight here after going to the village. I doubt very much he went to the market."

"I'd say he was dumping the clothes he had on last night, the boots and the cane." She thought of something. "That bloody suitcase in his workshop."

"We weren't to know."

"I realise that, but . . . No, I'm not going to blame myself."

"Glad you said that, because it's easy to look back and wish differently, but he had a plausible excuse, so what can you do?"

Voices out the back drew her attention to the door. Steven Timpson and his team had arrived and, as the kitchen was small, it'd be a squash with everyone in there.

"We'd better leave them to it."

She left the kitchen and stripped off her outfit on the patio. Lenny joined her to do the same so they didn't transfer anything else outside from the cottage. Steven was carrying a stack of bags over one arm, and peeled off a couple to deposit their dirty protectives in.

Anna popped hers inside and said to Steven, "We need to nip across to the pub and speak to the witness."

He raised his eyebrows. "Someone saw him getting shot?"

"No, but the suspect left the cottage via the garden, so you may want to concentrate on the gate down there, although if they were sensible they'd have had gloves on."

Anna realised they were right in the way, and moved to stand in front of the kitchen window. She saw blood spatter and a glob of brain on the inside of the glass. She turned her back on it. Took a deep breath. "We'll leave you to it, Steven."

"See you when I see you." He entered the cottage.

Anna walked down the side passage and out into the front garden. She signed the log and continued over the road, after picking up Lenny at the pub door.

She checked if it was unlocked, twisted the handle and went inside.

CHAPTER TWENTY-EIGHT

Several people in various kinds of bedtime attire sat close to the fire in the Jubilee, coffee cups on tables. Ian was perched on a bar stool nattering to a PC. While the officer had undoubtedly spoken to everyone already, Anna wanted it straight from the horses' mouths. She held up her ID in case not everyone here knew who she was. She didn't recognise two couples. The women looked similar, so were they the sisters and their husbands, the only ones in the village in their fifties?

She walked over. "Can we speak to Paul Shepherd first, please?"

A man in his thirties glanced at the woman beside him, who was holding a sleeping baby around five or six months old with ruddy cheeks. She nodded. He rose and followed Anna and Lenny to the table by the front window. She wanted to be far enough away from the others so the conversations could remain as private as possible.

They all sat.

"Hi," she said. "I've seen you in here a time or two. I'm Anna, and this is Lenny."

Paul nodded. He ran a shaking hand over the lower half of his face. "I've never been so scared in all my life."

Anna felt for him. "I can imagine. Talk me through what happened."

"We'd just got the little one settled. He'd been grizzly all evening — he's teething. He had a bit of a crying session before he finally gave in and went to sleep. More like screaming, actually. I looked at the clock, and it was half eleven. I put him in his cot by our bed, and just as I stepped away I heard the gunshot. I knew it was a gun because my grandad used to go hunting when I was little. I went with him a couple of times. So I ran to the window — our bedroom's at the back — and this man was strolling down Albert's garden. It was weird, how he just walked and didn't run."

Maybe because Toby can't bloody run. "Did you see where he went?"

"Through the gate down the bottom, and he turned right into the alley behind. I didn't see where he went after that because it's dark. I saw him clearly in the garden, though, because of the lights coming from Albert's cottage. He had a black coat on with the hood up. Dark trousers and shoes with a chunky sole. He had a shotgun and, weird as this sounds, he used it like a walking stick."

Definitely Toby — or someone pretending to be him? "Let's rewind to earlier in the evening. Did you hear anything iffy, as in someone breaking in? Through the back maybe?"

Paul shook his head. "No, like I said, our son was grizzly, and we were in the living room at the front all evening with the telly on."

"What height and build would you say the man was?"

"Five-six, slim."

"Thanks for that. Have you already given a formal statement?"

"Yeah, that copper over there took it."

"And your partner? Did she give one?"

"Yep. Hers is the same account as mine except she didn't see the bloke in the garden. She got up to grab the baby when

177

the shot went off. Thought someone was going to come in and shoot us."

"Poor woman. Who lives on the other side of Albert?"

Paul partially turned round to look at the others. "Edith and Fred. Those two in the matching grey dressing gowns."

"Okay, thanks for speaking with us. Would you mind sending them our way?"

Paul rose and spoke to the elderly couple, who came over and settled opposite Anna and Lenny. Fred appeared grumpy, his face twisted with irritation, but Edith seemed alight with inquisitiveness, her eyes wide, a child at Christmas.

Anna introduced herself and Lenny.

"We know who you are," Edith said. "We know you're a detective. I said to Fred that it's a sign of the times when a woman's got the job you have. About bloody time, I say."

"Let her get on with it, then," her husband grumbled, "so we can go home to bed."

"You'll have to wait for the go-ahead there," Anna said. "We need to make sure the offender doesn't come back. Your safety is our priority."

Fred chuffed out a derisive laugh. "What, you think he'd come back with you lot over the road? Not likely."

Anna was too weary to get into any debates with him, so addressed Edith instead. "As you live next door, did you hear anything?"

"The gun going off, yes. I'd got up for a wee." Edith clasped her hands in her lap and leaned forward, excited. "I ran in to Fred, woke him up and told him what I'd heard. He said I was hearing things and to come back to bed. I looked out of the window, our room's at the front, but no one was out there. Then Paul came just after I got into bed, and told us to come here."

"What about earlier in the evening?" Anna asked.

"Now that I *did* hear," Fred said. "I was making a cuppa, and there was the sound of breaking glass."

Edith slapped his arm. "You didn't tell me that!"

178

"Didn't feel the need to. You hear about do-gooders going off to the rescue all the bloody time, and they get hurt. Sod that."

Anna held back a sigh. "What time was this?"

Fred stared at the ceiling. "Half past nine or thereabouts."

"Did you do anything about it?"

He shrugged. "So long as it wasn't our place, I didn't give much of a stuff."

"Fred!" Edith shook her head. "Sorry about him."

"Don't apologise for me," Fred snapped. "I'm not about to go and put myself in danger, going snooping about a bit of glass. It could have been an armed robbery and all sorts."

"But we could have phoned the police," Edith said. "Then they'd have seen whoever it was in Albert's cottage."

"That would depend on what time the gunman went in," Anna said.

"It'll be Toby." Fred sat back and folded his arms. "It's obvious."

Anna couldn't resist. "Have you witnessed any altercations between Albert and Toby?"

"Yeah, the first one being at the factory when Toby got on his high horse. I said to my mate at the time, if a woman's left you for someone else, she isn't worth the effort."

"Oh, so you were at Cribbins?"

"My whole working life. Got a bloody nice pension off it an' all, *and* a watch for all my years of service."

"What about you, Edith?"

"Yes, I was there, too." She held up her wrist with a gold watch on it. "So many people from the village had jobs there years ago. Not so much now as they're all the youngers from Marlford."

"So you were both there when Lionel Kettering died?"

"God, do you remember that, Fred?" Edith stared at the table as if recalling the event. "I always said it was a bit weird that he'd killed himself there when he was a storeman for

179

Dobsons. That was nowhere near the factory, so why he drove there from work I don't know."

Fred appeared blank-faced. Had he schooled his features on purpose?

"Do you know anything about that?" Anna asked him.

"I've got my suspicions, but, seeing as she was eating lunch with Toby, there's not much else to be said."

"What did you suspect?"

Fred shook his head. "Let's just say I overheard Lionel talking the night before and what he said didn't match what he did."

"How do you mean?"

"He was leaving her. Had another woman on the go — she never came forward when he went up in flames, and I could understand why. Lionel said he'd be packing up and moving away with her when Elizabeth was at work. He'd taken the day off, so he *didn't* drive from Dobsons to Cribbins, Edith." He gave his wife a dirty look for getting her facts wrong. "I never understood why he drove there at all, though. It didn't make sense. Unless he'd gone there to pick his fancy woman up. She worked for Cribbins."

"Did you say anything to the police at the time?"

"Nah, I didn't want to get involved. Like with that glass breaking earlier. Not my circus, and it still isn't. I shouldn't have said anything."

"Why is this being raked up now anyway?" Edith enquired.

Anna couldn't answer. These two might tip Elizabeth off. *Mind you, they still could.*

Edith chirped up. "Elizabeth and Toby were thick as thieves afterwards, whispering away over there." She pointed towards the fireplace. "Personally, I thought he was getting in with her because Lionel was dead, if you know what I mean. Single man, in need of a woman."

Fred tutted. "Nah, he was besotted with Maureen, always has been. Like someone else I could mention."

"Who?" Anna asked.

180

Fred cleared his throat. "Is Albert dead?"

"I'm afraid so."

"Then I'll tell you, seeing as he can't come at me now." He caught Anna's admonishing gaze. "All right, I said it wasn't my circus, but that was before I knew I'd get in any bother."

"I never said a word." Anna smiled.

Fred smirked. "The woman Lionel was buggering off with was Maureen."

"What?" Too late, Anna had blurted out her surprise, and it drew glances from the others in the pub. She composed herself. Lowered her voice. "Um, and you know this for sure, do you?"

Fred nodded. "They used to go out the back of here on Saturday nights when Albert had had a skinful. Elizabeth was at home with the kiddies. They got a bit cosy in the yard, like. Besides, Lionel told me what they were up to. This is why I said I wasn't surprised that she didn't come forward when he died. She wouldn't have wanted to own up else Albert would have given her a beating for planning to leave him."

"Did you know she was also seeing Bruce Cribbins?"

"No. I found that out earlier when Toby announced it to everyone in here."

"Were you ever aware that Maureen was pregnant?"

Edith had suddenly become less animated since this little story had come out, and her cheeks had gone bright red.

"Edith?" Anna raised her eyebrows.

"I knew, yes, but she kept losing them. She was in such a state every time."

Fred gaped at her. "Well, she *would* be, wouldn't she! Bleedin' heck, woman. Look how you were when we lost our Cheryl."

Edith's eyes watered. "You know I can't talk about her."

Fred filled in the gaps. "Eight months pregnant. Stillborn."

"I'm so sorry," Anna said.

Lenny mumbled the same.

Anna pressed on. "How far along did Maureen get?"

"About six months with each one." Edith's bottom lip trembled. "She wasn't allowed friends, so she told me about it at work, on the quiet, like. I asked her about having to go in and give birth, but she just stared at me as if she didn't know what I was talking about. She *must* have known, because that's what you have to do by that stage."

"Like you, she might not have been able to talk about it." Fred tugged at his earlobe. "I said that at the time after you told me what had gone on."

"So you both kept it from Albert?" Anna asked.

"We did, although there's something else I'll tell you now he's dead." Fred took a deep breath. "The nights before Maureen went into work and told my Edith she'd lost the babies, there was shouting and screaming. Every time. If you ask me, he beat her up so she lost them kiddies."

Anna couldn't comprehend keeping that information quiet. "And you didn't report it?"

"None of my business. It was different then anyway. Men got away with that kind of thing."

"And we were scared of him," Edith added. "Albert had this way about him, and a certain look that told you to steer clear. I always thought he was one step away from doing someone some serious damage. I think he killed Maureen and Toby shot him for it."

Anna wouldn't disabuse her of that notion. If Toby hadn't murdered Maureen, he wouldn't have handed over completely the wrong clothes and whatnot.

"Is there anything else you can tell us that will be of help?"

"Nah." Fred stood and smoothed the front of his dressing gown. "We've said enough."

"Thanks for your time."

The old couple wandered back to their table, and Anna called the next pair.

The interviews dragged on. No one else had heard the gunshot, although two people had woken up without knowing why, so it must have jolted them from sleep.

They accepted coffees from Ian, who placed them on the table and left with a nod. Anna sipped, contemplating this latest turn of events, one question cropping up time and again.

Where was Toby?

CHAPTER TWENTY-NINE

Toby stood in Elizabeth's kitchen by the radiator to warm up. His journey here, keeping to the shadows and hiding from police officers wandering around, had chilled his skin and bones. At one point he'd thought they'd spotted him, and he'd backed up against a tree trunk and held his breath. How the hell he'd made it here without being caught, he didn't know.

"What have you done?" Elizabeth asked, her hair askew from being in bed. He'd woken her up by throwing stones at her back bedroom window. She patted it down on one side, then shoved her hands into the opposing arms of her ratty pink dressing gown, which she'd owned for decades.

"I need your help," he admitted.

"That much is obvious, what with that bloody big gun. Where the hell did you get *that*?"

"It was my dad's."

She tutted. "Do you want a cuppa?"

Toby nodded. He carried the gun to the table and placed it on top. Sat, weary. How could he tell her? Admit that he was just as bad as she was? He'd always had some smug kind of satisfaction that he was better than her, holier than her, because he'd never succumbed to his base instincts to kill Maureen and Albert long before now. Seemed he wasn't much better than Elizabeth after all.

I'll just have to blurt it out.

"I killed Albert."

Elizabeth stilled while filling the old-fashioned kettle, gripping the handle, the other hand poised above the tap. She stared ahead at the curtains over the window above the sink. Too many prints of teapots and saucepans on them. They'd always got on his nerves. She'd had them since the seventies. Said they reminded her of her mother.

She shut the tap off. "Oh my goodness, what on earth possessed you?"

"He got to me one time too many."

"You should have risen above it. I've always said that."

She had.

She popped the kettle on the Aga.

He stared at the floor. "The police were at my house earlier. They know it was me." He'd meant Maureen, and he hadn't planned on confessing that part, but it was too late to take the words back now.

She frowned. "When did you kill Albert?"

Toby glanced at the clock. "An hour ago."

"Then they weren't at yours for that. What's up with you? Has your mind gone funny? They've been there *hours*. And how come it took you all this time to get from Albert's to here?"

"I had to keep stopping and hiding. The police are everywhere, even them ones with helmets and guns."

"Oh dear Lord."

He had to give the woman her due. Elizabeth pottered about getting cups from a cupboard and taking milk from the fridge as if they were talking about the weather. It calmed him, her practicality, but was she scared inside? As much as he was?

185

"You know," she said, "you should have planned it better. Waited until all this with Maureen had died down. I would have worked everything out for you. All the pitfalls."

"I couldn't help it. I panicked when I saw them at mine. I knew I'd been caught, so I thought, what else is there to lose? At least I got the last laugh by taking her away from him."

Elizabeth stopped to stare at him. Then the penny dropped. "Oh, you didn't. Please tell me you didn't kill Maureen."

"It was an accident. One minute she was accusing me of stealing eggs, and the next my cane had landed on the side of her head. After the first wallop, I kept whacking her, couldn't seem to stop." This was true, so why did it feel like a lie? Something he'd convinced himself would fly when he confessed?

Elizabeth sank onto a chair. The kettle was rumbling. "Oh God. I understand how that happens, I really do, but you should have reined your temper in."

"How could I? It took me over. And you *planned* what you did. I only planned Albert, and even then it wasn't much of a plan."

"We need to get this sorted so you don't get done for anything. What, exactly, did they take from your house?"

"Clothes, shoes, my canes. Stuff without any blood on it. A coat, that tweed thing I used to be fond of until Maureen laughed at me, said I must think I was hoity-toity, gadding about in it. I told Anna I'd already washed what I'd been wearing, but she said it didn't matter. I had to give her *something* or it would have seemed weird."

"So they must have found something out to have been waiting at your house all this time. What can they know?"

Toby shrugged. "There was this woman. She drove past when I was on my way to the lay-by. She saw me."

"Right, so it could be that. Did she see you well enough?"

"I suppose so."

"Like the fact you weren't wearing the same clothes and shoes you gave to Anna?"

"Oh God."

"He won't help you now. I take it you didn't give Anna clothes even remotely like the ones you were wearing?"

"I got flustered. I just grabbed what was closest."

"You really are useless! I mean, for God's sake! She's a *detective*. Clever. They think differently to us." She closed her eyes for a moment. When she opened them, she turned glaring eyes on him. "Where's the cane you hit Maureen with?"

"In Jubilee Lake. I chopped it up. I put everything to do with the murder in a suitcase."

"That's something, then. What time did you go to the lake?"

"I left the village about eight."

"So someone could have seen you putting the case in the water and phoned in about it. All these people with smartphones. You could have been recorded."

Toby sighed. "Anna saw the suitcase in my workshop, she asked about it, so maybe she put two and two together."

The kettle whistled, and Elizabeth rose to make their drinks. "What's the plan now? You can stay here for the time being, but if the police come round you're going to have to get in the loft or the shed, and, if the worst happens and they find you, I'm going to lie and say I didn't know you were there. I have my own shit to hide, let alone yours on top."

Toby didn't think that was very fair, considering he'd covered for her with Lionel, but he understood where she was coming from. He'd feel the same in her shoes. And would it be so bad, living here with Elizabeth in secret? He'd miss his workshop, but she had the shed, and maybe he could go out there and create a few things, although he wouldn't be able to sell them. Not now. Then there was Joyce to think about. She came round here often, and she might hear him sawing and ask questions.

Elizabeth brought the teas over and sat, staring at the shotgun. "You'd have been better off setting his cottage on fire instead of using that. Make it look like an accident on his part."

"We're not all expert assassins like you."

Her eyes glazed. "I think about them sometimes. *Him* and Lionel. I wonder if I'd taken another route, moving away after Mum died, whether my life would have been better. I'd never have married Lionel. Cheating bastard."

"You never did tell me who he was seeing."

"No." She seemed to drift off in her head. "I pretended, you know, to miss having Maureen as my friend. Even earlier when I was asked about her, I was kind. But it was her. Maureen and Lionel."

The bottom seemed to drop out of Toby's world. "Pardon?"

"I saw them twice. In Marlford. When Albert was off fishing, she snuck into the city on the bus — it was before she'd learned to drive. I dropped my kids off with a neighbour and followed Lionel. They met up in a car park both times. Walked around the shops as if they didn't have a care in the world. Holding hands, kissing, *laughing*."

"I can't believe this."

"Maureen was a tart, you just couldn't see it. You had her on a pedestal because she was your first love. But she was free and easy — hid it well, too. And it seems she was also seeing Bruce. I never had him down as someone who'd do that. But that's the thing, isn't it? People do things behind closed doors. Folks only see what you want them to. I'm proof of that. Poor girl, her father hanging himself after he'd killed her mother, and then, of all the bad luck, her husband killed himself too. I kept my nose clean after that, as you know, but I'll tell you now, the amount of times I came close to getting rid of Maureen too, or telling Albert what she'd been up to."

Toby had trouble getting his head around this, so he let the information settle. And it made sense. Maureen had cheated on him with Albert, and she'd continued her adulterous ways after that. Why had she taken the risk? Albert would have clouted her if he'd found out. Hadn't she been able to help herself? Was she that insatiable?

Was the bitch he'd thought Albert had created an illusion, when all along it was in her to be that way from the start? Had she hidden it from Toby?

"What did I do wrong for her to leave me?" he whispered, more to himself than his friend.

"Do you want the truth?"

He nodded.

"She told me she was bored. Needed some excitement. I told her she ought to be glad to have someone like you. It wasn't you who had the problem, it was her. She thought Albert was exciting, and look how that turned out, so she copped off with Lionel. Plus she got her claws into Bruce."

"She only met him once a year."

"Then she was likely in bed with some other sap as well after Lionel died."

"If she was prepared to leave Albert and run off with Lionel, why did she never do that with anyone else?"

"Bruce would never have left Dulcie. Maybe men only used her for sex, so she stayed with Albert hoping to find another prat who'd go off with her, except none did."

"That's a long time to be abused while you're waiting for a better option. I always thought he had some hold on her and that's why she stayed." He was fishing to see if she knew about the babies.

Elizabeth sipped her tea. "He probably did." She sighed. "God, what a mess. When you think about it, how we used to be when we first started at the factory, so young and full of hope. How life changed, eh? We've both ended up as murderers."

"Except you got away with yours."

She nodded. "So far. But Anna's been asking questions. I doubt I'll get away with it for much longer. She'll be round at some point, you watch. But it's okay, I have a plan for that."

A loud banging on the front door had them both staring at each other.

"It might be the police knocking everyone up because of Albert," Elizabeth said. "Don't panic."

"But if it *is* the police, what if they ask to come in?"

She jerked her head at the door. "Get in the shed. Take the cup with you so they don't know I've had someone here."

Toby picked up the shotgun and the cup, and shuffled towards the back door. "Don't tell them where I am. *Please.*"

She smiled and nodded, and he walked out and quietly made his way over the spongy grass. It reminded him of the field where he'd taken Maureen, and hot tears spilled over his cheeks. He eased the shed door open and stepped inside. Closed himself in and patted around for somewhere to sit. He found what he thought was a stool and lowered himself onto it, a dusty scent going up his nose.

He'd reduced himself to this, a fugitive. He contemplated putting the end of the shotgun barrel in his mouth, but he couldn't pull the trigger a second time tonight. That stupid self-preservation kicked in, so he just sat.

And waited.

CHAPTER THIRTY

Elizabeth had to admit that, after years of hiding her truths, at her age she may well cave if interrogated by the police. Back then, she'd been so much younger, able to hide behind a facade of grief. The detective at the time — both times — had been easy to convince, a sucker for a crying woman down on her luck. And he didn't particularly want either case to drag out, he'd made that obvious.

Anna, though, she was another matter, and if Elizabeth had committed those same crimes today she'd have been caught quickly. Like Toby would be. If Anna was looking into the past, it was only a matter of time before she knocked on the door.

Elizabeth had lied to Robert earlier. That she'd be loyal to him until the bitter end. She had no intention of doing so. They'd left Diana to her rocking after Toby had stropped off, coming to the same conclusion at the same time. An easy way to save them from getting into trouble. A fly in the ointment, but she'd helped him with that.

Elizabeth had lots of pills from over the years, all stored in plastic tablet containers in her kitchen cupboard. She ignored the second lot of hammering on her front door and found a couple of bottles, tipping out the powder that she'd already created many moons ago by bashing at the pills with a rolling pin.

For a night like this. When all was lost and she'd reached the end of the line.

She'd had an inkling this would happen.

There was a certain satisfaction in choosing how it all panned out, now that the time had come to execute her final plan. Of course, she'd perhaps become complacent, especially the last few years, thinking she'd reach her death naturally, in a hospital bed maybe, all of her family around her.

Until Toby had been stupid enough to kill Maureen.

She hated him for that, but she'd get him back for it. He'd mentioned having the last laugh with Albert, but she'd have hers, too.

She stirred enough anti-depressants and God knew what else into half a glass of milk, forming a paste a bit thicker than pancake batter. She drank it down, gagging at the consistency, her body trying to reject it because her brain knew what it was. She paused for a moment, willing it to remain in her stomach, then poured some more powder and milk and forced that down the hatch, too. Calmly, she swilled the glass out and placed it in the washing-up bowl. Faced the hallway. A shadowy figure stood on the other side of the mottled glass panels in her front door, and whoever it was knocked again.

The letterbox flicked open.

"Are you okay?" a man asked. "Is anyone in there with you? Are you in any danger?"

So they were looking for Toby, then, not her. Anna hadn't joined enough dots to bring Elizabeth in, but she would. Tomorrow. Next week. It didn't matter when. Elizabeth had made her final choice, and there was no going back.

She took a second step forward.

"I'm so worried!" *Joyce?* "An ambulance was here earlier. She had a panic attack. What if she's had another one and passed out, banging her head?"

192

"No, no, she's there, I can see her. If you can go inside and speak to the officer, please, love. We're looking for an offender, and it's important you answer our questions. He's armed."

"Armed? But I haven't *seen* an offender."

Elizabeth smiled. Typical Joyce, asking questions. Wanting to know the ins and outs. She'd been such a good friend, but not good enough for Elizabeth to tell the woman her secrets. Joyce would probably find out everything soon, and she'd wonder how she could have been taken in by her next-door neighbour, the blue-haired woman who liked a bit of gossip.

I talked about everyone else so I didn't reveal things about myself.

But it wouldn't matter what Joyce knew. Elizabeth wouldn't be here.

"It's Elizabeth, isn't it?" the man asked. "Nod if you're being held against your will."

Nausea paid a visit, and Elizabeth swallowed several times to keep the drugs down. She anticipated getting drowsy soon — if she didn't vomit first, unable to control it. The body had a funny way of fixing whatever was wrong, didn't it?

Just a little while longer, that's all she needed.

"Do you have a man in there with you?"

She took another step forward.

Her head went floaty. The cocktail was working swiftly. Faster than she'd thought it would. Maybe because she'd had two glasses.

One more step.

"Nice and steady."

Two more steps.

"That's it, come towards me slowly and open the door."

She paused. Thought about her life, the happier times.

It hadn't been so bad after all. Underneath the veneer of who she'd wanted people to think she was had lurked the nerves, the worry that one day there'd be a knock on the door. Once a week, on a Friday night, she'd gone over what had happened, sure to cement it in her mind so she never forgot what was in those police files should she ever be asked about it again. A life spent rehashing what she'd done so it never left her. She'd never moved on.

All those years. She was tired of pretending now.

"Elizabeth, I need to know if you have a man in your house with a weapon."

Once she was sure she wasn't going to be sick, she opened the door. "He's in my shed. He's got a gun."

"All right, love, all right. You go with that officer over there now."

She let herself be herded to a car parked a few houses away and helped into the back.

A policewoman got in the front. "Are you okay? Did he hurt you?"

"I'm tired." Elizabeth rested her head against the window.

"Okay, you have a rest now."

If she was as lucky in killing herself as she'd been in murdering her father and husband, she'd drop off to sleep and never wake up. Fate had been kind to her until now. All she needed was one more little favour. Some would say she didn't deserve it, and she thought they might be right.

Her children would be upset, and their children, and then there were the great-grandchildren. This would hurt them. Bring shame down on them. Confusion. Embarrassment.

Too much for her to consider now.

She closed her eyes and prayed the officer in the passenger seat didn't realise something was up. Or that she'd be sick in her sleep and end up having her stomach pumped. She couldn't be alive anymore. Couldn't go to prison.

Her belly cramped, and she willed it to give up the fight and accept what she'd given it. To digest it and send the concoction through her bloodstream.

And she prayed she never woke up again.

That she wouldn't have to pay for what she'd done.

No, she'd pass that down to her family. That was her legacy.

She was a selfish woman, she knew that, but, as she floated into what she hoped was death's embrace, she didn't care. All that mattered was the end.

And no more worries.

CHAPTER THIRTY-ONE

With a stab vest underneath her coat, an hour after Elizabeth had passed on Toby's location, Anna stood in the garden at the top of the path closest to the house. They'd had to wait for a negotiator to arrive. Armed officers surrounded the shed, ready for when Toby relinquished the gun — if he even did. As the door was shut and there were no windows, there was no way to see him, to know whether he was aiming the weapon at the door.

How odd, to be standing here. Surreal, that was the word for it. Anna could get shot tonight. Any one of them could. Toby had asked to speak to her. No amount of wheedling from Bob, the negotiator, had changed Toby's stance on that. If she didn't come, he'd shoot whoever stood outside until she did. Anna had asked herself whether Toby even had enough ammunition, but she supposed someone who'd planned to go out and kill would have more in their pocket.

Whatever, they couldn't assume he'd put all his ammo through Albert's head.

Leaving Lenny behind her, she stepped down the path holding a full-body riot shield in front of her, as did everyone else in the close vicinity. The visored helmet had already brought on a sweat, and her head itched.

"I'm here, Toby," she said loudly, thinking of what Bob had told her to say. *Be calm. Let him speak. Get a rapport going.* "What did you need to talk to me about?"

"Elizabeth. Did she tell on me?"

It had sounded so childlike, a kid asking if he'd been ratted out.

Anna opened her mouth to spill the lie she'd been advised to use. "No, someone else saw you leaving the house and going into the shed."

"It'll be that bloody Joyce, I'll bet."

"I don't know who it was. I wasn't told. Can you do me a favour and speak up?" Her helmet had muffled some of his words.

"What for?"

"I can't hear you properly, that's all. Are you okay?"

"Like you care."

"I do actually." *I care that we get through this and you're taken into custody.*

"I'm frightened."

"I can understand that. Do you want to talk it through?"

"What's the point?"

"There could be extenuating circumstances that will go in your favour. Like Albert picking at you for years. And Maureen, too. It's a lot, isn't it? Putting up with all that? People snap when they've had enough."

"They were bastards. I always thought he was the biggest wanker out of the pair, but she turned out to be a right bitch, more than I knew."

Had he discovered something? Had she told him a secret before he'd hit her?

Why now? Why did it take him this long to lose his rag? "It sounds like she hurt you."

"She did, but I found out the worst of it after she was dead."

Nervous about messing this up, Anna blew out a long breath, and her visor misted. "What did you find out?"

"I can't tell you. It's not fair to Elizabeth."

Anna leaned towards a nearby ARU officer. "Can you get word to Lenny to go and have a word with her?"

"What's that whispering?" Toby said.

"I just asked someone to go and talk to Elizabeth."

"Where is she?"

"Asleep in a police car."

"How can she sleep at a time like this?"

"Some people get tired when they've had a shock. She had the police at her door, and it may have frightened her like it did earlier. We're letting her have a rest before we question her." In truth, with so much going on, the woman was the least of their worries. It was more important to arrest Toby than ask Elizabeth how he'd ended up in her shed.

"I can't believe she's having a bloody kip! After all I've done for her, the least she could do is stay awake."

Ah, we might be getting somewhere. "What did you do for her?"

"Ask her. I'm saying nothing."

Anna turned at the sound of murmured voices and footsteps.

Lenny beckoned her over.

"I just need to go and have a word with Lenny for a second, all right?"

"What for?"

"He went to see Elizabeth. I won't be a tick."

"You'll come back, won't you? You're not lying?"

"No, I'm not lying."

She moved towards Lenny, whose eyes hid in shadow behind his visor. They went out into the front garden and closed the gate. She handed him her shield so she could take her helmet off. He took his off one-handed.

"She's fucking dead," he whispered.

"What? I mean, how? In her sleep? Why didn't the PC watching her notice she'd stopped breathing?" Anna glanced down the street at a cluster of uniforms beside a car.

"Sorry, but if you think someone's asleep you're not going to keep looking at them, are you? And with all this going on, her being out of it was a blessing, one less person to deal with. The PC got out for a bit of fresh air about half an hour ago. I walked up, said I needed a chat, and she knelt on the front seat to ask Elizabeth to wake up. No response. Took a pulse, nothing. She's doing CPR on the road now. Ambulance is on the way."

"Shit. You couldn't make this up."

"Anna?" Toby shouted, the word faint. "Anna!"

She shoved her helmet on, took her shield, rushed into the garden and down the path. "I'm here."

"What's going on?"

She glanced at Bob for advice, mouthing, *She's dead.*

The shake of his head told her not to reveal that.

"It's all right," she said. "Elizabeth's being dealt with now."

"You're up to something. All of you."

Anna remembered what she'd been told. To distract if things got hairy. "Do you need a blanket? A cup of tea?"

"Like I'm going to open the door for you to give them to me. I'm not stupid."

"Can we talk about why you're in there? Would that be okay?"

"You know why I'm here."

"Shall we discuss it?"

"A confession, you mean."

"If that would make you feel better."

"Did you know Maureen was seeing Elizabeth's husband? Has she told anyone that yet?"

His change of tack could mean his allegiance towards Elizabeth was no longer important to him for whatever reason. Bob had explained that people in these situations often had erratic thought patterns; it affected their decision-making.

"Actually, sod this," he said. "She can stuff my loyalty up her arse. I want assurances before I say anything else."

"What kind of assurances?"

"One of those trades you see on the telly."

"Do you mean a lesser sentence if you tell me about another crime?"

"Yeah, that's it."

"That could help you, yes." *But you'll still see out your days in prison either way.*

"She killed him. Lionel. Because of the affair. He was going to run off with Maureen. I went out and had my lunch at the bin store," he prattled on, "knowing she was going to set his car on fire. I gave her an alibi. I don't even know why I did it."

Anna's heart thundered, and adrenaline surged through her. How on earth had Elizabeth managed to set the car alight, with Lionel in it, when the fire had begun in the driver's footwell?

We can't even ask her now. "Sorry she used you like that."

"Yeah, so am I, and I'm sorry she told me about her dad an' all. I had nothing to do with that, she just needed someone to talk to because Robert and Diana wanted to forget about it."

Anna resisted punching the air. "Her dad?"

"Yeah, he killed her mum, so she killed him. Robert and Diana helped her. Said there was blood, but I don't know where from."

While Anna was chuffed he'd confirmed the team's suspicions, he still hadn't confessed to what *he'd* done.

"Do you want to tell me about Maureen and what happened?"

"It was an accident, like I blacked out for a minute. She said I probably nicked eggs, didn't pay for them, and the next thing I knew I'd hit her. All those years of her being a cow to me, it all came back, and I *kept* hitting her. I felt sick after. I didn't mean it, I swear I didn't."

"Did you mean to kill Albert?"

Silence.

"Or was that someone else?" Maybe he'd be more inclined to answer if he thought she didn't know he'd done it.

"It was me."

"Where did you go when you left the village in your car at about eight?"

"Jubilee Lake."

"Why were you there?"

"I thought you'd have guessed. I put my suitcase in the water."

Ah, that bloody suitcase. "What was in it?"

"Send a copper to go and see."

She turned to find Lenny leaving the garden; someone must have passed along what Toby had said. The flash of the ambulance lights flickered through the open gateway, then they were gone as it closed.

She faced the shed again. "Can you let me have the gun, Toby?"

"No, not yet. I want to tell you something else so you get the measure of the man I killed. Albert murdered all of Maureen's babies. He kicked her until . . . He told me before I shot him. She buried them in their garden."

The horror of that nearly floored Anna, and she struggled to hold in a gasp. Trying to remain calm, she indicated for someone to pass that on to SOCO at the cottage. "Thank you for telling me. We'll sort all that, but my main concern is you. It's cold. We need to get you in the warm. Will you come out now?"

"Who's with you?"

Anna glanced at the negotiator. "Just the nice man who was speaking to you before me. Bob, remember?"

"Who else?"

"Only me and him."

The ARU officers peeled back a bit, some to the right to hide in the shadow created by a large pine tree, the others to the left, along the fence, all easily able to shoot if necessary. Those by the gate crouched.

201

Anna sucked in a deep breath, then let it out. *What did Bob tell me to say?* "I need you to open the door and put the gun down on the path, then put your hands up so we know you don't mean us any harm. Can you do that for me?"

"I'm scared."

"It's all right. We'll work everything out."

"What happens next?"

"I'll take you to your house." She wouldn't. "We'll get warm and have a cuppa. Is that okay? We can talk some more. Does that sound all right?"

"What about after that?"

"We'll discuss the terms of the trade. You've been really helpful there."

"And then?"

Bob nodded to her.

"We can go to the station, and you can get some sleep. Tell me everything again in the morning."

Silence.

The seconds stretched on and then, just as Anna was about to ask another question, the shed door opened a crack. Anna and Bob moved closer to get Toby's focus only on them.

"Me and Bob, see? We've got helmets on, but it's us."

Toby pushed the door a little more, to halfway, then three quarters. He appeared as a dark shape with a pale face. He lowered the gun, crouching, his eyes on Anna, and put it on the path, but kept his hand on it. Didn't he trust them? Her? The gun was his only bargaining tool and, if he let them take it, he was admitting defeat. He'd been strong throughout the years with Albert and Maureen, stubborn in a way Anna never would have been, keeping up the argument, taunting, biting back. He must know he couldn't do that once the gun wasn't in his possession.

He rose, hands up.

"I'm going to take the gun," she said. "I'm going to give it to Bob."

She stepped forward. Sensed her colleagues tensing in the darkness. She kept looking at the pale circle in the doorway, glad she couldn't see his eyes properly, the sadness and despair that undoubtedly filled them. She went down on her haunches and placed the bottom of the shield over the gun so he could no longer snatch it. She grasped the weapon and heat came through her glove; the stock was still warm where he must have been clutching it. She stood upright and passed it to Bob on her right.

"There. Can you come out now?"

Toby shook his head and took a step back. So did Anna. She took another and another, Bob doing the same, then the garden erupted in a cacophony of shouts.

"Put your hands behind your head!"

"Get down on the ground, now!"

Anna turned away, her heart a tad heavy at having to lie to Toby. But that was the name of the game. To get this result, she'd had to fabricate what was going to happen, and it didn't matter whether she'd upset him over it now he knew things wouldn't go as she'd said. This part of her job was done, securing the suspect, and she shouldn't feel bad about it.

A rumble of a voice came from behind her. "Toby Potter, you are under arrest for the murders of Maureen Frost and Albert Frost . . ."

Toby's loud crying chased Anna out of the garden.

* * *

The ginger cat had greeted them at the front door of Toby's house, wailing loudly and giving Anna the evil eye. An officer had arranged for it to be collected come daylight, but in the meantime Wilf from next door had taken it in. It was called Mr Baggins, apparently.

Suited up, a SOCO team went through every room of Toby's house. A shout came from the kitchen. The presence of blood. Anna waited for half an hour to see if anything else of significance was found, but, as the team would be going through absolutely everything, it could take a while.

A specialist team had been brought in to deal with the Frosts' back garden. Anna didn't feel compelled to be there if any bodies were unearthed. Some things, if she could avoid them, were just too sad to witness. Although she tortured herself with whether the babies had been put in the earth naked or Maureen had at least swaddled them in a blanket.

If it was even Maureen who buried them. It could have been Albert, lying until the end.

How must that woman have felt to place her flesh and blood in the ground? What kind of twisted person had she been to remain in that marriage? Maybe she'd had to stay because Albert had threatened her about the bodies. Had she indulged in affairs to give herself the love she wasn't getting from him? Or was she the type to revel in duping him, having secret liaisons as a way to regain some control?

All things that would never be answered because the couple were dead.

It was 3 a.m. and Anna was shattered. Should she take Ian up on his offer of coffee? He'd stayed up in the Jubilee, letting the officers use it as a hub. The residents of Albert's row had all been allowed to go home as soon as Toby was apprehended.

The resuscitation attempt on Elizabeth had failed.

Toby's car had been found by some council garages. A team were going to the lake in the morning as it would be better to search during daylight hours, although an officer sat in a patrol car outside the apartments to keep an eye out there. All Anna could think about was the contents of the suitcase being submerged for such a long time that any evidence would be ruined, but someone above Placket's paygrade had made the decision, so who were they to question it?

All that was left was to pay Robert and Diana a visit. Another officer waited in a patrol vehicle to make sure they didn't get in a car and drive off. Placket had told Anna and Lenny to get some sleep and to speak to the couple in the morning; he didn't feel they'd be going anywhere. Robert had opened the door earlier when the police had been searching for Toby and had let them check the farmhouse, though he'd asked them to be quiet so Diana didn't wake up.

I bet he bloody did. He wouldn't want her opening her mouth.

Fatigue pulled at Anna's shoulders, and she wandered over to Lenny in the living room. "I was going to try and stay awake, get some coffee at the pub, but d'you know what, I'm knackered."

"Same."

They left for her place.

She fell asleep almost as soon as she got into bed.

CHAPTER THIRTY-TWO

Anna had stayed asleep until seven, late for her on a workday, and she'd performed a quick test with Lenny before they'd set off for the day. Something that would come in handy later. They'd nipped to the Jubilee to get a coffee and a couple of bacon rolls each. Laura had served them, as Ian was in bed — the poor man must have been tired after staying up most of the night. While they'd eaten, Anna had familiarised herself with the main points of Jack Hudson's file. Sally had been researching late into the night and had sent Anna an email with some interesting information on it.

Now they were at Hawthorn Farm.

Belly full, and a little haggard from only a few hours' sleep, Anna stood with Lenny and PC Ollie Watson. Ollie had taken over from the officer who'd kept an eye on the farmhouse overnight. PC Parvati Jahinda covered the other side with another uniformed colleague in case the couple had a mind to run once they saw Anna — not that they'd get very far, but panic made people do desperate things.

"Ready?" she asked.

At their nods, she knocked on the door, the one she'd tapped on when visiting the Brignells in the autumn. If she remembered rightly, it led into a mudroom.

The door swung open, and a bleary-eyed Robert stared at them. It seemed he hadn't got much sleep either. "What now? I thought after the police had come here during the night that Toby would have been caught by now."

"He has been," Anna said. "We're here in relation to another matter. Best we come in and have a chat."

"I was just on my way over to feed the chickens."

"They can wait." Anna tapped her foot.

He sighed. "What's this about?"

Ollie stepped forward. "Can you just do as she says, please, pal?"

Anna hid a smile. Robert seemed more inclined to take notice of a uniform. He stepped back, and they filed in.

Anna walked through the mudroom and into the kitchen. "Officers are also round the other side of the property, just so you know. Where's Diana?"

"She's in bed. Not well."

"That's a shame. Still, we can talk to you first, then we can go and speak to her upstairs if she'd be more comfortable remaining up there. Shall we all take a seat?"

They settled at the table, Robert ramrod straight, his cheeks flushed, likely from anger. He wasn't in control, and he clearly didn't like it.

Anna waited for Ollie to set up the recording on his little device, then she mentioned who was present, the date, the time, the location.

"Okay, let me preface this by saying Elizabeth Kettering died during the night."

Robert paled, and his mouth worked, with no words emerging. What was going through his head? His friend had died, yes, but the news had stunned him in a different way. Something was iffy here.

And I'm going to find out what it is, even if it takes me weeks, months.

Anna laced her fingers on the table. "I can see that's a bit of a shock. Do you need a moment?"

"I . . . I . . . One second."

Anna waited for him to digest the news. He frowned, stared into space, and shook his head, flummoxed. Why did Elizabeth's death seem so confusing to him?

Anna had given him as much time as she was prepared to give. "Now, moving on. Toby was arrested after he confessed to a number of things. The one we're here about is your purported involvement in the death of Jack Hudson." She waited for the second blow to sink in.

Robert's frown disappeared. His eyebrows rose, then scrunched together. "I . . . I didn't have anything to do with that."

"Toby alleges that you and your wife helped Elizabeth Kettering, formerly Hudson, hang him from the ceiling by a noose."

"What? That's a lie!"

"We had reason to open the files on it during our investigation into Maureen Frost's death, so we're up to date with everything." She paused. Stared. "But I'd like you to tell me what happened."

He wiggled indignantly. "If you've read the file, then you know."

Ollie glared at him. Sighed. "If you could just do as she asked, sir."

Robert closed his eyes then gazed at the tabletop. Anna waited for him to relate his tale, guessing that, if he'd done something illegal, he'd either recall it easily or let slip some information he hadn't previously provided. Some people reminded themselves of their crimes often so they never put a foot wrong, others preferred to forget.

Which one would he be?

He seemed to have finished his contemplation as he took a deep breath. "We went round to Elizabeth's to listen to music in her bedroom. I wasn't even aware her father was at home. We had it on loud, the music, and I remember we had a bottle of beer each, which Elizabeth had taken from her father's drink cupboard. We were in her room for a couple of hours, we switched to lemonade — Corona, as I recall. Elizabeth had shaken the bottle without telling me, and it had sprayed all over us when she opened it. When it was time to go, we went downstairs. I was first, then Diana was behind me, and Elizabeth came after that. I opened the front door and stepped outside. Elizabeth screamed. I turned, bumping into Diana, and we rushed into the living room. Jack was on the floor, a rope around his neck, plaster dust on him. The ceiling light had given way. I went to the phone in the hallway and rang the police. We were told to wait outside until they arrived. That's it."

He's rehearsed it so much it's still the same account years later. Almost word for word with his statement.

Anna wasn't sure whether to be creeped out by that or admire him for covering his arse so well. "What would you say if I told you that Toby thought there'd be blood at the scene?"

"Blood? But Jack hanged himself. That doesn't make sense."

"So you didn't see any when you found him? The post-mortem revealed cuts on his wrists and broken fingers. As if someone had put pressure on his hands."

"He must have wiped it away or something, the blood. His fingers probably broke when his body fell."

"Forensic officers are at Elizabeth's now, and despite it being many years ago, if there's evidence there they'll find it. The post-mortem report states hesitation wounds, which at the time was put down to Jack trying to slit his wrists but changing his mind. Do you know anything about that?"

"No."

"How did you not hear the ceiling fixture give way?"

"I told you, the music was loud."

"I tried that out earlier at mine. I didn't pull the light fitting down, that would be a bit silly, but while Lenny had music on in my bedroom, the highest my speakers would go, I created a lot of noise downstairs and thumped the ceiling. He didn't hear those thumps but he *felt* them, and I'd say part of the ceiling coming down would create more vibration than that, wouldn't you? Say, if you were sitting on a bed with your feet on the floor."

"I don't know."

"Wouldn't you think that a father would go up to his daughter's room and tell her to turn the music down? The neighbours said they'd never heard it belted out like that before. So it's an odd coincidence that the music was so loud that day. And how on earth did you all speak to each other? You wouldn't have been able to hear yourselves think. Are you saying you sat in Elizabeth's room not talking?"

Robert looked Anna in the eye. "Maybe Jack was too upset about his wife to care about the music. He'd been bailed pending the post-mortem results. He was obviously in a state, otherwise he wouldn't have killed himself."

Anna smiled at him. "Did you know that the rope was a type mainly used by fishermen? Your father spent his weekdays over in Scudderton on his trawler and came home for the weekends, didn't he? That particular week he was poorly so hadn't gone into work. It says in the file that he thought Jack had stolen the rope from his shed, but I'm wondering now whether someone else took it."

Robert coloured up again. "I don't know what you're implying here."

"I think you do. I believe the music was up loud to drown out any screaming. Jack may have made a racket when his wrists were cut. He would undoubtedly have shouted when he was pinned down by his hands, when his fingers broke, and that noose was put around his neck. There was bruising noted on his stomach, which was conveniently put down to injuries sustained during the fight with his wife. Are we to believe that someone else came into that house and killed him while you were all upstairs?"

"I don't know. The music was so loud."

"Very convenient for the killer. Or killers."

"I didn't do anything. I swear."

"Elizabeth kept a lot of the old furniture when she inherited the property. We found a stool in the shed, as well as a stepladder, which someone could well have used to tie the rope to the light fitting. My colleague informed me of a case where fingerprints had been found on a surface that hadn't been touched for over forty years. I'm thinking, as the stepladder is right at the back of the shed, hidden, if you like, that we'll find some prints on there."

"Look, I can see what's going on here. Toby's told you a load of old rubbish, and you've believed him. I happen to have used that ladder a few times, so those prints will prove nothing except that I touched it."

"What did you use it for?"

"Oh, I can't remember now."

"Yet you remember the details of Jack's case as if it happened yesterday."

"Of course I would, it was traumatic. Using a stepladder isn't."

Unless you climbed it to hoist Jack up. "I noticed when we spoke to you and your wife before that you nudged her or stared at her in order to keep her quiet — that was my assumption anyway. Are you worried she'll tell us something?" Anna took out her phone and accessed the notes app where she'd jotted down the things Diana had said. "Your wife said the following things, which stood out to me as a little odd."

"I told you, she speaks gibberish."

Anna ignored him. "One: 'We're good people. We didn't do anything.' I'd only asked whether you saw Toby walking around the field. It was as if she was afraid. Guilty."

211

"You're skewing things to suit yourself."

"Two: 'We don't like screaming. No, we don't like that at all.' Why would Diana be so averse to screaming? Did something happen in her past such that it upsets her whenever she hears it again?"

"Lots of people don't like it. She's got sensitive hearing."

"Three: 'And we didn't like our house after—' This was about you moving to the farm. *Why* didn't she like your house after — after what?"

"She's never liked it there, even when she was a child. She swore there were ghosts in her room, which is ridiculous. She wanted a newer house when we got married, but I didn't want to move. I love that street. I have fond memories of growing up there."

"Yet you were happy to up sticks and come here to the farm. Interesting." Anna smiled again. "Four: 'It wasn't us. We didn't do it.' I couldn't ask her what she meant because you shooed me away. Something about having to feed the chickens, wasn't it? So . . ." She stood. "I'll be going up to ask Diana myself. Or if you'd rather I wait down here while you get her up, then we can take her to the station."

Robert sighed. "You can do it here."

She followed him up the stairs, Lenny and Ollie behind her. Robert entered a room and approached the bed. A gentle shake didn't wake the woman, so he pushed her arm harder.

"Oh my God, she's cold." He staggered back and bumped into a wooden wardrobe.

Ollie shot in and felt for a pulse. Anna went to Robert to hold him back should he have a mind to go to his wife. Lenny blocked the doorway.

"She's well gone," Ollie said.

Lenny phoned it in, retreating onto the landing.

Anna stood in front of Robert. "When was the last time you spoke to her and she responded?"

"Err, umm, last night. After I switched the telly off. I said goodnight, and she said it back. Ten?"

"Do you always make your side of the bed when you get up — *when your wife is still in it?*"

"What?"

"Did you sleep in here last night?"

"Yes! No!"

"Which is it?"

"Ah, I was on the sofa. Oh God." His face crumpled. "I *told* her this wouldn't work."

Anna's heartbeat sped up. "What wouldn't?" *Tell me, you bastard.*

"Elizabeth. She said Diana would just fall asleep and no one would think anything of it because of her age. That old people die in their sleep all the time, so it wouldn't seem unusual."

Die in their sleep all the time . . . Bloody hell, Elizabeth did that.

Anna glanced over at Ollie, who held the recording device towards Robert. Thank God, it would have taped the whole conversation since they'd come upstairs.

Anna glared at Robert. "What did you give your wife?"

"It was Elizabeth. She had tablets. She'd made them into powder and mixed them with milk." He broke down, ugly sobs wrenching out of him.

"Downstairs," Anna ordered and led the way.

She'd come here thinking she could grind Robert down into confessing, but the last thing she'd expected was to find his wife dead. And if Diana was cold, she'd been dead for a while. She may already have been dead when officers had come into the farmhouse to check whether Toby was there. Robert had said to the PCs that they needed to be quiet and not wake her up. God, what a devious bastard. If Anna, Lenny and Ollie hadn't turned up today, what had he planned to do, phone it in, pretending he'd found her dead?

In the kitchen, once Ollie and Lenny were present, Anna took the cuffs off her belt and snapped them around Robert's wrists. Cautioned him. Then she walked outside; couldn't

213

stand to be near him, sickened by the extremes that man and Elizabeth had gone to.

She took her phone out and rang Herman. "You've got another body. I've got a feeling the tox report will match that of Elizabeth Kettering. She drank some crushed pill concoction. Well, she was forced to."

"Okay. Glad you rang. I've finished Maureen's PM. The implement used left imprints of carvings behind."

"It'll be from a walking stick we've yet to drag up from the lake. Divers are over there now. Anything else?"

"The only news from the lab so far is ginger hairs, feline, attached to Maureen's coat."

"I thought that would be the case. Toby Potter's got a ginger cat. He's confessed anyway. You'll no doubt have Albert Frost's body in your fridge by now."

"Yes, he came in half an hour ago. You *have* been busy."

"Don't." She paused. "How are you?"

"Getting by. Today I feel the opposite to yesterday. Happy my grandmother had such a lovely life. Pleased I had her in mine."

"Grief is swings and roundabouts."

"It is, it is. Right, I shall make my way over to see the latest unfortunate, seeing as it's murder. Where am I going?"

"Hawthorn Farm. We might not be here when you arrive as I want to go and see what the progress is at the lake. I'm that cross because everything will be water damaged."

"Ah, you forget. The carvings on the cane. It'll have grooves. If the blood dried hard in those, we may still get something from them. The water might not have penetrated right through yet, depending on what else is in the suitcase. Also, if the carved bits weren't stained or varnished, it would have gone into the wood."

"From what I've seen of his other work, I don't think they would be." Anna thought of the cane stand he'd made, plus the kettle handle. The pale, untreated wood had stood out.

"How many hours of submergence are we talking?"

"Since around half eight last night."

"Ah. Still, we live in hope, eh?"

"We do. Oh, have you been warned there might be infant skeletons headed your way?"

"Yes. One's been found so far."

"Shit. I really wanted it to be a lie on Toby's part."

"Unfortunately not. I'll ring for a specialist to do their post-mortems when we know how many we're talking about and the remains are brought in. I'd best get going. Speak soon."

Anna instructed Parvati to take Robert into the station with her colleague. Lenny came out to say Ollie was staying with Diana.

In the car, feeling decidedly clammy from the latest events, as if Diana's murder was a tangible thing that had coated her skin, Anna drove them away from Hawthorn Farm wondering if it was cursed. The place had been connected to crime for years.

"Did he say anything else when I came outside?" Anna asked.

Lenny stretched his arms out and rotated his wrists. "Only that Elizabeth made the drug cocktail and he just agreed to her administering it. Diana has early onset dementia, and he tried to make me think it was assisted suicide."

"Bullshit. They needed to shut her up. And we can't prove he didn't do it because both women are dead. Bloody typical."

"He's culpable because he gave permission and was there when Elizabeth killed her. Joint enterprise, my friend. Even if we don't get him to crack under pressure for Jack Hudson, he'll go down for Diana."

"Poor woman. I wonder if Elizabeth knew she was going to kill herself when she forced Diana to drink that crap? She didn't tell Robert — he was genuinely shocked when I told him she was dead, did you see?"

"He must have been shitting himself, knowing she'd left it for him to take the blame."

Anna drove on, her mind in a whirl.

God, the depths some people would sink to.

CHAPTER THIRTY-THREE

Anna gazed out at the lake, an icy breeze wafting into her face. The suitcase still hadn't been found, which wasn't surprising, looking at the expanse of water before her. The divers were currently concentrating on the side closest to the treeline; someone was more likely to have dropped it in there as it provided some form of cover. A silhouette with trees and bushes as a backdrop was less likely to be seen.

She glanced over to the other side, and stiffened. Along with a bunch of residents who'd braved the cold to be nosy, Parole — she'd recognise his shape anywhere — stood beyond the cordon in the distance, chatting to a PC. The officer turned and stared her way, and she sighed at Parole possibly making up some stupid excuse so he could speak to her. Annoyingly, she hoped that was the case. Then she didn't. Then she did.

Sort yourself out, for God's sake.

Her phone rang, and she checked the screen. "DI James."

"Sorry to trouble you with this, but I've got a fella here claiming he saw someone putting something in the lake last night. He wants to talk to you."

Anna's tummy spasmed, and she swallowed a knot of excitement. "Okay, I'll come over now." She spun to face

Lenny. "Parole's seen something. Can you go over there with me? I don't want to be alone with him."

"Yarp."

"You sound like the guy off that film."

"*Hot Fuzz.*"

"That's the one." Anna chuckled, some of the tension leaving her, and she knew Lenny was trying to put her at ease. She was so lucky to have a friend like him.

They rounded the lake, Lenny talking about something and nothing, Anna giving noises as responses. Her mind was too focused on having to speak to Parole to be one of life's great conversationalists at the moment. Lenny probably realised; he knew her well enough to expect her to go inside her head every now and then.

They dipped under the cordon, and Anna gestured for Parole to walk with them. She wanted space between them and the other residents. With everyone so eager to put things on social media, she had to be careful. Two young women aimed phones their way, probably hoping Parole was a suspect and they'd get to see his arrest.

"You saw someone last night," she said to him.

"Straight to the point, no fucking about. I like it." Parole smiled.

Anna ignored the flutter in her chest. "Why didn't you phone it in?"

"Ah, see, I could only speak to you two about it. One of my little 'idiosyncrasies', we'll call it. I need to cover our backs before I offer any info to you."

"Right, so . . ."

"I was waiting to get word back from all the Kings as to whether it was anything to do with one of our jobs. Jobs that I didn't just admit we do, if you catch my drift."

"Why would one of your . . . I don't even know what to call them. Colleagues? Why would they dump something when you live here?"

"I thought the same, but some of them are a bit thick."
Parole smiled at her again. "Anyway, I saw him loitering and
came out to see what he was up to. I hid behind a tree and saw
him putting something in the water. Followed him when he
walked off. He was slow, seemed old. I shouted at him, asked
him what he was playing at, then I lost him."

"How did you lose him when he was slow?"

Parole shrugged. "He must have hidden."

"We know who he is, but thanks for passing that on.
Where was he when he put the item in?"

Parole pointed. "See that tree there that's fatter than all
the others? There."

Anna looked that way. "Okay, cheers."

"Fancy going on a date?"

Anna swung round and gawped at him. "Straight to the
point, no fucking about. I *don't* like it. Someone will come
by to take your statement." She strode off towards an officer
and let them know Parole needed speaking to formally, then
huffed off towards the other side of the lake.

Lenny caught up with her. "Nice response."

"Well, he gets on my wick."

"Why?"

"Because he asked me for something I can't give."

"But you had the perfect opportunity there for the undercover job."

"There isn't going to be one."

"Fair enough."

Anna rang the diver boss as he was too far away for her
to speak to him immediately. She explained where Parole had
witnessed Toby, and he thanked her for the information. No
sooner had the line gone dead than the diver team moved to
the spot.

Anna's phone rang. Sally's name on the screen. "All right,
Sal?"

"I wasn't going to say anything, maybe I'm just being
suspicious, but since you've been tied up at Upton and we've

219

been stuck here poking through the files I've been able to keep a closer eye on Peter. He kept getting phone calls yesterday — not on his personal phone or his work one. It's a smartphone but one of those cheap efforts. He checked whether me or Warren were watching, then he let the calls ring out. A minute later, he got up and made out he was going to the loo. I know the Kings team have a tail on him when he's not on shift and nothing's come of it, but those calls — a bit iffy, aren't they?"

"Was this what you were trying to tell me yesterday at the briefing?"

"I was trying to let you know I've been watching him. Sorry if that didn't come across too well. We need a code. Me pulling my ear or whatever."

"But we've all been watching him."

"I know, but . . ."

"What did he do when he came back from the loo?"

"Went on his computer, but he could just have been getting on with work. His monitor points away from the room, so I can't see what's on it."

"He's not stupid enough to use his own login details if he's up to something, we already know that because there's been a sweep on his access log. All of it matches the cases we've worked."

"I know, but how is he getting other people's passwords — I mean, he must be, right? Are there other Kings on the force?"

"Bloody hell."

"Also, he went out of the room yesterday, longer than going to the toilet. I assumed he'd gone down to the canteen or something, but he came back smelling of smoke."

"I thought he'd packed the fags in."

"Hmm."

"Did he offer any explanation?"

"I didn't ask because we said we didn't want him to know we were watching, didn't we?"

"True. What's he been like so far today?"

"Jittery. He jumps every now and then, like he did yesterday. I think he must have that phone on vibrate. And it looks like he hasn't slept very well."

"I'd say we could get Ollie in on this, but I'll have to run it by Placket first. He wanted to keep it between us because we don't know who we can trust, not that I think for one minute Ollie is bent. Do me a favour and go and see Placket. Tell him what's going on and pass on my suggestion. Also, let him know Peter might have left the station without being seen."

"Okay."

"Talk to you later."

A shout from the lake. Anna squinted over, and a diver's head popped up. He raised a hand and gave the "okay" sign. Happy they'd found the case, Anna swerved back to the car. It would be a while before the suitcase got to the lab to be opened, and she'd soon get word of what it contained. She hoped Toby hadn't lied about it. He'd confessed, but it was always a bonus to have the proof.

She nudged Lenny. "We'll go back to the station. I'll tell you what Sally wanted on the way."

CHAPTER THIRTY-FOUR

Trigger wouldn't leave Peter alone this morning. He kept sending messages, and, although the burner was on vibrate, Peter couldn't bring himself to ignore them. Not now he'd killed that kid. The previous messages had been taunts, he was sure of it. Trigger was torturing him over what he'd done.

> T: *Heard someone found him just after we left last night.*

> T: *His mum's devastated. Said she doesn't want to live without him.*

> T: *How does it feel to be the one who created so much grief? Good? Or are you going soft?*

> T: *I'll keep the clothes and trainers you had on. Insurance.*

Trigger and Wheels had gone into Peter's house afterwards. Peter had stripped and handed everything over without being told to. He knew the score. Then they'd fucked off to torch the vehicle, leaving him to stare through a crack in the curtains at the men outside in their car.

The burner vibrated again.

He got up and headed for the door.

"What the hell is up with you?" Warren asked. "You were like this yesterday. Are you ill? If you are, you shouldn't be here. I don't want to bloody catch it, thanks."

"I think I've got a pee infection."

Warren shook his head. "Get hold of a doctor, then."

"Cranberry juice helps women," Sally said. "Or you could have diabetes — you know, all that weeing."

Peter left the room, finding his colleagues' stares a bit much. He was paranoid, thinking they knew what he'd done when in reality they were probably just looking at him normally.

In the toilet, he accessed the message.

T: *Go and find out what's going on with Puppet.*

P: *I'm on a break. We agreed.*

T: *Do as you're told. The other person we have helping us isn't on duty until later.*

P: *Who is it?*

T: *Never you mind.*

Peter switched the phone off. Fuck what Trigger made of that, what he thought, how he reacted. Anna and Lenny would be back soon for a debrief. Peter couldn't cope if the burner kept vibrating. Anna was like a shark scenting blood, she'd know something was off. She might ask questions like she had yesterday when he'd jolted at the mention of a note. He'd have to tell her he thought he had a bladder infection. She'd send him home. Trigger would think he was pretending to be ill so he didn't have to do what he'd asked.

A surge of emotions swept through him. That feeling of being out of control again. Peter's life was being directed by Trigger, when all he wanted was to leave the Kings. He momentarily considered going to Placket, confessing, making out he'd been forced into everything, but nowhere in that scenario would he come out smelling of roses. He'd still lose his job and get sent down, and coppers didn't fare too well in prison.

Unless he cut off the head of the snake, killing Trigger — and Wheels, who was next in line to take over — he'd have to ride this out. Get his ducks in a row regarding a new identity. He'd already researched it — new bank accounts, new passport, new everything, and hopefully it would look like Peter Dove had disappeared off the face of the earth. Trigger didn't have big contacts he could get hold of to seek him out. The Kings weren't *that* kind of gang, like the Mafia. Unless Trigger employed a private detective. Which he might, because Peter was a risk — he knew too much.

But those men in that car would see him moving out. Report back to whoever had ordered them to watch him.

I'll have to pack a bag of clothes and leave everything else behind.

I could get a security job.

But National Insurance gets notified.

Then I'll have to get hold of that forger. Find his address on the system. Get fake documents.

Buoyed by making a firm decision, he left the loo and popped his head round the incident room door. "Just going for a cig."

"Thought you'd given up," Warren said.

"I *knew* I smelled smoke on you yesterday," Sally added.

Peter bit back the urge to tell her to fuck off with noticing things. "Yeah, well, that's my business."

"Touchy. Don't be long." Sally eyed him. "Anna and Lenny are on their way back."

It felt like a warning. One Peter didn't appreciate. What had she *really* been saying? He scratched his itchy inner wrist — he'd had the crown tattoo removed, waited for it to heal, then had a different tatt done. An eagle to represent freedom, the undersides of its wings triangle-tipped feathers, like the tops of the former crown, so it reminded him what he was free from. Or would be in the future, once he'd sorted everything.

He walked downstairs to the largest incident room, which was sectioned off for different teams. The one where the street crime team worked was on the way to the smoking area outside. In the far corner, DI Kev Clough stood in front of the interactive whiteboard, his team sitting facing his way. A debrief?

Peter paused to listen. Coppers — well, proper coppers — were invested in catching *all* criminals, not just the ones they were assigned to. They supported one another, no matter what. Him standing there wouldn't be seen as odd, thank God.

"So, we have Jamal Jenkins, street name Puppet. The two youth gangs, the Chiefs and the Loops, claim he didn't belong to them. They've made it pretty clear on their social media, saying Jamal sold drugs off his own bat, evidenced by the bumbags on his person. One contained cash — two hundred of it is counterfeit — one contained drugs. Coke, weed. No heroin, crack or spice. One stab to the femoral artery in his thigh — someone knew what they were doing. Found by a resident who heard a wheelie bin being knocked over and a car driving off."

"Any leads?" someone asked.

"None. Lack of CCTV and Ring doorbells. The homes down that street, people can't afford such luxuries. We all know the deal when it comes to Northgate, especially the Rowan estate. Low-income families, some on benefits, spice-heads wandering around."

"What about Molly Griffin?" a DC asked. "She usually knows everything that goes on there. Self-proclaimed queen of Northgate, she is."

Titters went round.

"She'll be spoken to today," Clough said.

"What's the general consensus here if he isn't in with the Chiefs or the Loops?" This from a woman tapping a pen against her cheek.

"No affiliation as far as we can see, so a lone wolf. Counterfeit money, so someone tried to scam him. Jamal could have got lairy about it if he noticed. Buyer shanked him."

"But the money was in his bumbag, so he must have put it in there — accepted it, like."

"Not necessarily. The buyer could have put it in there afterwards."

"What about the car?" Pen woman again.

"Found burnt out in a lay-by behind the factory. Completely ruined by the fire, so I doubt we'll get anything off it. CCTV will determine the route from the street to the lay-by, but let's face it, people are getting savvy. How many times have we found sweet fuck all from cameras?"

"So basically, this could go down as another unsolved gang murder?"

"I don't plan on it, obviously, but these teenagers, they clam up, close ranks. For all we know, the Chiefs and Loops are both lying and he *was* with one of them. They're covering their backs."

"So we're disregarding the Kings on this?"

"For the moment. Youths aren't their thing."

Peter had heard all he needed to. He went out the back and sparked up. No one else was out there, so he walked to the gate, his back to the door, and took the risk of switching the burner on. Two more messages from Trigger.

T: *Ignoring me isn't advisable, you know that. I tend to get a bit pissy about it. Makes me want to do someone some damage.*

T: *What the fuck are you doing? It's been ten minutes.*

226

Jesus, Trigger had not long asked Peter to go nosing. What did he expect, an immediate response?

> P: *Give me a chance! I had to make an excuse to get away. Before you ask, the Kings aren't in the frame. I have to go. Got a debrief.*

He switched the phone off, had one puff on the ciggie and stubbed it out.
Fuck my life.

CHAPTER THIRTY-FIVE

The debrief had gone well but had lasted a while with so much to cover. It had stretched past lunchtime, so Anna nipped to Brunch at three to collect everyone's orders. She sat at a table to wait for the baguettes to be prepared, sipping her favourite coffee and taking a moment to breathe, watching the shoppers go past the window, living life as best they could.

Prior to her leaving the station, Placket had asked her to go to his office and once again put the undercover scenario to her. Anna had held back the urge to snap at him. Why did he have to keep bringing it up?

"Listen to me before you go off on one," he'd said. "There's been a fatal stabbing. Sixteen-year-old lad."

"Another one?"

"Yes. It got me thinking. The Chiefs and Loops have both said he didn't belong to them, as they have done for other seemingly random youth deaths. And no one's stepped forward to claim the kill."

"If they've made claims in the past, have they been questioned?"

"Yes, but none of them have admitted they did it, obviously, and all have solid alibis. They like to announce what they've done but aren't so keen on paying for it. But when they say they *haven't* done anything, that left me wondering. What if those kills belong to the Kings?"

"Bloody hell."

"These are kids, Anna."

"You're trying to tug on my heartstrings. Underhand, in my opinion."

"I'll hold my hands up to that."

"Street crime isn't our remit. There's a whole team dedicated to it."

"Yes, but I've spoken to Clough and put it to him that Jamal Jenkins' death might be a Kings scenario. He'd already thought of that, obviously, as well as for all the unclaimed kills, and we got talking."

"I know what you're going to say. *Again.*"

"So will you consider it?"

"Because Parole apparently fancies me? Do you really feel he isn't going to think it's weird that a copper — one who's already refused his advances, I might add — suddenly changes her mind and goes out with him? *That* isn't suss. And what am I supposed to do, give him a ring? Turn up at his apartment?"

"Let it evolve naturally. Do it for the kids."

She didn't like being emotionally manipulated. "You can be a bastard at times."

Placket had smiled. "But for good reason."

Anna shook her head at the memory. At her agreeing to go undercover while working as usual, living her life as usual, except it *wouldn't* be usual, would it, with Parole in it?

The bell over the door jangled, and who the bloody hell should walk in but Parole himself. He came up to her table, his puffa jacket doing nothing to hide his physique. It pissed her off that he was so attractive.

"Have you been tailing me?" she asked, her chest a riot of butterflies.

"I might have spotted you driving past me, yes."

"And you followed me here? Creepy stalker much?"

He sat. *Lounged*, rather. "I like you. Sue me."

"I wish I could."

His laugh sounded deep. Dangerous. "So, as you knocked me back this morning, I'll try again. And everyone knows God loves a trier."

This was it, her chance. She wanted to take it but at the same time didn't. She wanted to find out if the Kings were killing teenagers but didn't like what she'd have to do to get the intel. Parole wasn't stupid, he wouldn't just give up information that would get the Kings banged up. It could take months for him to trust her. Unless she did what Placket had suggested and tell Parole she was a bent copper. That she'd filter information to him so he could pass it on to Trigger. Not only would they hopefully figure out who'd murdered the lads, she might also find out if Peter was involved.

It went against the grain to make out she was a bag egg among all the good ones at the station. The thought of eggs had her feeling guilty, considering Maureen had died buying them.

"Are you ever going to give up?" she asked, tagging a sigh onto the end of her words.

"Nope."

"Why me?"

"I've told you before. You intrigue me."

"You want to turn me into a King copper, more like."

"That as well, but I assume you're not for turning."

"Wouldn't you like to know," she muttered.

His eyebrows rose. "Really?"

God, his eyes. She was in trouble here. "I've been known to skew a thing or two at work. It's no big deal." She hated those words. Hated herself for uttering them.

"Well, well, well."

The lady behind the counter called out Anna's number.

"Excuse me a minute." Anna got up and collected the paper bag, then returned to the table. "Late lunch. We've been a bit busy."

"I imagine some of you have been *extra* busy."

What did he mean by that? Is he referring to Peter? "We all pull our weight."

"Some more than others, I'd imagine."

"You're being cryptic. That naffs me off." She was already forgetting what she'd been told. To act like she fancied him back. To not say things that would put him off her. But Parole would *expect* her to snap at him. It was better to behave predictably at first so he didn't suspect anything. "If you've got something to say, just say it."

"I'm not allowed. The Kings have rules."

"Right." She stood. "Anyway, some of us have work to do. We have to earn our money. We don't have grandfathers who fund our lifestyles."

He grinned up at her. "I bloody love your snarky attitude."

"I don't care whether you do or not." She strutted out and took her time getting into her car, leaving the door open while she pretended to look for something in her bag on the passenger seat.

As she'd hoped, he came out after her.

He crouched on the pavement, his body blocking the door. "One date. One night."

She made a show of glancing around in case someone saw them. "For fuck's sake, pack it in. I've told you, I'm a copper, you belong to the Kings. *Not* a good look for me."

"We'll go to York."

Anna thought of Bruce and Maureen. "I suppose your sort can afford the Spencer. I bet you all take women there."

"A dig at my grandad?"

"It wasn't, actually."

"Who'd have thought the old goat had it in him to play away? We didn't have a clue. My mum's shocked. She won't get over it for a while."

"He wouldn't have wanted to hurt your nan."

"Yet he shagged Maureen anyway. Took the risk." Parole smiled. "Though I have to say, some risks are worth taking. So what's your answer?"

231

She pretended to think about it. "One date. As for one night, if you mean us having sex you can bugger off."

"When?"

"Give me time to think about it. I'm busy at the moment, wrapping up the cases, and if another big one comes in it'll be overtime, no chance for me to get out, so you'll have to wait."

"Why did you agree?"

She flushed. "You know why."

"Because there's something there." He gestured from himself to her. "I *knew* I wasn't imagining it."

"This could get me in so much shit."

He rose, then bent down to poke his head inside the car, his face too close to hers. He smelled of fancy aftershave. His breath was warm on her skin.

"You forget, you'd be with a King, Anna. No one will find out. Wear a wig if you're that bothered. I quite fancy seeing you as a blonde."

"Piss off."

He stepped back. "So you'll message me?"

"I can't use my personal phone or my work one, obviously. I'll buy a pay-as-you-go effort and drop-call you. No idea when."

"I'll be waiting."

She closed the door without looking at him, couldn't, and drove back to the station. She'd done it, stepped over to the dark side, and, even though she'd been given permission, it still felt wrong.

Fucking Placket.

She entered the station and went to the incident room. Handed out everyone's baguettes and cans of pop. As Peter reached out for his Coke, his shirt sleeve moved up his arm and she spied his tattoo in full.

An eagle. The bottom of the wings like the tips of a crown. Had she been wrong when she'd glimpsed it before, thinking it was the mark of the Kings?

She headed to Placket's office with his lunch, sat at his desk, and let out a long breath. "One, Peter's tattoo is of an eagle, and two, I'm going on a date with Parole."

Placket opened his can of Fanta. "Thank you. I don't know what to make of the eagle, though. What's it like? I mean, could he have had a crown covered over?"

"It's possible. I didn't exactly stare at it too hard, in case he noticed."

"Okay. So when's the date?"

"I don't know. I kind of played hard to get, even after I'd agreed to it. I didn't know if you needed time to put surveillance on me."

"He'd spot that."

"So I'm going in alone? Can't you send two officers in as a couple to sit at a nearby table?"

"We don't know who the mole is. We can't risk word being leaked that you're only going on a date for your job." He sighed. "It has to look authentic, Anna, and I doubt very much you'll be in danger with him. He likes you too much."

She told him what they'd talked about. "So your plan might bear fruit."

"Good. You did well. How do you feel?"

"I'm shitting myself." *In case I fall for him.*

"You'll get used to it, I promise, and it'll be worth it if we can take the lot of them down."

Anna nodded. It would be best all round — and best for her especially — if Parole was out of the picture along with the other Kings. At least then he'd definitely be out of bounds and she wouldn't see him. Wouldn't get the tummy flutters.

In the meantime, though, she'd get plenty of those.

Ugh.

CHAPTER THIRTY-SIX

Five days had passed, and Anna still hadn't contacted Parole. She'd gone as far as buying the phone, though, drop-calling him as promised, then adding his number to her contacts. As she'd said to Placket, if she got hold of their target too soon he might think it was off.

Anna had occupied herself with work instead of what Parole may or may not be thinking and feeling. The lab had come up trumps. Both Elizabeth and Diana had similar substances in their tox reports, and the drugs matched the powder in the tablet containers in Elizabeth's kitchen drawer. Some were years old, so had she been storing them up, crushing them to use if she ever suspected she'd get caught for murder?

Blood found in the pieces of walking stick matched Maureen's. As Herman had predicted, the blood had gone right into the wood, and one minute speck had escaped the water penetrating it. So that, along with Toby's clothing and confession, meant none of the rigmarole of a trial, which was never a bad thing in Anna's opinion, although they still had to collate all the files and evidence as if there would be one.

Toby currently resided in HMP Wealstun, a category-C prison, as he was considered low risk of escape. Anna had checked on his welfare yesterday, and he was depressed and non-verbal.

Despite Peter's tattoo clearly being an eagle, she'd had time to think about the first time she'd seen it. She'd convinced herself it had been a crown, and Placket had agreed that Peter should still be monitored. Something about him screamed *dodgy copper* now, and Anna couldn't get that out of her head, although she did have a few thoughts that she'd kept to herself so far. She planned to discuss them with Sally to see what she thought before she brought it up with Placket.

Anna finished up for the day in her office, pleased she'd got a lot of filing out of the way. Peter and Warren were off to play squash this evening, and Warren had told Anna and Sally that, during their previous game two nights ago, Peter had taken off his long-sleeved sports top for the first time. Usually he wouldn't, whether he sweated buckets or not.

Showing off the eagle tattoo on purpose?

Anna and Sally hadn't had a chance to discuss that among themselves.

Anna left her office, leaving Lenny, Warren and Peter behind to shut down their computers, walking out with Sally by her side. At Anna's car, they paused.

"An *eagle* tattoo?" Sally said as if she'd picked up on Anna's thoughts. "I'd have sworn blind it was crown tips."

"Me, too. Placket suggested he's had it covered up."

"So do you think Peter knows we're on to him?"

"That or he's stopped helping the Kings. Could have even left them."

"But they're not allowed to leave."

"Wheels did to run the Kite, although I get your point, he's taken a step back, but he's still in with them." Anna sighed. "I don't know, but I'm sure it will all become clear once I've got in with you-know-who."

Only Anna, Placket, Lenny, Warren and Sally knew what she would be up to. Warren would continue to be pally with Peter so it didn't look weird if he said he wouldn't play squash anymore or go for a drink with him at the Hoof — Warren had been that disgusted with the suspicions about what Peter got up to that it had taken a while to calm him down. Anna had worried — and rightly so — that his protestations had been a front, because *someone* had to be filtering information to them if Peter had distanced himself, which he seemed to have done. The two different sets of men following him had reported that he did nothing untoward.

Warren's computer use had been examined on the quiet, as had Sally's. Only Anna and Placket were aware — apart from the tech bloke, who'd been sworn to secrecy and told to sign an NDA. That didn't mean he wouldn't go and tell Trigger, though. And those two computer searches didn't mean anything either, as Peter's had also come up with nothing to pin on him.

But Anna trusted her gut. She didn't think Warren or Sally were anything to do with it, and neither did Placket. Still, there was always that little niggle of doubt.

Sally glanced round to make sure no one could overhear. A few officers had come out of the station and chatted loudly about going to the Hoof.

"I'm that worried about you when it comes to *him*," Sally said, referring to Parole, her voice low. "What if he finds out what you're doing and turns on you?"

"Then I'll just have to make sure I'm careful, won't I?" Anna whispered.

The other officers got into their cars and drove off.

Anna sagged with relief. "I'm mostly doing it for those kids who keep getting killed, but having a mole on our team — ours, Sal — it makes me sick to my stomach. I trusted him, we all did, and he's used us, lied to us."

"*If* he's a King. It was the crown tattoo — or what we thought was a crown — that tipped us off to him possibly being dodgy in the first place. What if it was an eagle all along, he's innocent, and you're walking into the lion's den for no reason?"

"Okay, but what if those phone calls he kept getting were Trigger informing him that Jamal Jenkins was about to be offed? What if Peter told him he was leaving the Kings and Trigger forced him back in by doing one of those bloody loyalty jobs gangs are so fond of? What if, all this time, Peter's been forced to do a lot of things? We *know* he was in the Kings as a kid, then he joined the police. You said yourself, they're not allowed to leave. Our intel's told us that. Clough has said so, too. He's got spies on the ground."

"Whether he was forced to do things or not, he still did them." Sally shook her head. "Sorry, he knows what's right and wrong."

"But if you were threatened with losing your life, wouldn't you do whatever they said?"

"No, I'd tell the police and ask to be put in a safe house or something."

"Is that because you've got Ben to think about?"

"Yes, but I'd do it even if I didn't have a child. It sounds like you're defending him."

"Just playing devil's advocate." Now that Sally had confirmed Anna's thoughts on the matter, she smiled. Whatever Peter had done, the why didn't factor into it. "Anyway, I'd better let you go so you can pick the little one up from after-school club."

Sally bit her lip.

"Is everything okay?" Anna asked.

"Richard's being a dick again."

"He still doesn't get what being an ex means?"

"Unfortunately not. I'll have to see him later. He's coming to pick Ben up. He'll say the usual rubbish to wind me up so I have a crappy weekend, but I've been teaching myself to forget whatever he says as soon as he drives away. The problem is, I then have Ben coming back saying some weird things because his father doesn't know what he should and shouldn't say to a child. Or he does and says bad stuff to him anyway."

"You should write it all down. Make a diary of it. Then you can get the courts involved."

237

Sally nodded. "I think I will. Right, I'm off. See you on Monday if nothing comes in over the weekend."

"I bloody hope not."

Anna drove to Upton and parked outside her place, then walked to the Jubilee. It was weird not seeing Albert, Maureen and Toby there for quiz night. She ordered some dinner and a Coke and seated herself out of the way so she wouldn't be dragged in to join a team, not that she really thought anyone would ask her. If Lenny had been here, she might have entered them as a pair, but he wasn't. He was trying out a new dating app, meeting some woman or other at eight.

Her food arrived, and she tucked in. Her phone bleeped just as she'd popped the last piece of battered sausage in her mouth, and she fished about in her handbag and took it out.

No notification.

Shit, it wouldn't be her burner, would it?

She lifted it out and cringed at the screen. Opened the message.

Parole: I know I said I'd wait, but come on, Anna!

She took a deep breath. Composed her reply.

Anna: Okay, tonight, but I've already eaten. The Spencer, York, eight o'clock.

That would give her enough time to get ready, although, really, she shouldn't dress up and put make-up on because that wasn't her style. But if this was a date, wouldn't he expect her to at least put on a bit of lippy and eyeliner?

Parole: See you then.

She swallowed and switched phones to let Placket know.

Anna: Game on, boss.

THE END

THE JOFFE BOOKS STORY

We began in 2014 when Jasper agreed to publish his mum's much-rejected romance novel and it became a bestseller.

Since then we've grown into the largest independent publisher in the UK. We're extremely proud to publish some of the very best writers in the world, including Joy Ellis, Faith Martin, Caro Ramsay, Helen Forrester, Simon Brett and Robert Goddard. Everyone at Joffe Books loves reading and we never forget that it all begins with the magic of an author telling a story.

We are proud to publish talented first-time authors, as well as established writers whose books we love introducing to a new generation of readers.

We won Trade Publisher of the Year at the Independent Publishing Awards in 2023. We have been shortlisted for Independent Publisher of the Year at the British Book Awards for the last four years, and were shortlisted for the Diversity and Inclusivity Award at the 2022 Independent Publishing Awards. In 2023 we were shortlisted for Publisher of the Year at the RNA Industry Awards.

We built this company with your help, and we love to hear from you, so please email us about absolutely anything bookish at: feedback@joffebooks.com.

If you want to receive free books every Friday and hear about all our new releases, join our mailing list: www.joffebooks.com/contact

And when you tell your friends about us, just remember: it's pronounced Joffe as in coffee or toffee!